P9-DES-185

What the critics are saying...

"...*Cracked: Prelude to Passion* deserves a Gold Star Award because not only is it beautifully written but every element woven into the story: the characters, the plot, the pace, etc. is simply outstanding. It will surprise you, captivate you, and touch your heart. I recommend it to everyone..." ~ *Just Erotic Romance Reviews*

5 Angels! "The passion and romance starts from the very beginning and doesn't let up until the last page. Ms. Storm has created an exciting tale that has it all and shouldn't be missed!" ~ *Fallen Angel Reviews*

"...Ruby Storm does stupendous work with this most recent book! Between the earthy, unrestrained sex, the harrowing suspense and the absolute irony of fate, I could not stop reading...This isn't just a wonderful addition to your bookshelf, it's a necessary one!" ~ *eCataRomance Reviews*

5 Hearts "...A lustful and suspenseful story... if you are looking for a romantic suspense that will quickly set your blood on fire with desire, grab yourself a copy of *Cracked: Prelude to Passion* and start reading. This book is a definite keeper!" ~ *Romance Studio Reviews*

"...CRACKED: PRELUDE TO PASSION is one hot ride of sexual passion and intrigue..." ~ *Romance Junkies*

"Ms. Storm's exquisite prose keeps the reader in her thrall... amazed at the way this author can draw the reader in and captivate them from the first page..." ~ *Loves Romances Reviews*

Ruby Storm

CRACKED:
Prelude
TO
PASSION

ELLORA'S CAVE
ROMANTICA PUBLISHING

An Ellora's Cave Romantica Publication

www.ellorascave.com

Cracked: Prelude to Passion

ISBN # 1419953737
ALL RIGHTS RESERVED.
Cracked: Prelude to Passsion Copyright© 2005 Ruby Storm
Edited by Pamela Campbell
Cover art by Syneca

Electronic book Publication July 2005
Trade paperback Publication February 2006

With the exception of quotes used in reviews, this book may not be reproduced or used in whole or in part by any means existing without written permission from the publisher, Ellora's Cave Publishing, Inc.® 1056 Home Avenue, Akron OH 44310-3502.

This book is a work of fiction and any resemblance to persons, living or dead, or places, events or locales is purely coincidental. The characters are productions of the authors' imagination and used fictitiously.

Warning:

The following material contains graphic sexual content meant for mature readers. *Cracked: Prelude to Passion* has been rated E-rotic by a minimum of three independent reviewers.

Ellora's Cave Publishing offers three levels of Romantica™ reading entertainment: S (S-ensuous), E (E-rotic), and X (X-treme).

S-*ensuous* love scenes are explicit and leave nothing to the imagination.

E-*rotic* love scenes are explicit, leave nothing to the imagination, and are high in volume per the overall word count. In addition, some E-rated titles might contain fantasy material that some readers find objectionable, such as bondage, submission, same sex encounters, forced seductions, and so forth. E-rated titles are the most graphic titles we carry; it is common, for instance, for an author to use words such as "fucking", "cock", "pussy", and such within their work of literature.

X-*treme* titles differ from E-rated titles only in plot premise and storyline execution. Unlike E-rated titles, stories designated with the letter X tend to contain controversial subject matter not for the faint of heart.

Also by Ruby Storm

ഇ

Diamond Studs (*Anthology*)
Lucy's Double Diamonds
Payton's Passion
Perfect Betrayal
Twilight Kisses
Virgin Queen

*Check out Ruby Storm's Keeper Trilogy
at Cerridwen Press (www.cerridwenpress.com)*

ഇ

Keeper of the Spirit
Keeper of the Dream
Keeper of the Heart

Cracked: Prelude to Passion

ഇ

~ *Trademarks Acknowledgement* ~

The author acknowledges the trademarked status and trademark owners of the following wordmarks mentioned in this work of fiction:

Lincoln Continental: Ford Motor Co.
Discovery Channel: Discovery Communications Inc.

Chapter One

ಬಂ

Calli Lemont rushed through the front entrance to her home, spun and slammed the door behind her. As her cold fingers fumbled to click the deadbolt into place, her forehead settled against the warm, burnished oak that became the instant barrier between her and the uncertain world outside. Once again, an ominous shiver rippled across her skin because she couldn't shake the elusive sensation that someone followed her.

A deep breath preceded a swallow as the racing tempo of her heart slowed. She was behind a locked door now.

"Don't be foolish. It's just my imagination..." she murmured. Feeling safer than of a moment earlier, she turned to the security panel mounted beside the door and activated the system. Small red lights flickered, then stabilized, letting Calli know that the system was up and running.

Mentally shaking herself, she stepped further into the living room and ignored the same eerie notion she'd experienced on the way home tonight, no matter how hard she tried to push it aside. Her gray eyes clouded with doubt as her gaze shifted uncomfortably past the edges of the lamp's soft glow to the darkened corners of the room. Was she really the only person in the house? The fingers of one trembling hand raked through her straight chocolate-brown hair from her temple to the back of her slim neck, then she wrapped her arms about herself.

Her life was a contradictory kaleidoscope. On one hand, the fear that some insidious terror had crept inside the house sent a shaft of fear straight to the pit of her stomach.

But if that intruder was something else?

Not something, Calli. Someone... Are ghosts real?

Her harried gaze settled on her piano.

She could attempt to reach him. It had happened before.

What if it didn't happen tonight? What if it never happened again? Could she live without him?

She had to, because there was no other choice. Ghosts weren't real, only a figment of a troubled person's mind—a wonderful, sensual fantasy.

Her gaze flicked anxiously about the room.

One more time. She would allow herself one more time...

Crossing hesitantly to her baby grand piano, she ignored the chill in her blood when she brushed her fingers tentatively across the ivory keys. Blue-tinged lids fluttered shut momentarily as she worked up the nerve to sit on the shiny bench before the keyboard. Finally, drawn like the moth to the flame, she sank slowly to the hard surface, uncurled her fingers and reached out, powerless against the overriding need that filled her. Soft resonant tinkling filled the room.

She hovered on the edge of reason.

How can life be perfectly normal throughout the day, and then I come home to...

Her heart pounded harder with each touch of her fingertips against the smooth ivory as the music enveloped her like a warm blanket. Her lithe body swayed to its gentle rhythm. Her brow furrowed, and then flinched as she moved deeper into the sound. Images of Raine trickled through her mind. With each stroke, Calli felt a breath closer to him. He'd come to her. It had happened before...

Raine...

As the music calmed her weary mind, her thoughts shifted back in time. Nearly one year had passed since he'd left her to fend on her own. Almost three-hundred-and-sixty-five days of sadness that no one should ever have to experience. Days of wretched loneliness filled with a yearning so powerful that it nearly suffocated her and weakened her soul.

But then, in the quiet romance of her music, he at times would appear. Some would shake their heads at her foolishness.

They would tip their heads, eye her speculatively, and whisper with piteous frowns that turned down their mouths.

Let them. I don't care.

Calli had lost that ability on the day of the funeral.

She played on, a poignant smile curving her full lips upward in defiance, as she moved deeper into the music.

Let it happen tonight…

Then, in the quiet comfort of the melody, silky soft strains of a whispering bow against a violin's tight strings wavered sweetly behind her, settling into a familiar, harmonious accord that she'd only found with one man.

She prayed for the moment to stand still in time and fought the insistent urge to tilt her head to glimpse her dead husband holding the violin in his masculine hands, playing the instrument as if it were an extension of himself. To do so might equivocally change the course of the night.

Her brow knit further over her shuttered eyes as she recalled how those same hands could make her own body sing like his beautiful violin. The soft touch of his warm fingers caressing her body, his moist lips tugging at a nipple to tease it into a hard bud, his breath whispering across the taut skin of her stomach in perfect promise as his head lowered between her open thighs.

She waited.

She prayed.

And like the early morning sunrise that slowly inches its way onto the horizon to warm the land beneath it, the chilling vulnerability she lived with since his absence from her life, lessened. Unearthly warmth cloaked her shoulders, filling her heart with joy.

If this was madness, so be it.

"Raine…" Calli was unsure whether she had actually uttered his name aloud or if it had only resounded inside her brain. Her hands danced crazily across the ivory keys, forcing the haunting melody from the piano as if the power of her playing could strengthen his presence at her side.

One melodic note hung in the air behind her, then echoed away to nothing. A spiking jolt of heat raced through her blood when the quiet was replaced with a gentle touch of callused fingertips playing against her cheek.

"Oh, god…Raine…" she choked out.

His silent, spiritual presence surrounded her. Calli's hands stumbled over the keyboard when the heat of his lips pressed close beneath her ear causing the hair to rise upon her neck. His tender strength guided her up from the hard bench. Gentle hands turned her to face him.

Mesmerized, Calli stared into his dark eyes, lifted a trembling hand and caressed his masculine cheek. Her loving gaze followed the line of his straight nose to where her fingers now rested against his lips—lips that weren't icy in the grip of exacting death, but were filled with a strange, momentary warmth.

She had memorized his noble features the day she'd sobbed beside his casket, the cold gray skin of his cheekbones, the full lips that looked ridiculously feminine when the morticians had colored them slightly for the viewing. She'd pleaded with them not to close the coffin as she had draped her body across his. Then her father's firm grip had pulled her away. Horrified, she'd watched through blurred vision as his loving face disappeared for what she thought would be the rest of her life.

A shaft of pain pierced her heart with the recollection, and then quickly receded. She was in Raine's embrace now. Whether he was a ghost or some insane figment of her imagination, it didn't matter.

Her fingers fluttered across the line of his jaw. "How?" she asked in wonder. "How is this possible?"

Raine's ethereal smile flashed above her. Silently, he guided her body to the soft carpet at his feet, gently pushed her to her back, and then reclined beside her. Immediately, the cool air of the room rushed across the bare skin of her midriff as he stripped the sweater from her body.

A small whimper left Calli's lips when his hand slid beneath her bra to cup a breast. Her eyes frantically sought his. "Sometimes you don't hear me playing for you. Raine..." The lump in her throat silenced her briefly. "Raine...what happens when I can't reach you anymore..." Even as the words left her mouth, Calli fought the realization of how things would be. She would be forced to accept his total departure from her life and finally move on.

A moment later, deft fingers undid the clasp between the small, firm mounds, dragging her conflicting thoughts from the future. Her nipples puckered in expectation as his lips hovered only a kiss away. Raine dipped his mouth to suckle the hard bud that crested one breast, an unspoken command that he needed her. One hand slid teasingly down across her stomach, dragging the zipper of her slacks with it as he went on to search for the heat between her thighs. Calli's body arched sensuously in response as her knees fell apart. Raine massaged her feminine lips outlined by the silky material of her pants as his mouth slid up to capture hers.

A hungry pant languished on her lips. She slid her fingers through his soft dark hair, slanted her mouth, and met his tongue with a desperate ferociousness. Calli didn't understand the why and the how, only relished the moment of Raine within her embrace.

"Don't make me wait," she murmured against his mouth. "Fuck me, Raine. Make me forget that tomorrow I'll be alone. Love me before you're gone..."

His determined fingers slid off her pants and sheer, lacy underwear in one bold move. A flame built between her thighs as her eyes batted open. Raine's body was wonderfully naked as he slid atop her.

"Now, Raine. Now..." she breathed. The soft walls of her pussy clenched in expectation.

His lazy, sensuous smile widened as he clasped her hands and guided her arms out across the carpet. His knees forced her legs wider. His simmering gaze pinned her to the floor as his lips lowered to capture one swollen nipple. Raine rolled the sweet nubbin between his teeth before his mouth slid to its twin to do the same. As he straddled her, his fingers drifted from hers to cup her breasts, and then he licked the warm satiny space between her aching mounds.

Calli's moan broke the silence when his lips followed a soft invisible line to her navel. His tongue darted inside the tiny cavity, swirling and prodding until the action produced another groan and a flood of moisture between her legs.

She knew where he was going. Raine's tongue persisted on to lap through the soft tuft of dark pubic hair until he reached her inner thigh. She strained beneath him, her dripping sex searching for orgasmic satisfaction.

Raine's fingers tenderly parted her lightly furred lips, exposing her clit to the cool air of the room. Calli's muscles clenched desperately, tingling, twitching with what would be a massive orgasm if he would only fill her.

"I love you, Raine," she breathed softly. Her head rolled from side to side as her cunt surged toward his mouth in a soundless plea, her body jerking fitfully when he flicked the tip of his tongue at her wet entrance. "Oh, god, Raine..." The heat of orgasm teetered on the edge of her restraint.

As he slipped two fingers into her wet hollow, his teeth gently latched onto her clit.

It happened all at once. Calli's lower body reacted with a swinging pitch forward. Her pussy clamped around the thickness of his fingers as her body pulsed wildly. She struggled for air. Her lungs constricted as the magical heat spread through her blood.

"Raine!" she gasped out. "Oh, god, Raine, I love you."

The waves of orgasm poured over her like scalded water. The sweet quintessence of his love cloaked her body even before he slid up her slender length and cupped her face to kiss her gently as his cock slid easily inside her dripping sheath.

Calli writhed uncontrollably. The motion of her hips, her clawing fingers, her legs wrapped tightly around his trim waist, signaled her still-vital need to be taken roughly. Raine responded immediately by pulling back and then penetrating deeply into her body, filling her as his cock swelled further, straining to stay buried. Her pussy clamped around him yet again as her orgasm continued to rip her sanity to threads. She could feel Raine's fingers biting into the flesh of her buttocks as he gripped her cheeks tightly to hold her in place. He pounded time after time, grinding into her, then rammed forward with an intense ferociousness. The heat of his cum filled her…

* * * * *

Quinn Morgan's hips jerked forward and cum spewed inside his boxer shorts. His eyes snapped open to the darkness as he gasped for air. His cock throbbed to a rhythmic release and there was absolutely nothing he could do about it. A strangled groan whipped across his lips as the shudders raked through his body, the spiked heat radiating in all directions. The warmth of his semen shocked him to his core.

He lay beneath the sheet, knowing it was useless to fight the euphoric sensations and waited until the jolts of his orgasm lessened and the tight knot in his gut receded. A sheen of perspiration covered the sinewy muscles of his upper body, soaking the sheet beneath him and the pillow his head lay upon, as the pulses diminished and his breathing slowed. Finally, ignoring the stickiness in his shorts, he swung his legs over the edge of the bed and stared disgustedly about his darkened bedroom.

"What the fuck's the matter with me?" he uttered as he heaved himself up and headed for the shower. When he flicked on the bathroom light, the glare blinded him momentarily. With a flick of his wrist he had the hot water running. Careful not to smear semen down the length of his long legs, he finally managed to kick off his boxers. Checking the water first, he adjusted the temperature and stepped into the pelting spray to rinse the milky cream off his crotch and upper thighs. Quinn's head tipped back wearily as he closed his eyes.

Wet dreams. He was twenty-nine years old and had just had another wet dream. What the fuck? Maybe he should see a specialist, but just the thought embarrassed the hell out of him. He grabbed the soap, worked up suds and lathered his crotch.

Christ. He hadn't had a wet dream since he was fourteen. That is, not until about six months ago. That's when the problem had started.

Silver eyes flashed through his mind. His hands became suddenly still. His brow dipped as the water pelted his taut skin.

Who in the hell is she?

Quinn didn't have a clue. But every time she appeared the same thing happened. He dreamed every detail of making love to her—and only her. Even now the remembered silkiness of her thick straight hair prodded his mind. She was a brunette. Well, if that's what you could call the shade. He must dream in color because he knew with certainty that her hair reminded him of the color of rich milk chocolate.

And those eyes...

Silver. No, maybe closer to the shade of burnished pewter. In the misty vestiges of his brain, she would beg him to take her as he played his hands over her small, supple breasts and down to the heavenly hot crease between her legs. Every intimate detail of her beautiful face was as clear as a new photograph in his mind. She possessed high cheekbones. Almost Asian. Exotic. Thin eyebrows feathered over those piercing eyes and round full lips glistened only a breath away from his mouth above a tiny cleft in her round chin.

She was sensual perfection—and a complete figment of his imagination. His cock hardened as he washed himself. Quinn jerked his fingers away from his lower body. He dropped the soap and inhaled the humid hot air of the shower to try and think his burgeoning hard-on away. Expelling a troubled sigh, he leaned one hand against the ceramic tile, tipped his head back to let the water run over his head—and almost won the battle. He couldn't get this last sexual episode to vanish from his mind.

Piano music. Whenever he made love to her in the dreams, the soft tinkling of ivory keys would drift around him, suffusing his body with the magical sound. Whenever he was pumping inside the mystical woman, the feel of her skin was just too real, too potent to disregard.

Quinn winced hard. The imagined sensation of her wet heat wrapped around his cock, sucking at him with each frantic glide was just too good to be true. It was more than a man could take.

He shut off the water and stepped onto the rust-colored mat covering the tile beside the shower. Grabbing a clean towel from a built-in shelf, he angrily shook it open and rubbed his hair until the dark strands were a mass of curls.

"This bullshit's got to stop," he murmured as he swiped the beads of water from his arms and legs, flung the towel over the edge of the vanity and headed back to his bed, not even stopping to don another set of clean boxers.

Once beneath the covers, he rose to an elbow, punched the fluffy softness beneath his head, and sank back onto the pillow. Drawing in a long breath, he forced himself to lie still. It was even a bigger struggle to try and keep his mind blank. Finally, he gave up because the mysterious vision of his dreams refused to leave.

"Great. Now she's hanging around when I'm wide awake…"

The erotic dreams were entirely crazy. It'd be different if Quinn hadn't had any sex over the last six months. He'd had plenty. Real sex with real women. In fact, he'd gone looking for it on a regular basis lately in an effort to expunge the silver-eyed vixen from his mind. He'd hoped that pounding senselessly into some other woman's body would be the answer to these sporadic bouts of wet dreams.

It wasn't working.

He flopped onto his stomach, angrily punched the pillow one more time, and buried his head into the fluffy softness.

Chapter Two

∞

Calli's eyes fluttered open to the early morning sunlight that streamed through her living room window. Dazed and confused, she dragged herself upright and shook her arm to rid it of the tingling numb sensation. Still squinting with the fuzziness of deep slumber, she glanced down as she swiped the curtain of hair from her face.

Her lips parted. She was stark naked. Again. Her clothes from the night before lay in a heap beside the piano bench. The time spent within Raine's arms flooded her brain.

"Oh, god... Raine..." she murmured as her eyes welled with tears. She crawled across the carpeted floor to where his once-prized violin perched within a gilded iron stand beside the piano. The violin was—had been—his pride and joy and an instrument that he had retired shortly after purchasing. With a trembling hand, she reached out through the iron bars to stroke the burnished mahogany of the violin's belly.

Her fingers moved to the delicate strings, across the ebony fingerboard, then followed the cool outer curved edge of the instrument, her teeth biting into the flesh of her bottom lip to stifle a small gasp of lonely pain. A Dutch manufacturer had crafted the hand-fashioned instrument especially for Raine three years earlier. She could almost hear his deep voice telling her how he'd always thought the outline of the violin reminded him of the sensuous dips of a woman's body—her body. Because of it, a carved wooden likeness of Calli's face decorated the neck.

An instant lump of overwhelming sadness tightened her throat. The magic of their music had always bound them.

Calli forced her gaze away, scooped up her wrinkled clothes and clutched them tightly against her chest. She detested the limbo his death had tossed her into. Her lids drifted closed. Last night the music had once more crossed the imperceptible line of her sanity and brought them together. It was something that had started months after the funeral, but Calli was unsure if she should believe that the evening had really transpired or not. The night before, she had desperately wanted Raine to come to her when she played the music, or at least experience again the touch of his body against hers.

She shook her head. His lovemaking had been so vivid and had helped to erase her loneliness if only for a short time.

Brushing her knuckles softly across the violin one more time, she forced herself to her feet and trudged up the curving staircase to the second floor. Once inside what used to be both her and Raine's master suite, she tossed her clothes onto a chair and hurried to the shower.

Her motions were automated as she flipped on the faucet and waited for the water's temperature to adjust. She purposely kept her mind blank until she stepped into the spray and the hot water pelted against her skin. Only then did she return to thoughts of the past and how they'd met four years earlier at the Sanders Theater in Boston.

A sad smile curved her mouth as she remembered the first time she'd seen him…

It just so happened that they both had walked through the doors of the institution to audition for the Boston Philharmonic on the same day. Since their appointments were scheduled so close to one another, they'd waited together for their individual interviews. By the time his name had been called, she'd already fallen half in love with his deep voice, his sexy brown eyes, which were pierced with flecks of gold, and his quiet, comfortable demeanor. The hardest thing she'd ever done was to leave the empty chair beside her a few minutes later and follow the concierge when it was time for her audition. What she'd really wanted to do was to wait for him to appear once more through the double doors at the other end of the room.

Calli had hit the mark that day during her audition and was immediately offered a position within the orchestra. She had played the piano beautifully despite a part of her mind that lingered on the earlier conversation with a dark-haired man named Raine Lemont, hoping that they'd both be offered a chair so she might see him again. Once the interview committee had given her their decision, she had thanked the panel, gathered her purse and left the audition room in a flurry of panic. To her elated surprise, Raine waited for her just outside, also ecstatic with the news that he'd made the cut.

That was the beginning. Only one week had passed before they'd found themselves caught up in the wondrous aura of the Philharmonic, both doing the one thing they'd always dreamed about. Those first weeks of practice, Raine was situated across the stage, but in a spot that gave her an unobstructed view from where she sat at the piano. As she'd played, she'd watched the flow of emotions cross his rugged features. His violin was like an extension of himself, drawing the depth of sadness one second from the notes on the page before him, and then instantly switching to a lighthearted melody of rapture, mesmerizing and hauntingly exquisite.

And that was how he'd always made love to her.

Calli ran the soap over the length of one arm, ducked her head beneath the stinging spray, and finally found the nerve to delve deeper into her thoughts.

They had known each other a little less than a month before the first magical explosion of the lust that simmered between them. After countless lunches, practice days spent together at the institute, and long, late suppers after a performance, he'd seen her to her apartment one night, reached up and taken the key from her hand, and kissed her while he'd unlocked the door.

A small pain pierced her heart when she thought about that first night in his arms. There had been no discussion, no preamble to the torrid sex they'd shared. They hadn't even made it to the bedroom. Once Raine had started to kiss her, she'd somehow found herself inside her apartment still locked within his embrace. As he'd stripped the clothes from her body, his mouth had worshipped her skin as each inch became bared to his gaze. They had sunk to the floor and made hot passionate love. He'd done things to her body that no one else ever had and coaxed a song from her heart with the sensual world he'd only begun to introduce her to. Raine had quickly become the heady drug she couldn't live without.

That was the night he'd first called her his blossom. Calli was a perfectly unique combination of two heritages. Her American father had met her mother during the Vietnam War. Calli was Eurasian, possessing lighter hair and gray eyes from her father, but the high curve of her cheekbones below rounded eyes, honeyed skin, and a petite stature would always be her mother's traits, lending an enchanting, exotic look. Raine had always said that Calli reminded him of a delicate hothouse blossom.

They were married six months later. Purchasing a home in an upscale neighborhood, they had lived a fantasy life of love and had gained prosperity by opening a private music studio for wealthy students who clamored to their doors.

Her slender fingers covered her face as she turned her cheeks upward. They'd had four wonderful years together, days of playing their music. And at night? Their bodies had become living instruments of sexual pleasure that had left them even more breathless after every encounter.

That was until the phone had rung one evening to let Raine know that the special gift he'd ordered for her was ready to be picked up. He'd left with a promise in his gold-flecked eyes and a fervent kiss against her lips that he wouldn't be long.

Calli had never seen him alive again.

She turned off the water and stepped onto a thick bath mat, steeling herself to relive that horrible night. She remembered how she'd constantly checked the clock, finding it odd that Raine hadn't returned home—especially after assuring her he'd only be an hour or so. As each hour had passed and the clock had finally struck ten, Calli hadn't known if she should be angry or worried with his delay. She'd played the piano and worked on a piece she'd been composing when the doorbell had finally rung at ten-thirty. With a smile, she'd jumped up thinking that he'd left his keys and couldn't get in. Instead, two burly detectives filled her doorway, introduced themselves, and asked if she was Mrs. Raine Lemont.

Even now with just the memory, Calli again experienced the same sick thread of trepidation that had curled in her belly that night like a snake waiting to strike, the same unexplainable fear she'd felt when she'd lifted a shaking hand to her heart and responded that yes, she was the person the detectives were looking for.

The rest was a blur...days of reeling in the abject grief of a horrible nightmare. Raine had been in a fatal car accident on his way home, driven off the road to avoid a head-on collision. Witnesses had watched a van leave the scene and disappear into the night. The police had tracked the vehicle only to discover that it had been stolen weeks earlier. The case had been closed only days after the funeral.

Even though thick steam still rolled around her head, a shiver raced across her flesh.

The funeral.

Somehow she'd survived that horrible day with the help of her parents and many friends. Upon returning home, however, she had been plunged into yet another nightmare. Nothing seemed out of the ordinary when her father had pulled his car into Calli's driveway. A few close friends had followed. They'd walked up onto the porch and when she'd slipped the key into the front lock, to her surprise the door had swung open.

What met their eyes seconds later was a house in total disarray. Personal articles had been strewn about. Every drawer to every cabinet had been flung open and the contents emptied. Her buttery-soft leather divan and two chairs had been overturned, the chair's cushions lying haphazardly on the floor. The same chaos had extended throughout the entire house. Someone had broken in and turned her home upside down. The police were called and hours later it had been determined that nothing had been stolen, but someone had definitely searched for something specific. It had taken days to clean the mess and even longer before Calli had found the courage to leave the safe haven of her parents' home to move back into the sprawling house, much to their dismay, even though a state-of-the-art security system had been installed.

That first night back inside the lonely walls and alone with her grief, she had been driven to her piano to fill the house with sound, anything to get through her fear of being alone. Every evening after had been the same.

Calli donned a terry robe and headed for her bedroom as she toweled her thick hair. Sinking to a window seat, she stared out into the blustery night, unable to do anything but return to the past.

Finally, she had returned to Sanders and her commitment to the Philharmonic. To date, she hadn't resumed the private lessons. Months had passed and then one late night at the end of summer, a ghostly apparition that defied logic had appeared as she'd pounded out her grief upon the piano. At first, the touch of his fingers against her arm had raised goose bumps. At the time, she'd been convinced that the sensation of his touch was born from a tremendous imagined longing to have him by her side. But when she'd looked up it wasn't dead space she'd seen but, instead, his handsome features smiling down.

He'd taken her hand and pulled her into his arms. She'd been in such a state of shock since his untimely death that her numb mind had refused to register the impossibility of his presence. When she'd awakened on the floor the following morning, the first thing that had gone through her mind had been that his death had taken a complete toll on her sanity. A month later, however, it had happened again under the same conditions. He only appeared when she played the piano, but not at every instance. Some nights she had played for hours, praying and pleading to no avail, only to crawl into her bed alone and crazed with despair.

Calli shook her head, took a deep breath to rid herself of the sick feeling that had resided inside her for the last year, and left the window seat wondering if her life would ever move forward.

Chapter Three

ဢ

Quinn stomped up the steps of Precinct Six as the cold winds of March plucked at his jacket and whipped his wavy dark hair around his head. Yanking open the door, he marched across the foyer and down the hallway past the many offices of the Boston Police Department.

His hurried flight, tight jaw and squared shoulders caused more than one brow to rise, because Quinn didn't offer his usual morning platitudes or nod of the head.

He ducked into his office and sailed his coat across a cheap plastic chair before rounding the corner of his desk, still finding it difficult to believe that once again he had physically reacted to a mere vision in his dreams like a high school boy. Flopping down into his chair, he stared at a pile of paper. With a disgruntled sigh, he scooped up the first sheet and started his day. It was difficult at best, because every time his instinctive armor fell, his haunted thoughts traveled back to soft strands of chocolate and silvery eyes.

Danny Briggs, his best friend and partner on the force, sauntered by a few minutes later and lingered in the doorway. Quinn cast a cursory glance upward from where he sat flipping through the pile and immediately returned his attention back to the disorderly stack, still battling to keep his attention where it needed to be.

Danny leaned against the doorjamb and studied his friend. "I thought you were going home last night."

Quinn continued to shuffle papers. "I did."

His friend snorted. "Liar."

Danny's response made Quinn glance up again. "What's that supposed to mean?"

"Have you looked in the mirror? You look like you were on an all-night bender. Bags under your eyes, which by the way are pretty bloodshot." He tipped back his head and studied Quinn for a second through narrowed eyes. "So, spill your guts, partner. I was a good boy and went home to my wife and kids. Who'd you end up with?"

Quinn rolled his eyes. "Always trying to live life vicariously through me, aren't you. I'd exchange mine with yours in a minute."

A deep chuckle rumbled in Danny's chest. He strolled into the office and flopped into a chair that faced Quinn. "What? You'd rather be changing dirty diapers, going to grade school plays and spending entire nights awake with screaming kids?"

Quinn leaned back, pursed his lips and shook his head. "You don't fool anyone. Everything you just listed is what makes you get up in the morning. Every time Maggie pops out another kid you're like a fuckin' peacock around here and talking about the next pregnancy." He glanced up at the ceiling—one that needed a paint job—and squinted. "Let's see. It's been…a little over a year since Danny Junior was born. Wouldn't by any chance have some news for me, would you?" He watched incredulously as the smile spread across his partner's face and it dawned on him why. "Jesus Christ, Maggie's pregnant again, isn't she?"

"What can I say?" Danny replied with a wide grin. "Maggie's from a strict Catholic family. I was just coming in to tell you."

"Well, congratulations—again." Quinn straightened in the chair, picked up a pencil and scribbled a note on the paper in front of him. "Although, I don't think Maggie's religious persuasion is the only reason she keeps popping out babies. You two are on each other constantly."

Danny ignored his comment and pressed on. "Well, come on, stud. Fill me in on the details. I'm not letting you out of this office until you do. Got a little hot ass last night, didn't you?"

Now it was Quinn's turn to snort. "It seems to me you're getting a lot more ass than I'll ever see. Like I said. I wasn't with anyone. I went home." *And made love to a figment of my imagination...*

"So why do you look like hell?"

Quinn shook his head and tossed the pencil to the desk, knowing he wasn't going to get anything done as long as Danny lounged in the chair across from him. "Christ, you're not gonna let it go, are you? Did you learn that trait from your kids?" He watched his partner's goofy smile widen as the man fished around inside his pocket, pulled out a cigarette and lit it.

"You know you're not supposed to be smoking in here," Quinn warned.

"Can't do it at home. Maggie has a fit if I even smoke outside on the porch. So, until some asshole around here calls me on the carpet, I say fuck the rules."

"You're taking seven years off your life with that habit," Quinn returned.

Danny merely shrugged. "Yeah? Well, those last seven suck anyway so I may as well enjoy myself now." He blew a stream of white across the room, totally unconcerned with a possible reprimand. "By the way. You can run, but you can't hide. Eventually you'll tell me who you were with. But for now, I suppose it's back to business. McMartin called a meeting in fifteen minutes in the conference room."

"Something coming down?"

"Got a great lead on a shipment of cocaine supposedly coming through North Rail Station of all things."

Quinn tensed. "The rail depot?"

"This is a big one, Quinn. Those bastards are bypassing the Mexican border, floating the shit in with illegal aliens under darkness, and landing on the San Padre beaches. The IA's either bury it in the dunes for future pickup or haul the stuff inland. The Texas DEA has been after this specific cartel for sixteen months. Their mole also discovered how the organization smuggles the shit across the country. Apparently, coke is packed into drinking straws, and then the straws are wedged into the spaces of corrugated cardboard boxes. And I'm not talking a shoebox full. They've got a regular manufacturing plant in an as-yet-undetermined location in Texas. Shit, we're looking at close to two million in street market value—and that's just this one shipment. Supposedly these bastards are shipping across the States every other day."

Quinn shook his head disgustedly. He and Danny worked for the Department of Drug Enforcement in Boston. As the war on illegal drugs escalated year after year, new ways to smuggle drugs into the United States also progressed. It was always the same. As they fought against current suppliers of illicit drugs and made headway, someone was always waiting in the wings. Quinn didn't care to dwell on the many horrific things he'd seen and experienced because of the Colombian pipeline of cocaine that never ceased to spill across borders into Mexico, then on into the States.

He shuffled the papers into a stack and stood. "They always discover a new venue, don't they? Well, let's go hear what McMartin's got."

Danny stood and joined his partner as they headed for the conference room.

* * * * *

Calli parked her car, gathered her purse and briefcase, then raced up the steps of the Sanders Theater. When the automatic door opened, the melodic strains of Stravinsky's Symphony in No. 1 E Flat met her ears.

"Damn," she muttered as she hurried across the marble floors with a quick nod to the receptionist sitting behind a glass enclosure. She was late. Rehearsal had already started. As she rushed through the open double doors into the theater proper, she hoped Maestro James wouldn't take her to task. The Philharmonic orchestra was a mixture of professionals, amateurs, and interning students. Since Calli was already an established paid performer within the group, she knew she wasn't setting a very good example by being extremely late. But she'd lost track of time earlier when she had returned to the window seat to rethink the night before.

She quickly tossed her belongings onto a chair, shrugged off her heavy coat, and rushed up the side steps to the stage with her sheet music clutched in her hands. She didn't even have to glance to her left to know what was happening. The feel of the maestro's eyes boring into her as she seated herself on the piano bench and settled the music in front of her made her wince. Listening intently to the familiar music around her, it was only a matter of moments until her fingers began to move.

At the end of the composition when the hollow beat of the tympani echoed across the hall, she lifted her gaze and cringed inwardly at a pair of angry eyes.

"How wonderful that you could join us today, Mrs. Lemont. Sleep in, did we?"

Calli wet her lips. "Sorry, Maestro James. It won't happen again."

"I should hope not. We have a performance in less than three weeks." Tapping his baton against the stand before him, the maestro glanced around. "We will go over that composition again — this time with our pianist in attendance for the entire opus. How fortunate we are."

Heat suffused Calli's cheeks with the man's pointed comment. She watched his hand and commenced playing on the second downswing. Soon though, as she was drawn into the beauty of the melody, she let her mind empty of everything except the music. Her body swayed, her fingers danced across the ivory keys, and for the next two hours she set aside her pain and anguish of the last year.

When the rehearsal concluded, Calli strolled with a few orchestra members off the stage, agreeing to go for a late lunch before returning home. Stuffing her music into her case, she gathered her purse and coat and waited for the group of women to do the same. Once they were ready, the small entourage headed for the outer hall.

Calli was just slipping on her coat when the receptionist's door opened and the elderly woman stepped out.

"Mrs. Lemont?"

Calli glanced over her shoulder. "Yes?"

"There's someone here to see you."

"To see me?"

"Yes, ma'am. I asked your…um…visitor to remain in my waiting room until I saw you come out of the theater."

"Oh, okay," Calli responded and then turned to her friends. "Why don't you all go on and I'll catch up shortly." Once the group decided where to meet, she turned back to the receptionist. "Thank you for taking care of my visitor. There wasn't any need to put him in your office waiting room, however. That was very nice of you."

The receptionist stepped up to follow Calli. "Well, you see, Mrs. Lemont. I just wasn't sure we really wanted this person hanging around in the outer hall. And your visitor is a woman, not a man."

"A woman? Did she give a name?"

The receptionist wrung her hands. "Well, at first she wasn't looking for you. She came up to the window and asked for…for your husband. She was looking for Mr. Lemont."

At the sound of her dead husband's name, Calli's stomach did a quick roll. Somewhere in the back of her mind, she wondered if she'd always have that initial reaction of feeling sick whenever someone spoke Raine's name aloud.

"I didn't tell her, ma'am, that Mr. Lemont di— That he's no longer with us. I didn't know what else to do so I told her that you were here. She really wants to speak with you."

"That's very strange. Well, I'll go in and see what she wants."

"Mrs. Lemont…there's one more thing. This woman is…" The receptionist wrung her hands again. "Well, I'm not one to point fingers, but I put her in the back office because she's rather unkempt. I was afraid Security would escort her out because she looks like…like a vagrant."

Calli's step faltered momentarily. Why on Earth would someone like that be asking to see her husband? Apparently some sort of stranger because the woman had no clue that Raine had been dead for nearly a year. "Thank you. You did the right thing. I'll go check this out."

As Calli strode once more toward the office, the receptionist called out a final time. "Mrs. Lemont. Just so you know, Charlie from security is on the floor if you should need him."

Calli wasn't sure if she even wanted to open the door after the woman's statement, but she took a big breath and turned the knob. Nothing could have prepared her for what was waiting inside.

An unpleasant odor, one that resembled cooked cabbage mixed with the mustiness of old clothes, assailed her senses. An older woman sat hunched on the edge of a chair, her scraggly gray hair pulled back into a jumbled knot. She wore no makeup on her sunken eyelids or lipstick to color her pale lips. Her shoddy coat's hem was ripped and hanging and missing one button on the lapel. When Calli's visitor glanced up, something akin to fear and surprise blazed momentarily in her dull eyes.

Calli was going to close the door, but thought twice about it. Instead, she only swung it halfway shut. Hesitantly, she turned back to face the woman. "Hello. My name is Calli Lemont. The receptionist said you were looking for Raine?"

The woman swiped the back of her hand across her nose. "You his wife?"

"Yes, I am." She was, wasn't she? Just because Raine was gone didn't mean that she wasn't still married to him, did it? Calli mentally shook her head and focused on the stranger.

"Do you think you could tell me where he is?" The woman's eyes suddenly blazed hopefully. "I'd like to talk to him."

Calli seated herself in a chair on the opposite side of the room. "You haven't told me your name. Why don't we take care of that and then we'll get to other details." She smiled gently, wanting to set the disheveled woman at ease.

"Um, yeah, where are my manners. Name's Jenny. Jenny Johnson." She fiddled uncomfortably with the worn lapels of her coat.

"Well, Jenny Johnson, is there a reason you were looking for Raine?"

Jenny's hand dropped limply to her lap. Her bloodshot gaze darted about the office as she swallowed. Sudden indecision glowed in her eyes. Nervously, she fiddled with a loose button. Finally, she brought her gaze back to Calli.

"I... I just needed to see him. Maybe I'll just come back another time..." She started to rise from the chair.

Calli wasn't about to let her go anywhere until she discovered an answer to her silent question. Why would someone like Jenny be looking for Raine?

"He won't be here if you come back." She steeled herself to say the words aloud. "Raine...my husband...was killed in a car accident nearly a year ago."

Jenny's body instantly sagged into the chair as if someone had punched her, her ashen cheeks making her round, lifeless eyes appear larger. Calli was amazed when the woman's hands began to shake. Her news had affected the woman deeply.

My god, what is the connection?

"Did you know Raine at one time? I don't recall him ever saying he knew someone named Jenny Johnson."

Jenny straightened with a trembling hand smoothing the thinning gray hair at her temple. Carefully, she used slender fingers to tuck errant strands behind her ear, the movement baring her slender neck to Calli's gaze for a quick instant as her coat gaped open. The gesture, for some odd reason, reminded Calli of a dainty butterfly flitting from one flower to the next, a strange vision in light of the woman's present state.

Jenny's head wagged slowly as she batted away the sudden tears in her eyes. "I knew Raine a long time ago. A long..." Her words trailed to nothing. "Those people said I could find him here. But he's dead. How come they didn't know that?" Her eyes closed and her body swayed slightly in reaction to the news. "All this time and now...he's dead."

Calli had to lean forward to hear the woman's whispered lament. "How did you know him? You really need to tell me." She watched Jenny's slender fingers tipped with dirty, chipped nails, crawl up her face in slow motion as a small moan left her chapped lips. Rising from her chair while ignoring the malodorous aroma that surrounded the upset woman, Calli reached out to gently clasp her thin shoulder. "Ms. Johnson...Jenny...please, can you tell me why you're so troubled? How did you know Raine?"

The distressed woman's hands finally left her face, giving Calli a clear view of the utter pain and remorse burning in Jenny's eyes.

"Because...because he was my son..."

Calli's hand flinched with the shocking revelation. Impossible. Her lips parted, but no words would come. Her head swam as she sank weakly to an empty chair beside Jenny's quaking body.

Raine's mother? Calli knew Raine's mother, and it definitely wasn't the woman crying quietly beside her. But even as she refused to believe the possibility, her eyes found the partially opened door. The receptionist was just outside.

Calli rose shakily, crossed to the door and peeked out to see the theater's security guard talking inaudibly with the woman behind the desk. They both turned their heads in her direction. Calli forced a smile to her lips. "I'm just going to close the door for a little bit. Everything is fine." Before either could say anything, Calli clicked it shut.

She steeled herself to turn and face Jenny. The woman blew her nose into a piece of ragged paper towel she'd just dragged from a torn pocket. Calli took a deep breath. "Why do you think Raine was your son?"

Jenny wadded the paper in her palms before she glanced up again. "I don't think. I know. Because I gave birth to him. Raine was born twenty-nine years ago. August twenty-third. I gave him up for adoption."

Calli's hand swept up to rest against her chest momentarily before she could find her voice again. Jenny had nailed Raine's birthday—and his age. Feeling nauseous, she cleared her throat and crossed the room to sit. If what the woman stated was true, Raine had died without the knowledge.

"Mrs. Johnson...Jenny. You have to understand that this is a little hard to digest and even more difficult to believe. Raine was an only child. His parents never said anything. Who told you that you could find him here?"

Jenny swiped at her nose with her coat sleeve before she answered. "The people from the agency. The people that stole him from me. I—I wasn't married. Only sixteen."

As she spoke, Calli quickly calculated her age. Forty-five? Unimaginable. The woman, in her bedraggled state, didn't look a day under sixty. Lines etched deeply into the mottled skin around her eyes and mouth. Gray, scraggly strands of hair stuck to her wrinkled forehead.

"My ma and pa didn't have a lot of money. They were embarrassed that I got pregnant. Insisted that I give up my...that I give up my baby. I didn't know anything then. I had no say anyway. I was so sick I could hardly get my head off a pillow."

"Sick?" Calli asked.

Jenny nodded. "Sick with fever and something I couldn't understand. They took my son by caesarean. I said I'd never forgive my ma and pa for letting the agency have their way with my…" She used the edge of her scarf to swipe at a tear as her head shook. "Two years later, I was set to marry a boy I'd met working at a café. I told my pa he'd never see me again, that I'd never bring shame on his or my ma's head, because I'd be gone. Oh, he was mad at me. I told him to hell with you. Just to hell with you. It's the first time I ever swore at him. I said I'm leaving the dump I lived in for better things. Me and my Eddie were gonna have babies and be happy living in a nice house. I was going to make my life right. My old man just started to laugh at me. That's when he told me I was so sick for so long because the doctor that birthed me also gave me a hysterectomy. My pa was gonna make damn sure I never had another baby." Jenny's chin lolled against her chest as she struggled with the past. "Looks like I still don't know anything exceptin' that after all these years, I needed to see what kind of man my baby became. Before I die, I wanted to talk to him. Tell him it was a good thing to be raised by fine people instead of someone like me. I could love him, but I couldn't give him anything else." Hesitantly, she raised her watery eyes.

Calli sat in a state of stunned shock, silent and pale.

"I couldn't take care of no kid…neither could my parents. So I hounded those agency people once me and Eddie got on our feet. They wouldn't tell me nothing, not where my baby was, nothing. I kept going back for years, but they refused. I just decided over the last year that I had to know. When no one would talk to me, I started spending days sitting on the bench outside their door. One day not long ago when it was raining, I got up and headed back to the place where I stay. I don't have a house. I stay at a shelter when it's winter."

Good god, she's homeless. Where is Eddie?

"That night, a young lady who worked at the agency came there and found me. Said I could come here and ask for Raine Lemont. Said he had my eyes because she met him a few years back after a concert. That's all she said because she could get fired if anyone knew she told me that much."

Calli studied her more closely than of a moment before, trying to discover Raine within her features. Looking past the red rim of Jenny's eyelids, she suddenly found the same color eyes as her husband's. Deep brown with flecks of shimmering gold.

Calli nearly quit breathing. Up to now, she hadn't even noticed them. Memories of Raine's eyes shining down at her tore at her heart. She used to tell Raine that his eyes were powdered with gold fairy dust…

A wave of nausea washed through her stomach. She had to get home. She had to contact Raine's parents and ask them if what Jenny touted was true.

Her breath hitched in her throat. No, she couldn't, could she? What good would it do now to cause them even more agony? They'd aged horribly since Raine's death. In fact his mother, Margaret, was just starting to rejoin the living after suffering a nervous breakdown. Calli rubbed her forehead. To approach Margaret now would only cause her more heartache and send her deeper into the tailspin of grief. She had to wait until her own shock wore off and then make some sort of decision. After all, Raine was dead.

But is he? Is he really when someone, a ghost perhaps, comes to me at night?

His parents must have had their reasons for never letting the truth out. That is, if what Jenny said was true.

Calli's head began to pound. She glanced up when Jenny dragged herself out of the chair. "Where are you going?"

The woman shrugged dejectedly. "Back to the shelter. He might have died a year ago. But to me?" She shook her head. "It's been only minutes." Her whispered response floated on the air when she turned and trudged toward the door.

"Wait! Don't go." Calli leapt up. "At least give me the address of where you and Eddie are staying."

Jenny swiped at a tear. "There ain't no Eddie anymore," she said while still shaking her head. Finally, she met Calli's eyes.

"Why would you care where I live? What would a lady like you want with me?"

The look on Jenny's face was one of total defeat.

"I... You just can't drop the information you did and then leave."

Jenny shrugged. "I got things I gotta do." She turned away again. Her waif-like body trembled beneath the ragged coat.

"Wait!" Calli grabbed her purse from a table. "Wait. Let me give you something." She dug inside the bag and yanked out her wallet. If Jenny was Raine's mother—and even if she wasn't—Calli had plenty of money. The other woman looked like she had absolutely nothing. "Take this." She grabbed Jenny's rough-skinned hand and shoved a fifty-dollar bill into it.

Jenny's mouth gaped open. "You're giving me money?"

Calli's head nodded. "Yes. Take it and...and buy anything you like with it. Please, could you tell me where I could find you if I needed to?"

"Why would you need to?"

"Just because. Just because you're Raine's mother. Please." Calli still didn't know quite what to think, but she wasn't going to let Jenny walk away, never to be seen again. She held her breath, then sighed. "Please?"

The other woman's features finally softened slightly. "I'm at the women's shelter on Fourth and Fifty-Seventh."

Callie nodded. "Okay. Thank you. Do...do you need a ride?" Putting a complete stranger in her car was something she wouldn't have even thought about an hour ago. But now? For some reason, she didn't fear Jenny. "I could drop you off."

"No...that's not necessary. I got a city bus pass." Jenny folded the paper bill carefully and tucked it inside her coat pocket. "Thank you for the money." Without another word, she turned, opened the door and walked out of the office.

Chapter Four

ജ

That same night, Quinn eased his long length out from behind the wheel of his car. Glancing across the yard at Danny's house, he reached back in to grab a bottle of wine from the seat. At first he hadn't wanted to accept the Briggs' invitation to supper, but as he slammed the door, he was glad he'd changed his mind. It had been a long week at work. And spending an evening with Danny and his family would get his mind off the recurring nightly bouts with the silver-eyed vision, which were quickly overtaking his days, too. He stepped onto the covered porch, readjusted the bottle and rapped his knuckles against the front door.

The commotion from the interior of the house only intensified as the door swung open. Danny welcomed Quinn with his grinning daughters, Maria — perched on his shoulders — and Deena, who had her arms and legs wrapped tightly around her father's shin.

"Hey!" Danny chuckled. "It's a about time! The kids just about drove me and Maggie nuts when they found out you were coming."

Maria clutched her father's head with chubby fingers and leaned to the side. "Hi, Uncle Quinn! Did you bring us a treat?" Her dark brown eyes blinked as she waited.

Danny peeked between his daughter's splayed fingers. "Maria! Can't you at least wait until he's in the door?" Danny stepped back, dragging Deena along with him. "Hey, Quinn. Take this one off my leg and I promise to get you a beer. Supper's a little behind schedule — as usual."

Tucking the bottle of wine into his jacket pocket, Quinn bent and plucked Deena's fingers one by one from his partner's shin until he'd loosened her grip. He chuckled when the little dark-haired girl screeched in delight as he hoisted her onto one shoulder, and then followed Danny into the kitchen. The smell of garlic permeated the air as did the smell of warm fresh bread. Danny Jr. sat in his highchair munching on a cracker. When he saw Quinn, his legs began to kick and his crumb-covered mouth widened with glee.

Maggie glanced up as she measured pasta into a pan of boiling water. Her dark eyes twinkled in welcome. "Hi, Quinn! Supper won't be too long. Every time I plan to eat at a certain time, things go haywire. It's been hectic around here. Danny, get Quinn a beer, would you?"

Her husband strolled behind her, his hand trailing across the curve of his wife's ass as he passed by. "Already on my way there."

Maggie flashed him a look that completely floored Quinn — even though he'd seen it pass between the couple a thousand times. It was a look that gave him the impression of a woman totally and completely in love, a warm lingering glow and one that belonged more in the bedroom than over a pot of boiling water. He was surprised how quickly his mind jumped to a vision of silver eyes glowing in just such a manner. With a mental shake of his head, he set Deena on a chair and plopped down beside the little girl.

Danny placed a beer in front of him a moment later, but it took a second for Quinn to get his bearings. Now the exotic image of his dream lover was invading his waking hours, and he could feel his cock stir against his zipper. He sucked in a big breath, letting the family atmosphere in the kitchen pull him back to the present.

"I hear congratulations are in order, Maggie."

A happy smile split her face as she stirred the noodles. "I'm so excited, Quinn. Although, with all the noise around here tonight, I did have a few qualms about the coming months."

Someone tugged on the sleeve of his jacket.

"Psst. Uncle Quinn. Did you bring a surprise?"

Quinn's gaze swung downward to meet Maria's round, inquiring eyes once more. "Have I ever forgotten?"

"No," the little girl giggled as she covered her mouth with chubby fingers.

Quinn smiled, reached into an inside jacket pocket and pulled out three candy bars. Digging in another pocket, he found a small package of animal crackers. "Here. The candy is for you and your sisters and the crackers for your brother. Why don't you put these on the counter until after, though? I think your mom wants you all to eat your supper first."

Maggie watched her daughter tramp to the counter with her loot, and then raised a slim eyebrow. "You spoil them rotten, Quinn."

He shrugged. "I enjoy them, Maggie. You've got a great bunch of kids."

Danny chuckled quietly as he swung a leg over a stool at the snack bar. "So, get some of your own, Quinn. In fact, I'll lend you mine any time you want. It would give me a chance to spend some time alone with their mother. And I know exactly what I'd do."

"Danny," Maggie admonished with a becoming flush. "Quinn's not even their real uncle, and there you are trying to pass off your kids. Although..." she stated as she set a bowl of salad on the table, "it would be nice to have a date with you— somewhere nice and quiet. You're always working lately."

"I wasn't thinking about somewhere nice and quiet," Danny teased.

Maggie headed back to the stove, but stopped to press a quick kiss against her husband's lips. Before she could get away, his hand snaked around her waist. She sighed and leaned into him as she glanced over her shoulder to assure her guest she wouldn't hold him to anything even though her words were for her husband. "No way would I do that to Quinn, though. If we tossed our four monkeys at him, we'd never see him at the altar."

Again, the feeling of sitting on the outside looking in flared in Quinn's blood. Danny and Maggie's love for each other brightened the room, and not because they worked at it. Their relationship was just like that. It would be easy for even a stranger to realize the deep commitment between the two of them. Quinn wondered if he'd ever find a partner and a love like the Briggs' had in one another. He sighed inwardly. First, he'd have to get rid of a haunting vision and find a living, breathing woman.

He was shocked out of his reverie when Deena stood on her chair and hung precariously in the air as she tried to jump across to him. Catching her, he then tucked the little girl into his lap. "Hey, I'll watch them anytime you want. Alexa can help me. Speaking of which, where is she tonight?"

Maggie removed Danny's hand from where it had slipped to her plump ass and wiggled out of his embrace. "She's upstairs practicing her lines for a spring play that her class is putting on. Lexi's going to be a daisy—big stuff for a second-grader. I'm sure you're going to get an invitation."

"Well, I'm sure I'll be there. Hey, why don't you two set a time and I can watch the—" Quinn's words were cut off when Deena sneezed. Evidence of her sneeze trailed down to her top lip in two thick strips. His stomach lurched at the sight, but he grabbed a napkin and wiped at the girl's nose and mouth. "How in the h— How do you two do this all the time?"

Danny burst out laughing, took a swig of his beer, and sauntered over to the table to take the napkin from Quinn's hand. "And you wonder why I drink and smoke. You should see what it's like some days. Thanks for the offer, but I think the teenager next door is better suited to babysitting. Once you have a couple of kids, then we'll talk." He tossed the napkin into the garbage, washed his hands, and opened a cabinet door. After pulling out a stack of plates, he yanked open a silverware drawer, grabbed a handful of forks, and headed for the table. When he began to distribute plates, his eyes met Quinn's.

"Since I had to leave early today, anything new on the coke case? Hey!" He made a grab and took away a fork from Deena before she poked Danny Jr. in the eye. "Goddammit, they're quick. Gotta keep an eye on them all the time. Deena! Sit down before you hurt yourself or your brother."

"Dammit, daddy!" the little girl squealed delightfully. "Dammit, sit!"

Maggie marched across the kitchen and set a bowl of meatballs none too gently on the table while sending her husband a querulous look at the same time. "Don't swear in front of the kids or you can go to the school and explain why they talk like a bunch of sailors."

Quinn hid his grin. It was always like this when he came to the Briggs' home. Organized turmoil, Danny called it. Better than organized crime. He watched Maggie head back to the stove, wondering how she managed the place and always appeared so unruffled. "Yeah, more news," he finally answered. "This cartel isn't only bringing in the shipment, they're planning to stay."

"Stay?" Danny questioned as he walked across the kitchen and stopped at the bottom of a narrow staircase. "What the hell for?" His hand shot up in front of him. "Wait. I want to hear the whole thing. Lexi! Come down and eat your supper!" he called up, then headed back. "Okay, now you've got my full attention."

"Well, it seems that a big shipment came through a year or so ago. We don't have an exact date, but the stuff was dispersed. And the money disappeared."

"Whoa, are you telling me that the bad guys are screwing each other?"

"Danny!" Maggie hissed. "Come on. Not in front of the kids."

"Ah," he waved with a snort. "They don't know what I'm talking about."

"Uh-huh," Maria piped up. "You ask mommy to screw all the time."

Maggie stopped dead in her tracks, raised her eyebrows and frowned at her husband. She lifted a warning finger and shoved it right under his nose. "You're going to the school. I refuse to do it when they call."

Danny winced before he leaned in his daughter's direction. "I ask Mommy all the time if she wants me to screw in a *light bulb*. That's what we're talking about."

Maggie looked heavenward, made the sign of the cross and shook her head.

Quinn was simply happy he didn't have any beer in his mouth when Maria had stated the obvious, or it would have sprayed all over Maggie's clean table.

* * * * *

Across town, Calli paced the length of her elegant living room, her eyes darting constantly to the darkening sky framed by a window. She sighed, switched on a lamp and sagged into a chair. Her fingers played with one dangling earring as she went over the conversation with Jenny Johnson for the hundredth time.

Raine's mother? Never in her wildest dreams would she have thought such a thing. More than once since she'd arrived home, she'd grabbed the phone to call his parents, but always ended up placing it back into the cradle.

Her fingers drummed the soft, buttery leather stretched over the arm of her chair. The entire situation was a nightmare. Her lids lowered as she pictured Jenny's eyes, and then her dead husband's.

Too similar to disregard the possibility. It didn't matter that Raine was a large man in comparison to his mother. He could very well have inherited his real father's stature.

Her thoughts drifted back to her husband's eyes once more, ones so different from his parents'. Another possible clue from the past. Margaret had blue eyes and Harold's were green. It was a family joke that somewhere in the past, an ancestor had possessed the eyes of a lion and Raine had inherited them.

Calli left the chair and refused to glance at the piano as she crossed the room to the kitchen. Switching on a light, she set about making a salad for her supper. Her mind roiled constantly about the fact that Raine could have been adopted. Then she would tell herself that it didn't matter. He was dead.

Her fingers clutched the counter's edge as she struggled against a shaft of pain. *But, he's still in my life!* How was she to ever move on if he continued to haunt her? Her eyes darted about the room in search of his ghostly figure. Was she really alone?

"Raine... You know the real answer, don't you? Are you here?"

She waited. Nothing. Absolutely nothing.

* * * * *

Calli shot up into a sitting position, her eyes darting about her darkened bedroom. She'd been dreaming about her wedding day, the quaint service with those she loved standing witness as she pledged her life to Raine.

Taking a settling breath now, she leapt from the bed and raced from the bedroom. Her feet padded down the carpeted steps as she headed for the living room, and then stopped short as her gaze fell upon the piano. Raine knew the truth.

Don't be foolish. He came last night...or you dreamed that he was here...it won't happen again...not so soon after...

Her hands flew up to cup her face. Calli almost screamed aloud with frustration. Finally, gaining a hold on her tumultuous emotions, she marched resolutely across the shadowed room, sat at the polished bench and stared at the keys. She would play. And if he didn't come to her, she would play again. He had never appeared twice within a twenty-four hour period, only weeks and weeks apart. But she didn't care. If she had some kind of connection with him, then she was going to demand his presence. It wasn't going to be Raine's choice tonight.

Closing her eyes and rolling her neck to loosen her muscles, she finally reached out. Her fingers skimmed across the ivory, coaxing a haunting melody until her body swayed and her nerves began to calm.

Thirty minutes later, Calli still played. Not a soft gentle touching of the keys, but a frenzied pounding, the sound leaping from inside the piano as picture frames vibrated on the polished surface of the baby grand. She wouldn't stop. She couldn't stop. Somewhere in the back of her mind, she knew she would dissolve into a fit of tears if she remained alone.

Her heart slammed against her ribs as a stringed note echoed in the room.

A finger trailed down her cheek.

Calli's body jerked and her fingers stumbled momentarily. Shivers raced across her skin. Her heart continued to hammer. The hair rose on her neck and arms as she squeezed her eyes closed, but she forced herself back into the melody, hardly daring to believe.

A warm masculine palm slid down the length of her arm and stilled one hand. Her smooth skin prickled beneath the fleeting touch.

Hoping beyond hope, her eyes fluttered open when her opposite hand came to a standstill. She stared down at his familiar fingers entwining themselves with hers.

"Raine…" she gasped out. Calli swiveled on the seat, seeing him through watery eyes. "Raine, you came." She leapt up into his embrace, loving the feel of his arms about her. As he played with the silky strands of the hair trailing down her back, she tightened her hold around his body. "Please don't leave me tonight. Please don't let me wake alone. I don't know how much more of this I can take. You're dead…and yet you're here." Swallowing the lump in her throat, she leaned back and stared up at his gentle smile. "Do you know what happened to me today?"

Raine simply continued to let his fingers drift through her hair. Silent. Always silent.

"A woman came to the theater to look for you. Raine, she believes she's your real mother. Did you know that? Did you ever know that? Why?" she whimpered achingly. "Why can't you talk to me? I need to hear your voice…"

The smile wilted from his lips as his gaze scurried across the high cheekbones and down to her full rose-colored mouth. His eyes lowered to her breasts. He reached out and began to loosen her blouse, one button at a time.

Calli's breath caught in her throat when his fingers slipped beneath the silk and parted the edges. Raine languorously dragged one fingertip along the exposed skin above the lacy border of her bra. Her nipples tingled with anticipation, ached horribly as she forgot anything but his sweet touch. The pressure of her bra against her skin disappeared when he flicked open the catch between her breasts. Cool air rushed across her hardened nipples. His hands cupped the firm roundness instantly.

Calli shrugged the blouse and bra from her shoulders as Raine continued to fondle her nipples and massage her breasts. She fought the urge to close her eyes and be lost within his touch when he bent his head and his lips covered one erect bud. Instead, her eyes drank in the soft wave of his hair as his tongue swirled gently, time and time again as she leaned into his demanding lips. Her knees trembled, her hands shook. Cream dripped from her cunt making her clench and unclench her sex as his hands slid to her waistband, the action fanning her desire to be fucked.

She could hardly breathe.

Raine.

Slipping to one knee, he drew her pants inch by inch over her hips and down her legs, leaving an all-consuming trail of heat wherever his knuckles grazed her goose-bumped skin, quickly building her need with his slow, drawn-out motions. Calli clutched his shoulders tightly as she stepped from the heap at her feet. Raine's hands danced a slow waltz up the length of her trim leg, around her hips to massage her bare ass cloaked in only a silky thong, and then back to her flat stomach.

Calli slowly expelled the air in her lungs as her head lolled back. So familiar. So wonderful to have his smooth fingertips coax her body to a delicious shiver of anticipation. When he hooked his fingers beneath the lacy strings at her hips, Calli was certain he would pull down the last piece of resistance and toss it away.

Instead, he hooked his fingers inside the thong and followed the line of lace over her hips to her crotch, teasing and scorching her skin wherever he touched until she shuddered violently with increased anticipation. Calli's head rolled forward as she reached down blindly to force his fingertips further inside her thong. Her legs were parted, her covered clit swollen and painfully throbbing for release. The fire swept through her blood as her pubic mound pitched forward. She had to have something hard and probing inside her. She had to be fucked. She wasn't so sure if only his fingers inside her slit would be enough to quench the passion she felt. She wanted his throbbing cock. But Raine only withdrew his hand from her clutching fingers and gently forced her to sit on the piano bench.

"What? What do you want? Don't do this to me. I need your cock in me. I want to be fucked. Please, Raine, please before you're gone… Maybe for the last time…"

He smiled as he forced her to lean back against the piano, then clasped her hips and pulled her lower body to the edge of the bench. Calli's elbows fell to the keyboard, producing a cluster of crazy notes as she balanced herself. Her mouth sagged open when he forced her knees wide and brushed his hand up her inner thigh. Only a small strip of lace lay between her painfully swollen clit and the tips of his fingers as he teased them against the material.

"Take them off, Raine. Please. Fuck me. Don't make me wait any longer. Please..." Her hips jerked when he slipped a finger inside her panties, using the back of it to brush her wet, swollen, feminine lips, purposely leaving her clit untouched. She waited on the edge of a precipice, waited for him to slip it inside her clenching sheath but, instead, Raine hooked his finger around the material and pulled it away from her pussy. The motion caused the thin strip of lace between her ass cheeks to tighten and grate against her anus. He continued the action and the pressure nearly drove her crazy. Her anal muscles throbbed against the force. When her hips began to jerk, Raine slid the material to the side to expose the full length of her feminine lips.

The uneven, pounding notes of the keyboard echoed around Calli's head as she grappled to stay on the bench by curling her hands over the ivory keys. The breath shot from her lungs when his fingers spread her lips wide. Her hips continued to sway forward, an instinctive urgency that she had no control over.

She watched in a trancelike state as his face drew closer between her thighs, his tongue curling over his lips as his flecked eyes locked with hers. Once again, he tantalizingly licked his upper lip to tease her.

"Please..." she whimpered. Her eyelids fell shut as she waited breathlessly for the touch of his mouth against her. Her cunt throbbed before him.

When the tip of his tongue traced its way through her wet slit, small uncontrollable shudders coursed through her belly. Calli couldn't spread her legs wide enough. She couldn't grind her clit against his mouth hard enough. She rocked forward in quick little jerks, feeling the flickers of an orgasm eating at her insides.

A thick finger slid past her entrance and buried itself as deeply as it could go. His teeth clamped over her clit.

Calli wanted to scream. She wanted to suck air into her lungs, but her throat tightened. She shuddered around his finger as she drew in one strangled breath after another. Raine clamped down harder on her clit, sending her orgasm to an even higher level of pain and pleasure. The waves rolled through her body, tightly constricting the muscles of her belly, swelling her small breasts, and sensitizing her clit further.

Raine slipped another finger into her, slid in as deep as he could go and pinned her spine against the piano as he sucked at her clit, drawing it deeper into his mouth.

It was only the breadth of Raine's shoulders that kept her thighs parted when he released her bud and lapped through her slit. She was weak and perspiring as the jolts of the orgasm lessened. Her body slipped downward as her arms weakened, but Raine caught her and kissed his way up over the silky skin of her abdomen, on to suckle a breast, and then to her mouth. He licked his way into the sweet cavern, sweeping across her tongue, urging Calli's to dance with his.

Her arms wrapped around his shoulders as she tilted her head and passionately met his seeking mouth, licking her own juices from his tongue. She was barely aware when he lifted her from the bench and carried her across the room. Setting her gently on the carpeted floor before the unlit fireplace, he carefully, but firmly rolled her to her belly.

Her eyes drifted shut as she listened, waiting to feel his hands upon her once more. The room was silent, but she knew he hadn't left her. The warm aura of his love cloaked her securely. The carpet was rough against her cheek and the air cool against her naked skin as the light sheen of perspiration dried.

Suddenly, his fingers were back, firmly grasping her hips. Raine guided her to her knees and pressed a palm between her thighs until she spread wide. When Calli tried to rise to her hands, gentle pressure between her shoulder blades settled her cheek back to the floor. Just knowing that she was spread for him, that her pussy was opened to his gaze sent a shaft of heat to her womb. She was ready again. The flame began to intensify once more. Her pussy throbbed between her legs.

Something brushed against her, the pressure slowly increasing until her silent mind screamed. Her body trembled. Was it a finger or the tip of his cock sliding through her slit? Ever so slowly—teasing and slipping easily through the slick wetness. Never entering, never pulsing inside her, only taunting her pink slit, stopping to roll against her clit, and then back through the line of her pussy. The moistened tip pressed against the entrance of her ass, a taunt of what was to come.

Calli's forehead rolled against the rough carpet. Raine had introduced her early on in their relationship to the joy and pleasure of being fucked in the ass, but in all the times he'd come back to her since the car accident, he'd never done it. And if he had? She wouldn't know because Calli had always fainted, and then awoken alone on the floor the following morning.

Her clit throbbed to the beat of her heart.

"Now, Raine. Fuck me again—now—before you're gone..." Her muffled voice scraped against the thick carpet.

The pressure increased. Only his cock could make her tunnel widen like that as he slipped the end of it into her tight, dark passageway. His fingers gripped her ass cheeks tighter as he stroked forward, filling her ass, stretching her open and making her cunt drip hotly.

"Oh, my god, Raine..." She surged back to force him deeper.

Raine's hand slipped between her legs in search of her sensitive bud. Flicking it twice, he then pinched it hard between his fingertips as he began to thrust with a quick steady tempo, holding her in place as he continually rammed her ass with staccato jerks.

Calli squeezed her anal muscles to suck his cock in further, needing to feel completely stretched tightly around the pounding shaft.

She exploded… Her clit throbbed against the tight pinch of his fingers, her muscles spasmed around Raine as he pumped hard…

Sparks of light flickered behind her closed eyelids, the sound of Raine's groin and balls slapping against her backside became muffled, as if she listened to it from beneath the water… She couldn't feel her legs or her arms, only the waves of heat that scorched through her blood…

* * * * *

Piano music swirled inside Quinn's head. His cock swelled, painfully throbbing between his legs. His fingers flinched as they wrapped around hips encased with warm burnished skin, more velvety than anything he'd ever caressed. He stared down at the wealth of straight chocolate strands that whipped across the center of a slim, feminine back.

It was her. Even though she knelt before him, her silver eyes hidden, he was certain. Just as he was certain that those eyes flashed, and then darkened by the second with sensual heat, turning to a deep color of pewter as he gently placed his palm between her shoulder blades and forcefully pressed her chest to the carpet.

The skin of his knees burned with the friction of the rough-napped carpet he knelt upon. Small beads of sweat trickled down his naked back. His eyes traveled down her spine, touched upon his hands, which clutched her surging hips, and moved to where her ass cheeks were spread wide in taunting acceptance. Incredulously, his cock slipped past the puckered hole. Inch by inch. The thick shaft of his penis disappeared as her ass stretched around it. Her body adjusted itself, the movements meant to suck him deeper.

His heart hammered in his chest. He'd never fucked a woman in the ass—had never found a sex partner who was interested in what he instinctively knew would be a passionate and pleasurable act.

She wanted him buried inside her. The silent thrusts backward, the quiet mewls from the back of her throat and the squeezing pressure was the way she let him know. She wanted him.

And only him.

He rocked his hips forward and was rewarded by the sensitizing squeeze of her quaking muscles and harsh pants that rent the air.

"Fuck me now before you're gone..."

Gone? He wasn't going anywhere. Not when her ass sucked at him forcefully, milking his shaft with a sexual plea to come hard.

He could feel the first flickers of heat flaring inside his groin. He didn't want to come until she joined him. He wanted her ass shuddering around him as he exploded inside her. Reaching down, his hand slipped between her legs and brushed against the smooth silkiness of one inner thigh, until he found her swollen clit. She was wet. Dripping hotter and wetter than he could have imagined.

And it was all because he was fucking her like she yearned to be fucked.

The tips of two fingers slipped through her wet folds in search of her clit. Swirling a fingertip around the throbbing little bud, he pinched it between two fingers, the act sending a shaft of pleasure through him when she started at his touch...and then moaned low in the back of her throat.

He was going to come and there was no stopping it. He stroked hard, his skin making contact with her ass and sounding as if he were spanking her. Perspiration rained down over his temples. His knees burned. His ass muscles clenched as he pumped wildly.

Suddenly, the deep shudder of orgasm rippled through her cunt. The muscles of her ass pulsed, squeezing his cock tightly until...

Quinn's groan preceded a shot of milky cum that was followed by stream after stream. His body emptied itself with a rhythmic flow.

His eyes snapped open as he gasped for air, his hips rocked upward as warmth filled his underwear, and his heart pounded in his ears. It was useless to fight it. Overwhelmed, he continued to pump against the material of his boxers, the image of her spread ass cheeks clear and sensual in his mind. He let himself go until the overpowering heat of orgasm slowed, allowing his hips to finally fall motionless against the cushions of the couch.

He sucked breath after sharp breath into his lungs as his eyes darted about his living room. The room was dark except for the sparkly glow of the television. The only noise was the heavy sound of his breathing and the near-muted sports announcer on the set. Quinn's right arm dropped limply over the edge of the cushion as he stared at the ceiling. It had happened again. Another quick flash of her bouncing ass wrapped around him made his cock jump slightly against his body. He flung the wrist of his left arm across his closed eyes and ground his teeth.

"Christ almighty…"

He stayed that way until the beating of his heart slowed to a near-normal tempo and his breath came easier. Disgustedly, he swung up to a sitting position, doing his best not to disturb the milky cream in his shorts. Other than a quick glance at the clock on the coffee table, he remained motionless. Twelve-thirty.

He'd left the Briggs' around nine o'clock, came home, flipped on a basketball game and hit the couch. He'd fallen asleep and, once more, the ghostly vixen had haunted his dreams. There was no doubt in his mind who it was. The color of her hair and the honey-colored hips were imprinted in his mind's eye for what would most likely be a lifetime.

And he'd fucked her in the ass. Something he'd never done with any woman.

Quinn raised his hands in front of him, clenched his fists, and then slowly wiggled his fingers as he stared down. He could still feel the satin of her skin as he held her hips in place. Just thinking about sliding into her tight ass caused an instant rise between his legs. What was going on? Quinn was proud of the fact that he was always so keen and in charge of his emotions.

Used to be. The hair rose on his arms. Now all he wanted to do was fall back into a deep slumber and fuck her again. Two nights in row the Aphrodite of his dreams had appeared—and along with her some of the best sex he'd ever experienced. His hand scrubbed over a stubbled jaw as his eyes closed. She was there, flitting at the edges of his mind. Her chocolate hair, the skin that looked like it was suntanned, and those strange haunting eyes.

Quinn swallowed back a sick feeling of aching desperation and gave in to the heady euphoria of having someone extraordinary in his life. She wasn't even a real woman, yet there was a special connection to her heart. Just because she wasn't physically in the room with him didn't mean a thing. He could feel the pulse of her blood pounding in unison with his. He could smell a perfume that was familiar, but a scent he'd never sniffed before.

Along with it, however, was something tangible and just out of his reach. Grief? A silent call for someone to take away her pain? Her undiscovered sadness permeated his soul. If he could, he would take her pain away, soothe her rattled emotions and bring a smile to her mouth. He wanted to protect her always. No matter the infrequent nightly bouts of adolescent longing—it hit him that his world was a little less sour because of the silver-eyed vision.

His eyes snapped open. What he'd just described to himself was akin to the emotions of love, or at least what he'd always thought it would feel like once he discovered it. Love? He shook his head. Was he falling in love with a phantom?

That discovery unnerved him more than the strange dreams did. It grabbed at him. How was it possible to love someone who wasn't even real?

"That's it…"

Scooting to the edge of the cushion, Quinn carefully rose and cringed when the cream in his shorts shifted and drizzled down one inner thigh. He headed for the shower, thanking his lucky stars that it was Saturday and he didn't have to work in the morning, because there was no way in hell he would chance another encounter with the haunting woman in his dreams and a glimpse into his own psyche by going back to sleep.

Chapter Five

⅏

Quinn shook his head to rid himself of the weariness he felt, pushed himself away from the desk in his home office and shoved the stack of papers he'd been studying into a folder. Flipping it shut, he rose and headed for another cup of coffee. As he passed by a mirror, he caught sight of the bags beneath his eyes and the tousled dark hair that made him look like he'd just awakened. A short derisive snort erupted from his throat. *Or on a bender as Danny would put it.* He looked so damn awful because he'd forced himself to stay awake after his last encounter with the mystic woman in his dreams.

After showering, and true to his late-night resolution, he'd worked for hours trying to put together the information he and the department had obtained in regard to the Colombian cartel. That alliance was heading toward Boston like a thunderstorm on the horizon, and if he and his colleagues didn't discover where the missing links were, there would be hell to pay. Gunfights, dead bodies showing up out of nowhere and innocent people being caught in the crossfire, plus the hundreds of thousands of dollars worth of coke on the Boston streets. There was no code of ethics as far as the drug lords were concerned. Everyone was fair game. The cartel's motive was simple. Whoever stood in the way of profit would be disposed of neatly, but not cleanly. The "white gold" was too precious a commodity. And when the suppliers couldn't find buyers for the expensive coke, they brought out the meth, the marijuana—it didn't matter. As long as sales continued and the cartel lined its pockets with the souls of addicts.

Quinn's unit had collected names. Lots of them. Some suspects were alive and some were dead. As he poured himself a mug of coffee, his eyes flicked to the calendar on the wall. Today was March twenty-third. To the best of the department's knowledge, it looked like everything would come down in thirteen days. Normally, the bosses who spawned the evil white dragon and manipulated the underground operation stayed worlds away. They let their henchmen handle any initiatives and let the translators set up the various networks that fed the pipeline from South American jungles to the streets of the United States, as they lounged in luxurious surroundings and watched their illegal coffers grow. Word had it, however, that Enrique Palacios, one of the biggest bosses in South America, was going to slither into the United States and oversee the recovery of the money that had disappeared a year earlier. Just his personal attention to the matter meant death and destruction. The man was only one arm of the insidious underworld of drug trafficking, but was portended as one of the most ruthless drug lords to come out of the jungles.

As he sipped at the coffee, Quinn continued to sift through the information. The official report stated that it wasn't apparent that last year's missing shipment had ever made it to the street. That was good, but the drugs were somewhere and eventually would find a way into the hands of the pushers and on to the addicts. In order to discover the whereabouts of the missing coke and keep future shipments from being dispersed, every departmental maneuver needed to be planned out to the tiniest detail.

April fifth. Thirteen days was not a whole hell of a lot of time when so many lives could be at stake and so many facts were still undiscovered.

* * * * *

Another hour passed as Quinn worked diligently, drawing up lists with names, matching dates, and trying to discover the common denominator between the cartel, his list of illegal aliens, and the known distributors within the United States. When the doorbell rang, he greeted the interruption with a fair amount of satisfaction. He needed a break from all the unconnected facts.

Grabbing his mug of stale coffee, he got up and headed into the living room. As he reached for the doorknob, the bell rang again.

"Yeah, yeah, I'm coming."

When the door swung open, he stared in total surprise at an older woman with graying hair. She stood huddled and shivering against a cold blast of wind. The gentlemen in Quinn wanted to usher her into the house, but detailing her appearance in his quick mind, he didn't think it was a smart thing to do.

The woman finally looked up. Her eyes bored into his before they darted across his features. The ragged scarf wrapped around her face drooped slightly, partially exposing her stunned expression.

"Can I help you?" Quinn asked as a streak of wariness in his gut raised the hair on the back of his neck.

Her fingers slowly reached up to completely remove the scarf from her mouth. She tucked it beneath her chin, her dry lips moving soundlessly as she continued to stare up through a misty haze. The blood drained from her cheeks.

This is all I need — some old woman fainting on my doorstep. "Ma'am? Ma'am, is everything all right?"

Finally she nodded.

"Yes… Yes, I think it is. I think everything's probably all right for the first time in a long time."

Quinn hadn't been sure what to expect, but her comment was as far from what he'd anticipated as it could be.

To hell with it… The woman shivered uncontrollably.

"Would you like to come in for a moment and warm up?" He stepped back and opened the door wider, wondering what the consequences would be for letting in someone who looked to be a vagrant.

She nodded and cautiously entered the house. Untying the scarf, her guarded gaze moved slowly around the interior of the masculine living room.

Quinn tried to place a possible age as he watched her closely. Her gray hair was laced sparsely with deep brown strands and pulled back in a messy knot at her crown. The skin around her eyes was heavily lined, yet he could still detect a flicker of youth shining from their depths. His eyes darted to her hands when she slipped off her thin gloves, revealing slender fingers with chipped nails. But her hands weren't the hands of an elderly person. Definitely not youthful, but no age spots of brown. Baffled, he was just about to ask her to sit for a moment when her next question caught him completely off guard.

"Are you Quinn Morgan?"

How in the hell does she know that?

"Should I know you?" Christ, his stomach churned crazily.

"M-my name is Jenny Johnson. I've been looking for you for a long..." Her words drifted off to nothing as she simply stared in awe of his presence.

Quinn watched her swallow as if gathering courage. She blinked once, and then blinked again. For the first time, he noticed the flecks of gold in her brown eyes. The tempo of his heartbeat picked up. His stomach continued to roll.

He didn't like this. He didn't like at all the fact that he was having some sort of knee-jerk reaction to the woman and didn't have a clue why. Instinct told him, however, that he wasn't going to like anything she had to say.

Jenny took a deep breath and exhaled slowly.

Quinn felt the soft rush of air swirl up around him even though his stature dwarfed the woman. Oddly, his heart thumped even harder against his rib cage. His fists clenched slightly. He watched her mouth open as if in slow motion. In the deepest part of his being, he was certain that whatever she said next would forever change the future. How? He was at a loss to explain it. But it was there, waiting to be released, waiting to strike.

"I've been looking for you for a long time because...because you're my son."

Quinn's head snapped back as if she'd punched him in the face.

"What?" His eyes narrowed imperceptivly once his head quit spinning. He struggled against the urge to reach out and steady himself against the door.

"That's impossible." He couldn't think of anything else to say. He couldn't even race to the phone — as he wanted to do that very second — and call his parents, because neither was alive any longer. He had no one — no brothers, no sisters.

"I imagine that shocks you." Jenny's hand drifted up to swipe nervously at wisps of gray hair lying against her cheek. "But it's true. I gave you up for adoption when you were two days old. Or rather, you were taken from me."

Quinn looked everywhere but at the eyes that so mirrored his own, refusing to acknowledge the possibility, his mind racing in a thousand directions at once. He ran a hand through his tousled hair as he struggled to gather his thoughts. "You've got to understand why..." Finding it difficult to even mouth such a thing, he simply stood with his arms held out in supplication.

"Why you find this hard to believe?" Jenny finished for him.

Silently, with dread curling inside his belly, he nodded.

"Could you give me a little time to explain? I'm sorry to just show up on your doorstep, but I had to see you. All these years have gone by and I've always wondered about you."

He should kick her out the door, slam it, and flick the lock. She was a fruitcake, some derelict street person trying to get warm, and possibly pull him into a financial scam.

Get rid of her...

One large hand scrubbed his shadowed cheek. He stared. He should listen to that inner voice that screamed in outrage at such a ridiculous assumption. How could he, though? She'd just dropped a bomb at his feet.

"I guess I have few minutes. Why don't you follow me to the kitchen? I'll put on a fresh pot of coffee."

* * * * *

Quinn reached up into the cabinet for two clean mugs. Jenny sat perched on the edge of a kitchen chair, looking totally out of place in the tidy room. She hadn't said much, only quiet answers to inane questions that Quinn scrounged for, anything to delay the real issues that swirled about them. He turned with two filled cups in his large hands, flicked his gaze over her disheveled appearance, and joined her at the table.

"Do you take cream or sugar?"

She reached for her mug. "No. Black is fine."

Quinn observed her closely as she lifted the rim to her thin lips, blew across the surface of the hot liquid, then sipped carefully. An instant later, a sigh akin to a small moan was heard. It was enough of a noise to let him know that she was more than savoring the robust taste of his expensive coffee beans.

"Mrs. Johnson…"

"Please, call me Jenny."

Quinn settled back in the chair. "Okay. Jenny. I guess we may as well get down to brass tacks. First off, I'd like to know how you knew my name and where I lived."

"A lady from the agency told me."

"What agency?"

"The Children's Services. The place that handled your adoption."

His stomach jumped at her reference. Quinn had heard of the place. It was a small private adoption agency in Boston that had been in business for years—with questionable ethics at times. His eyes closed for a second.

Impossible. With a troubled sigh, he took a sip of his coffee and organized his thoughts.

"So, putting this together in my mind, you're telling me you walked into the Children's Services building and they just handed over information of what should have been a private adoption—no questions asked? Give me a break. What kind of scam are you trying to pull?"

Jenny set down her cup and unbuttoned her shabby coat. "Quinn. I can call you by your first name, can't I?"

He shrugged his acceptance, but remained silent while he suspiciously eyed her.

"It wasn't as simple as that. They refused to tell me anything, but I'd decided that I wouldn't give up until someone opened the adoption records. I went there every day for the last year. One of their employees finally came to me. She told me that she'd traced the adoption on her own, and gave me your name. She said it took a bit to figure out where you lived because you're not listed in the phone book. Finally tracked you down through the state computer system. You're a cop?"

Christ...so much for fucking obscurity... Rather than give her any other information in regard to what he actually did for the state of Massachusetts, he nodded. "What do you mean this person came to you? Why would someone do that?"

Jenny's finger traced the rim of her cup. She shrugged. "She felt sorry for me, I guess, because she'd seen me at the agency every day. When no one was around, she pulled my records from old files. She took the chance of losing her job by coming to me at the women's shelter." She glanced up to gauge his reaction at her pronouncement. "You look surprised. I don't have a residence, Quinn. I live at a shelter." Her eyes closed when she wagged her head slightly. "My life is..." She sighed heavily and met his surly gaze once more. "Let's just say that even though I fought the idea of you being taken away from me when you were born, it was for the best."

When she stated that fact aloud, another rush of shock rattled Quinn's brain. He'd opened the door only minutes earlier and everything he'd believed as fact had flown right out across the porch. "You have to understand that I need more proof. You just can't show up on my doorstep and expect me to accept this. My parents never said anything. I've been searching my mind since you walked in here, trying to remember something that might have pointed to a secret like this. There's nothing. Absolutely nothing." His startled gaze met hers. "Why are you staring at me?"

A sad smile curved Jenny's mouth. "You've done well for yourself. I always wondered about that. You have a beautiful home that shows off your success. Are you married?"

Christ, he didn't want to discuss his bachelorhood or his personal life with a complete stranger, one who'd just stated minutes earlier that she was his birth mother. He wanted fucking answers. "No, I'm not married. We shouldn't even be talking about that. I want some proof."

Her head tilted as she studied him. "I really debated about coming here today. I'm glad I did. Proof? Go look in the mirror. You have my eyes. It's nice to know that."

Quinn ignored the leap of his heart. "Real proof, Jenny. There must be hundreds of people out there who have eyes like yours. Where is it?"

He watched her hand slide to the coat pocket at her side. His mind screamed his denial. He might have just demanded the evidence, but in his heart of hearts, he didn't want to see it.

She slid a handful of folded papers across the table.

"Everything you need to know is right here."

Never taking his eyes off the bedraggled woman, he reached out and pulled the folded mess closer. With a tight jaw, his gaze finally swept to the sheets as he unfolded them.

He read. And then he read some more. Only the hum of the refrigerator's motor broke the uncomfortable silence. Quinn laid the first piece of paper facedown, the official adoption record, and continued to read the second, which outlined Jenny's story in bits and pieces. A sixteen-year-old girl. Pregnant. Her parents with no financial resources to help care for two—

His head snapped up as he struggled for air. For the first time in his life, he felt like passing out. His hand shook, but his jaw clenched tighter. Two? There were two babies. Twin boys. His life as an only child flashed through his head. His parents telling him when he was older that as much as they wished to, they were never able to give him a brother or a sister.

"What the hell is this," he gritted out, then swallowed the bile in his throat. His nightmare deepened by the second. If he really was Jenny's son, then there was so much more to this lurid tale than he'd first thought.

"Is this true?" he croaked out when the spinning inside his head slowed. "You had *two* babies you gave up for adoption?"

Her eyes misted, deepening the brown around her pupils and making the gold flecks shimmer brighter. "Yes. Identical twin boys."

Quinn tossed the scrunched papers to the table's surface. His forehead dropped into an open palm as he massaged his brow. He had a brother somewhere? A twin brother? It was almost too much for a person to handle.

The touch of Jenny's hand on his forearm was strange. Not a motherly touch, but soft and understanding nonetheless. He refused to look up.

"I know it's a lot to take in, Quinn. I'm sorry to upset your morning so, but I had to meet you once I found out that you lived in Boston."

Finally, his hand fluttered from his brow. Tentatively, he met her gaze. "I imagine that if I keep reading, I'll discover where my supposed twin is?" His eyes widened when a tear slipped down Jenny's cheek. She patted his arm and withdrew her hand. "What? Do you know where he is?"

"His name was Raine Lemont. I went to see him yesterday."

Quinn's brain flashed into overload. Yesterday? That had to mean his brother lived here in Boston or close by. Jenny didn't look like the person who possessed the resources to travel far.

Jesus Christ— Wait a minute...was? He held his breath as he waited. Then something else hit him. Raine Lemont? He knew that name.

"Too late," she continued with a shake of her head. "I visited too late, Quinn. Your brother was a violin player for the Boston Philharmonic." A pang of undisguised astonishment continued to shoot through Quinn's gut as he listened to Jenny. Raine Lemont. His brother. His stomach clenched. He knew the name not because of the Philharmonic, but because it was listed in the report he'd studied throughout the night.

"I went to the Sander's Theater yesterday and discovered that Raine died in a car accident last year. I did speak to his wife. Calli Lemont is a real nice lady."

Quinn shot off the chair. His fingers raced through the thick waves at his temple as he began to pace. Insane. Unbelievable. He struggled to concentrate on Jenny's voice as it drifted across the kitchen.

"I looked in the phone book when I got back to the shelter. I put her name and address on the back of one of these sheets." As Jenny spoke, she straightened the adoption papers into a pile, flipping over the one with Calli's information so Quinn would see it when he was ready. "I don't know why, but I thought that maybe you would want to meet with her. She can tell you much more about your brother than I can." When Quinn continued to pace, she rose and buttoned her coat. "She doesn't know about you. I left Sanders yesterday, not knowing if I should tell her or not... I'm going to go now. I want you to read everything in the report. If you want to find me, I'm at the Women's Shelter on Fourth and Fifty-Seventh."

Quinn stopped his restless wandering, rested a hip against the counter, but didn't say a word. The last thing that Jenny Johnson saw before she left the room was the glittering flecks of gold in the confused depths of her son's wary eyes.

Chapter Six

ဢ

Sunday had dawned with bright spring sunshine spreading its warmth, but now only a few hours later, ominous clouds built, casting a gray gloom across the city of Boston. Calli's gaze flicked tiredly through the kitchen window as she finished her breakfast dishes, noting how her fingers and upper arms cramped if she straightened them too quickly. Her back and neck muscles protested her upright position beside the counter. She'd spent hours the evening before at her piano, playing...praying that Raine would come to her for the third night in a row. But the music had failed her. She'd finally given up, tossed down sleeping pills and slept undisturbed.

Her brain still blurred with drug induced weariness as she wiped the last of the dishes. With a heartfelt, lonely sigh, she slumped into a chair, wondering what she would do for the rest of the day. Leaning her head back, she closed her eyes and thought about past Sundays when Raine had been alive.

The weekends had always been so special. They'd participate in performances at Sanders both Friday and Saturday night if the Philharmonic was presenting a concert in Boston. It never seemed like a job because they loved the hours on stage doing what they both loved to do. Then, Sunday would roll around. They would frolic beneath the covers when they awakened...

Calli's heart pounded out a quick beat as she thought about those long ago passionate days. Making love with Raine had always been wonderfully heady, a feast for the sexual senses. But those mornings with sun streaming through the windows onto their naked bodies had only heightened the level of erotic pleasure. There was nothing to hide the many emotions playing across his features as he fucked her, bringing Calli to a sexual peak time after time while playing with her body. It was as if nature's light opened his mind to the many possibilities of how he could coax yet another mind-numbing orgasm from his wife.

Raine had always told her how much he enjoyed her body without the shroud of darkness. At first, Calli had been embarrassed about granting her husband the many things he requested. He wanted her on her back with her thighs spread wide so he could see every intricate part of her femininity. His hands would brush across her skin, his fingers dipping into her wet slit before tunneling inside her pussy or her rectum. Time after time, her body shuddered beneath his sexual manipulation, writhed with uncontrollable lust and, when one orgasm was complete, she would beg for another. And Raine always responded. Whether it was a new position, or his tongue bringing her to unimaginable heights, or the use of a host of toys, he always had some secret pleasure to surprise her with. Nipple clamps, clit clamps, vibrators, his mind never ceased to think of ways to pleasure Calli. She had soon discovered how intensely she looked forward to seeing his every emotion glitter in his eyes as he worked her body into a peaked frenzy. Soon, it had become a matter of course to always leave the lights on when they made love and to welcome the sunshine's brightness in the middle of the day...

Calli hadn't even realized she'd unconsciously opened her bathrobe while she drowned in the many memories of Raine. Her hands massaged the flat line of her belly and moved lower with a will of their own.

Her clit tingled with expectation.

Her thighs parted.

Dripping moisture wet her fingertips as she lightly ran a finger down her slit, then back up to touch her swollen bud. Her body jumped. This was something she'd never done. She'd never masturbated. Not when Raine was alive, because he had satisfied her every need. And certainly not after he'd died. Normally, she'd toss the thoughts as far as she could, stumbling in the nightmare of his death instead of becoming aroused. Then there were the times his ghostly apparition had returned…

She had to come. There was no denying the subtle surge of her hips and her clit throbbing against her fingertips.

As if in a sexual trance, she rose from the chair, suppressed the urge to come on the spot, and stepped purposefully up the stairs to the second-level bedroom. The silky bathrobe slipped from her shoulders and floated to the thick carpet as she crossed the room. Opening the closet door, she sank gracefully to her knees. Pulling a heavy cardboard box from the back, Calli lifted the cover with a trembling hand. Her teeth nibbled on her bottom lip as she dug through the many sexual toys that had been locked away since the day of the accident.

Calli was of a determined mind. The sexual need that coursed through her blood intensified as her nerves tingled and her breath became short pants of eagerness. Nothing was more important at the moment than the yearning to quench the sexual desire that Raine had created inside her from the first day they'd met. Reaching deeper into the corrugated box, her fingers wrapped around a soft anal plug. She pulled it out, mindlessly acknowledging how her rectum clenched as she held it in her hand. She continued to dig until a thick lifelike vibrator lay on the floor beside the plug along with a tube of lubricant. She dripped with anticipation now. Her hands flew to gather up the toys.

She didn't care. No one would ever know. No one would ever understand the driving force that spurred her on.

Hurrying to the bed, she dumped her playthings onto the surface. With a shaking hand, she reached for the lubricant. Heat suffused her body when she squeezed a generous amount onto her fingers, leaned over the mattress with one hand and spread her stance.

A shot of pure delight raced up her spine when her fingertips touched her ass. Her eyes closed as her teeth captured her lip in response to the cool gel she dabbed around her anus.

Her hips arched upward as the walls of her pussy and ass clenched.

There was no stopping now. Her breathing shallowed with each surge of her body. Raine had created the sexual woman she'd become, and she'd been left alone to deal with it.

Calli let herself flow with the sensual moment, but her mind raced ahead, already anticipating the feel of the anal plug sliding into her rectum. She continued to stroke the fine line of her ass, teasing herself mercilessly.

With a rattled breath, she straightened once more, subtly enjoyed the feel of slipperiness between her cheeks and prepared the plug. Bending over the bed once more and bracing herself on one arm, she rubbed the tip of the plug against her tight opening. A gasp sounded along with the jolts of pleasure that ripped through her belly, knowing instinctively that she would orgasm shortly. Bending further to widen her ass cheeks, she pressured the plug past the puckered rim. Her knees began to shake as she gently forced it in, inch by slick inch. The plug widened her rectum, filling Calli with incredible bliss.

A small moan escaped her lips as her shoulders swayed downward until her swollen breasts flattened against the mattress. Her nerves stretched taut. Her fingers crawled across the silky texture of the bedspread, clawing for a better hold as she squeezed her muscles tightly. The first wave of orgasm hit her, making Calli squirm mindlessly as her hips bounced to a rhythm all their own. Behind her tightly closed eyelids, she imagined Raine's body cupping her own as he fucked her in the ass. Her stomach muscles bunched tightly as she shuddered through the torrent of pulses radiating through her lower belly.

Scrunching the bedspread in her grasp, Calli's forehead rolled against the mattress. A low mewl sounded in her throat when her knees gave out. She lay there, half draped across the bed, kneeling on the floor with the plug still inside her ass and cream trickling down her inner thighs. She gasped and sucked in one breath after another to slow the pounding of her heart.

But she yearned for more. She needed to be lost within the release, to be mindless and numb to the loneliness that clung to her heart. Starved for more of the scorching fire to consume her, she finally crawled onto the bed, rested a moment on her side, then reached out for the vibrator to pull it closer. The moment was now all about being lost in the sensual pleasure of a massive orgasm. She squirted more lubricant onto her fingers, carefully rolled to her back so the anal plug would stay in place, and spread her raised knees.

Her entire body spasmed when the cool gel coated her swollen clit. Spreading her silky folds, she dipped inside her hot pussy, realizing there was no need for the lubricant. Calli was dripping wet and ready to be entered. The vibrator was clutched in her hand a moment later. She pressed a button and immediately the thick shaft began a low hum and shuddered in her tightly clasped palm. Taking it in both hands, she massaged her clit with the pulsing tip, applying pressure against the throbbing bud until her hips thrust back in response. Her knees came up as she drove the hard rubber tip into her welcoming sheath as far as it would go.

Calli went wild with the instantaneous heat that bolted through her. As she rocked against the ramming thrusts of the vibrator, the rhythmic movement pressured the anal plug in and out of her body. She was filled tightly, heating with the first impending shudders of another orgasm.

She screamed when it hit. Every muscle in her body constricted as the waves tore through her, heating her breasts and filling her mind. The fingers of one hand jerked through her slit and pounded against her clit. The quaking jolts continued, scorching her insides with their intensity as the contractions literally stole the breath from her lungs.

Her arms and legs fell limply to the bed's surface. She gasped, her body trembling involuntarily as the pulses slowed. It was an effort to simply run the tip of her tongue weakly across her lips. Reaching down, she shut off the vibrator still imbedded inside her. Her hand finally stretched out and her fingers grabbed the edge of a folded quilt. Dragging it over her perspiring body, she fell into a deep slumber, her desire utterly slaked. Flecks of gold sparkled out from darkened eyes in the recesses of her mind.

* * * * *

Quinn's gaze moved from one house to the other as he studied the expensive homes in the neighborhood. He still couldn't believe that he was driving down the street where his brother used to live, ready to meet Raine's widow and discover what the man's life had been like.

He shook his head in amazement. A brother. The notion was odd and difficult to think about.

He'd gone over the adoption report from Jenny a hundred times yesterday and into the middle of the night. He'd paced like a caged lion, but was always drawn back to the crinkled sheets of paper. The information he'd read had finally begun to sink in and assuage his disbelief. An older, childless couple named William and Charlotte Morgan had signed the final papers. It hadn't even been necessary to study the signatures. He knew them both by heart because he'd lived and seen them a thousand times as the son of the loving couple. Then there were pages of information about a couple named Lemont who took his twin sibling into their home. By this morning after another sleepless night, he'd had to admit that his adoption by a wonderful childless couple was true. The knowledge had driven him to the shelter where his biological mother lived. When he found her, he'd invited her to breakfast. She had agreed to accompany him, and she had answered a ton of questions he'd thrown her way.

Jenny Johnson. She'd lived a hard life forever, a woman now forty-five years of age who looked like she was in her sixties. Road-worn and weary. Pregnant at the tender age of fifteen, gave birth when she was sixteen, a botched hysterectomy that left her ill and near death for months, and parents who really didn't give a shit about her or a meaningful life to share with their grandchildren. When Jenny had met a boy named Eddie and decided to run away with him, the world had seemed right for a time. Until Eddie had begun to beat her on a regular basis. Bleeding and near death one night, a friend of hers had called an ambulance. Eddie had been tossed into jail and Jenny had been put in contact with county agencies to help get her world back on track. There had been a series of men throughout her life and situations that had always ended up with his biological mother being put out onto the street. She owned nothing except the clothes on her back even though she held a part-time job at the shelter's kitchen.

Quinn's knuckles turned white as he gripped the steering wheel. Jenny didn't have a goddamn thing because she was also a junkie—a fact that she'd tried to hide from Quinn. Her pittance of a salary most likely all went to buying illegal drugs to keep her addiction fed. He knew the symptoms, because he'd seen them too many times. Bad skin, twitching limbs, facial tics, rotting teeth—and eyes that continually darted to a clock because the effects of the last needle, pill, or line were beginning to wear off. She blew her nose steadily, sniffed and squirmed with agitation. Cocaine, crack, meth—she most likely did it all. And Quinn hated to think how she obtained it when her small monthly salary from the shelter was exhausted.

One thing at a time, Quinn…

Which meant Jenny hadn't seen the last of him but, for now, he needed to meet his brother's wife. The urge was stronger than anything he'd ever experienced. Until he had that little bit of uneasy business over and done with, his mother—god, it was so strange to think of the woman in that manner—could wait. But soon, very soon, Quinn was going back. No matter what it took, he was going to get help for her.

And what of Calli Lemont? He'd reread the various reports from work. Not anywhere in the many pages was there an indication that Raine Lemont had left a widow behind. Why? There should have been a number of follow-up visits after the accident even if at the time the man's connection to the cartel was unknown.

He pulled the car up beside the curb and stared at a red-bricked home sitting in the middle of a manicured and spacious lot. The sheer size of the two-storied house and varying roof levels left no doubt in his mind that his late brother was no pauper. An attached three-stall garage curved along the cement drive. Putting the car in park, he dumped the keys into his pocket and got out.

"This is it, Quinn," he mumbled as he forced himself to walk up the sidewalk. "Get it over with." His stomach flipped with agitation. He also wondered what the hell his dead brother's wife would think when she discovered she had a brother-in-law.

He stepped up and crossed an elegant porch with expensive outdoor furniture and thick rugs that ran its length. Taking a deep breath, he rang the doorbell and waited, surprised that in one sense he couldn't wait to meet the woman on the other side of the door, yet he wanted to run like hell. Shifting his weight to one leg, he tipped his head and listened. No muffled voices or footsteps could be heard. After about a minute or so, he rang the bell again. Once more, no response.

"Come on," he muttered angrily. A part of him wanted someone to answer, because he didn't know how soon if would be before he could put himself through this again. Another two minutes passed. Once more he rang the bell and waited.

"No one home. Just my luck." Shrugging, he turned away just as the doorknob rattled behind him.

* * * * *

The sound of the front bell reached Calli where she lay in a stupor upon her bed. The quilt still covered her, but the vibrator lay on the floor. When she'd awakened thirty minutes earlier, she'd pulled the sex toy from her body and had flung it angrily away. She'd then spent the last half hour going over the fact that even though she'd found gratifying release, the ache of grief had not receded. She lay staring at the ceiling, knowing she needed to put her life back together and move on.

The doorbell rang again, spurring her from her reverie and forcing her from the bed. Picking up her bathrobe from the floor, she slung it over her naked shoulders and hurried from the room as she tied the sash around her waist.

Her steps quickened at the bottom of the staircase when the bell rang for the third time. Racing across the living room, she stopped to first look out the peephole to see who it was.

A gasp left her throat as she fumbled desperately to open the lock.

* * * * *

The door swung wide behind him.

Quinn swiveled back.

His jaw sagged open. A streak of lightning-quick shock bolted through him. His broad shoulders jerked in response to the tiny woman framed in the doorway.

She stood in a bathrobe with her chocolate brown hair, familiar honeyed skin and piercing silver eyes, which widened in distress with each passing second as she stared up at him. Her slim hand jumped to her throat as if she couldn't breathe. Her lips worked to form words, but nothing except air escaped them. As her body sagged against the doorjamb, the blood drained from her face and she began to crumple to the luxurious rug she stood on. Sheer instinct made him jump forward to catch her wilting form before she hit the floor.

"What the hell—" The sensitive skin of his palms burned wherever he touched her, sending strange signals of disbelief to his brain. Quinn adjusted her dead weight, lifted her against his chest, and stared unbelievably at the dream turned real within his embrace.

It was her. Calli Lemont was the woman who haunted his dreams. His twin's wife. He blinked against the lightheadedness of adrenaline charging through his veins.

Quinn's heart rapped crazily when he strode into the house and shut out the outside world with the heel of his foot. He rushed by a piano looking for a place to lay her down, ignoring how his body physically reacted to the sight of the shiny baby grand. Blood roared inside his head.

Piano music. Always a piano playing in the background when he'd made love to her.

Christ almighty...

Ignoring the buzz in his ears, Quinn hurried to a leather couch, sank to one knee and gently laid her down. His gaze darted over her feminine features, knowing that he'd find a small freckle just above her full upper lip. Brushing familiar thick strands of hair from her face, he couldn't help but touch the soft curve of her cheek because he'd already experienced the pleasure of the velvety texture. He'd done it so many times over the last months.

What in hell was going on?

Quinn's breath caught in his throat when her eyelids fluttered.

Her head rolled slightly against the pillow before her eyes opened completely.

Neither breathed a word as they gazed at one another.

"I wanted you so badly beside me," she murmured as she reached up, slid her fingers through the hair at his temple and pulled Quinn's lips to hers.

He was still in a state of shock as her warm tongue urged his mouth to open. Undeniable memories of flashing silver eyes, sweet warm breath, the feel of her full lips against his made his cock swell between his legs. Lost in the emotion of finally having the real woman in his arms, he angled his head to deepen the kiss.

God, she was real, so very warm and real—and not the enticing temptress of his dreams.

Her fingers moved to massage the hard strip of muscle at his shoulders, then caressed the length of his powerful biceps, down his forearms until her hands found his as they gently cupped her face. A tiny groan accompanied the quickened dart of her tongue across his lips.

Sweeping the inside of her mouth, Quinn was drawn like a moth to a flame. Her perfume clouded the air. He groaned with delight as images of her slender legs wrapped around his waist flickered through his mind. He deepened his kiss further. Their intimate dance of tongues had his heart pounding and his body in a full state of arousal. Totally lost in the sensual moment, he eagerly looked forward to the sensation that her wandering hand at the hard bulge between his thighs evoked—until her seeking fingers covered his hard, jeans-covered cock.

Sanity returned like a cold blast of water. His head jerked back, and he leapt up from the floor. The expression on her devastated face further unsettled his already shaky emotions. It was a look of surprised hurt, desperation, and was so forlorn that it tore at his gut.

He shook his head to clear it. What the hell had he been thinking, to kiss a complete stranger so intimately? But she wasn't a stranger—they'd met many times before this.

Quinn scraped his fingers across his skull. The action stopped him from pulling her against his chest once more. "I-I'm sorry. That won't happen again. It's just that you...you kissed me and I couldn't help myself." His gaze steered away from her gaping robe and the expanse of a slim thigh.

"You don't want to kiss me?" she murmured quietly while sitting up. She never gave her open robe a thought.

Her voice. It rang inside his head. Quinn stared at her hair in an effort to block out one small breast whose nipple was barely covered.

"What's the matter, Raine? Did I do something? I think I fainted, didn't I? I'm sorry. I...it's just that you've never appeared before unless I played the piano. And never in the light of day." She gasped and her eyes rounded. "I can hear your voice...that's never happened...not until now."

"Who? What did you say?"

"Oh, Raine," she exclaimed as she pushed herself up from the couch. Tears glistened in her eyes. "I can hear you!" she sobbed out happily. Her arms immediately snaked around his shoulders as she forced his mouth to hers once more.

Quinn grabbed her tiny wrists firmly, broke the sizzling contact of their mouths and set Calli away from him. He spotted the confusion in her eyes. How was he going to tell her? For some strange reason, she thought he was Raine. Christ, Raine was dead. He had no choice but to tell her because her body swayed forward as she struggled to get closer to him.

"I'm not Raine. We really need to talk. You are Calli Lemont, aren't you?" He let go of her and stepped back quickly, ignoring the reckless heat that sizzled in the air.

"But..." Her eyes darted about before settling once more on Quinn's face. "Of course I'm Calli Lemont. Don't joke with me, Raine. I've been through too much."

"Mrs. Lemont, I think you'd better sit down. I'm not Raine—I'm not your husband. I'm Quinn Morgan, Raine's twin brother."

Instantly, her cheeks turned ashen. Quinn grabbed her arm and guided her down to the couch when she swayed precariously. He started to sit beside her, then thought better of it. Stepping back, he settled uncomfortably in a velvet-covered chair.

Panic suddenly blazed in Calli's eyes. "I-if you're not Raine, then what are you doing in my house?" She wrapped her robe tighter about her body and scooted to the far edge of the couch, ready to run if needed. "What kind of horrible joke is this?"

"Don't be frightened. I wouldn't be inside your home if you hadn't fainted. I didn't know what else to do but get you somewhere comfortable."

She didn't look like she believed him because her eyes continually darted from his face to the door as if she was measuring an escape route.

"I came by because I wanted to ask you a few questions. Honest to god, I won't move off this chair."

Calli struggled to maintain her balance even if she was still sitting down. He'd said he was Raine's twin. She eyed him more closely. He most certainly could be, because even as she stared, she had to convince herself that the man across from her wasn't her dead husband. The likeness was uncanny and made her queasy. But he was a stranger sitting in her house... A wave of lightheadedness rushed through her all the way to the tips of her toes.

Madness... Calli swallowed her terror and struggled to think clearly.

Quinn's fingers curled around the chair's armrests. Nausea washed through him, then pierced his gut. The question of why she haunted his dreams swirled in his head, but he shoved it away. He couldn't tell her about that. If he did, she'd probably call the cops on him.

He nearly burst out laughing hysterically. He was a fucking cop for chrissakes.

Quinn shook his head. One thing at time.

"Mrs. Lemont..."

Her body jerked in reaction to his voice.

This was crazy. How could he be so formal when they'd just shared one of the most sensual kisses of his life?

"I think you'd better leave. Now." Calli clawed her way through the conflicting emotions the man across from her had elicited. She wanted answers, because clearly Quinn Morgan had to be related to Raine. The set of his jaw, the sound of his voice, the glowing eyes that were so familiar... But she was too vulnerable sitting naked beneath a flimsy bathrobe with nothing to protect her. Her eyes darted to her security system. A lot of good it would do her now if he decided to attack her.

"Calli. Please just give me a minute. I'm here because I had a visitor yesterday. The same one you had a few days back. Her name was Jenny Johnson."

Calli visibly stiffened. "Jenny? Raine's mother?"

"Yes. She surprised the hell out of me. She showed up at my door, stating she was my mother and that I had a twin brother."

Calli peered at him closely, the suspicion in her eyes lessening a bit. What he said had to be the truth—as far as meeting Jenny. How else would he know any of those details? She fought an internal battle. The fact remained, however, that he was a stranger in her home. But, one side argued against the other, he hadn't done anything that would lead her to believe he was dangerous and out to hurt her. She eyed the door once more. If she had to, she could leap up and race outside screaming. Ignoring the warning bells urging that she get as far away as possible before something happened, Calli took a deep breath instead. She had to know more. She met his gaze squarely.

"I did meet the woman. Of all things, she stated she was Raine's mother, something he never knew about—if it is true. Now…now you're telling me that you're his twin? Jenny never even hinted that my husband was a twin. She kept saying *my little boy*. One. That's all." Overwhelmed, Calli clutched the arm of the sofa. Silently, she rubbed her forehead with the trembling fingers of the other hand. When the door opened and she'd seen him standing on her stoop, the force of her emotions had been strangling. She'd thought it was Raine, a breathing real-life Raine come back…not the nighttime apparition who…

She sucked in another breath, trying to sort out the facts. Jenny Johnson had come to Sanders in order to meet her son, but had never stated that Raine was a twin. Why hadn't she? Then the woman had gone to Mr. Morgan.

Calli's head came up. Her heart acknowledged the quick disbelief at Quinn Morgan's likeness to Raine with a rush of emotion. "Why didn't Jenny tell me about you? Did she tell you where I lived? I never gave her that information."

"She said she looked up your name in the telephone book."

Calli rubbed the back of her neck, feeling the first pangs of a horrible headache. "I can't believe this."

Quinn nodded in agreement, still stunned that he was in the same room with her. "I didn't want to believe it myself. I still don't know if I completely do just because this whole thing is so bizarre. I demanded proof, however, and she gave me copies of the original adoption. The information was pretty hard to dismiss. She also told me that my twin is no longer living." He reached inside his jacket pocket to withdraw the papers as evidence and noted how Calli's body flexed beneath the flowing robe as if ready to run. Who could blame her? She'd be a fool to completely trust him when he was really nothing but a stranger to her.

He sat forward, held out the papers until she carefully took them without touching his fingers, and then sank back into the chair to put her at ease. He didn't want her to bolt. "It was quite a lot to take in when I've spent my entire life thinking I had no siblings."

He watched how the curtain of her hair drifted over one shoulder as she silently studied the adoption papers, knowing how the soft texture felt as it slipped between his fingers.

Calli read a few sentences, then darted a quick glance at him before returning to the pages. A clock ticked somewhere as she flipped to the second sheet.

Figuring that she must surely have reached the adoption information about Raine, he finally broke the silence. "Were Geoffrey and Margaret Lemont the names of Raine's parents?"

Calli's hand shook when she glanced up. "Were? You mean *are*. They're very much alive."

"Have you spoken to them about this?"

"No," she shook her head. "My god, I've only known about this for a few days."

"Did Raine know he was adopted?"

Her head wagged. "I don't think so. He never said anything. I know my husband. He would have told me something like this had he known."

"Are you going to tell his parents?" Quinn had to keep asking questions. It was the only way to help him steer clear of the fact that he knew what it was like to have her naked body in his arms, of the fact that even now he was rock-hard just looking at her.

"I don't know if I'm going to tell them about this or not. Please. You won't approach them, will you? Margaret hasn't been very healthy, mentally or physically since Raine was killed. She's just coming around. Something like this will set her back terribly, and I don't want to take that chance." She folded the papers, but didn't hand them back. Glancing up, she met his shuttered eyes, surprised at how the sight of them warmed her cheeks. "Let me ask you this. Have you contacted your parents — your adoptive parents?"

"My parents were older. They're both gone now." He glanced about the room in order not to drown in the silver pool of temptation across from him. His jaw tightened when his gaze rested on the baby grand. He had to ask, even though it was like leaping into the ring of fire.

"Do you play the piano?"

"What?" She looked confused at the quick change in his questioning.

"Do you play the piano?"

She watched his eyes darken as he waited. The damn gold flecks glittered, making her want to reach out because they were so familiar. She ignored the stab of pain in her heart and the tumultuous emotions raging inside her chest. Good god, she wanted nothing more than to caress his firm jaw. "Yes. I'm a concert pianist. I play for the Philharmonic, as did Raine. Why?"

He damn well couldn't tell her why, so he grabbed at the first thing that came to mind, struggling against the lustful urge to join her on the couch. Christ almighty. When had he turned into a sex fiend? All Calli Lemont would have to do is kiss him one more time and any good intentions he'd ever had would fly right out the window. "I noticed the piano when I first carried you into the house." His gaze moved to the violin taking up its stately corner of the room. He nodded in its direction. "Is that violin Raine's? Even from here I can see that it must have been handcrafted."

She followed his line of vision. "Yes. It was very dear to his heart. Having that meant so much to him. He only played it on special occasions and never on stage. It was just for our enjoyment. A few years back, he decided to retire it." She turned back to him, feeling slightly more comfortable, but continued to stay on guard. "You seem like you know a little about music. Not everyone could casually look at a violin and know its worth."

Quinn shrugged, glad that Calli was finally more at ease. He just wished he felt the same. "As unbelievable as this is, I studied the violin for years. I've never played in the professional venue, though. That violin isn't any run-of-the-mill instrument. I'm surprised that Raine did what he did. Mind if I take a look?"

Calli used one hand to flip her long hair over her shoulder. "I suppose it would be all right."

She watched him ease his long length out of the chair, shocked beyond belief that he moved exactly like her dead husband. The set of the shoulders, the way his stroll seemed lazy as he crossed the room... Her eyes fluttered shut momentarily to regain her equilibrium, then she shifted her position to look directly at his back. Unbelievable. He could be Raine.

Quinn stood before the caged violin imagining his brother playing. His brother. Raine Lemont. It still blew his mind. To think they had lived their entire lives only miles apart and had never met personally—especially when he was a DEA officer and Raine had drug connections. "Why did your husband quit playing this particular instrument?" he asked over his shoulder.

"He was always concerned that someone would steal it, so he purchased another for everyday use." A soft sigh left her parted lips. "He always said he would serenade me with it when we were old and gray."

Quinn's gaze followed the curve of the main body, then moved back up over the strings until they rested against the wooden likeness of Calli Lemont's features. This was no ordinary violin. The exquisite hand-carved violin must have cost thousands of dollars.

His entire body stiffened. Names, places, tons of written information about missing money and drugs hit him full force. His dark eyes snapped shut as he struggled against the nausea that unexpectedly weakened him. He locked his knees so they wouldn't shake. He didn't want to ask, but he had no choice. Was Calli Lemont involved? Somewhere there was a missing link because it seemed no one knew of her.

"Your and Raine's line of work must be very lucrative," he stated again over his shoulder. "This is quite a house and quite the neighborhood. I didn't think the Philharmonic paid that much."

"For your information, Raine comes from money, plus he had a good head for business. He played the stock market wisely." Her round eyes narrowed. Her hands began to tremble again. "You know, how we—how *I* live is none of your business." She stood, her back stiff and her shoulders squared when he turned to face her. Unconsciously, she tightened the sash of her robe further as if the gesture would protect her from the stranger in her living room and the bizarre feeling of déjà vu that choked her.

Is he a stranger? I thought he was Raine…

"I think you should leave, Mr. Morgan. I'll thank you to keep all this to yourself until I can sift through this information and figure out what needs to be done or *not* done."

He simply stood there and stared at her. Finally, his big body shifted as if preparing for something. She wondered if she would have to run screaming to the front door.

"Why did you kiss me?" His eyes drew her in like a swirling eddy of water.

Mr. Morgan's question caught her completely off guard. "I-I thought," she stammered, "I…"

"Did you really think I was Raine? Do we resemble one another that closely?"

She let out a defeated sigh and nodded at something over his left shoulder. "Look at the picture behind you."

Quinn swiveled to look at a picture he hadn't noticed before. The photo she spoke of was a professional portrait. Calli sat in a cream-colored chiffon gown at her piano, poised, and exotically beautiful with her tinted skin and burnished hair. It was the strangest thing he'd ever experienced as he stared at his brother who stood beside her with the violin in his hands. Quinn could have sworn he looked into a mirror. His eyes moved to the softness of Calli's bare shoulders above the dress's bodice. A flash of a naked, petite body burned inside his brain.

He had to get out of this house.

He turned back.

Their eyes met, each wary of what the other might say or do next.

"I'm sorry that I've upset your day. When you're ready, I'd like you to contact me. I'd like to know more about my brother, but maybe we need to step back for a bit and digest all the facts." He reached around to a back pocket, pulled out his wallet and flipped it open. "Here's my card. My home address isn't on it, but you can call me at work when and if you think the time is right." He held out the card. When Calli refused to take it, he tossed it onto the coffee table. What would she think when she discovered what he did for a living?

She stood quietly in her bathrobe, her full lips and petite body clouding his mind. If he didn't get the hell out of her house, he might very well scoop her into his embrace. "I'll let myself out."

Without another word, Quinn crossed the carpet, opened the door and left.

Callie raced across the room to peek from behind a heavy curtain as soon as the latch clicked. He resembled Raine so much as he marched down the bricked sidewalk. The same wide shoulders, the auburn tint hiding within the thickness of his dark hair, the same stride. She pressed her knuckles against her mouth to keep from calling him back.

* * * * *

A gray Lincoln Continental was parked halfway down the block from Calli's manicured lawn. The fancy car was in a fancy neighborhood. Blending totally with the affluent surroundings was a given.

Suddenly, the two men who lounged against the rich black leather seats shot forward with incredulous eyes. Both the occupants' gazes followed a dark-haired man marching from the front door of the Lemont home to his vehicle.

"What the hell?" Diego Trejos squinted. He snagged the sunglasses from his face and tossed them to the seat. His partner's breath hissed across the small space between them. Jorge Cardez had just experienced the same shock of recognition.

They turned to stare at one another.

Silently, Diego grabbed a set of binoculars and studied the man down the street who now dug inside his coat pocket for his keys.

"He's alive," Diego muttered. "That two-timing *bastardo* is alive…"

Dark eyes watched, one set looking through the tinted windshield as the other squinted through a camera's lens. The shutter clicked crazily as one picture after another was taken.

Quinn opened his vehicle door and got in. A moment later, the car pulled away from the curb and drove past where the two Colombians were securely hidden behind the dark windows of their car.

"Where in hell has he been hiding?" Jorge responded with astonishment.

Diego gritted his teeth ominously, his mind scurrying back to nearly a year earlier. A mangled car, an ambulance…a body being carefully pulled from the wreckage.

Raine Lemont was supposed to be dead. Diego had confirmed it with his own eyes. The cartel's spies had confirmed it. And because of the connived accident and stepped-up heat from drug enforcement agencies, he and all his compatriots had fled the United States to bide their time in Bogota, Colombia. He and a handful of men had only arrived a few weeks earlier to begin surveillance once more on the defector's wife. The drugs and money were still hidden. This time, the group would not be leaving without their rightful property.

Diego flipped open a padded box that housed the car's satellite phone. He hit speed dial, the speaker button, and then waited with fingers drumming against the expensive leather.

Finally, a voice crackled on the other end. "Hello?"

"This is Diego. Let me speak to Enrique."

Diego waited impatiently, knowing his employer would be incensed when he learned of this most recent discovery.

"What is it, Diego?" Enrique Palacios' gruff voice filled the car.

"He is alive."

"Who?"

"Raine Lemont."

Silence. Then…

"What do you mean he is alive?" Enrique's question was clipped. His evident wrath seethed through the car's interior with just the few spoken words.

"I do not know how, Enrique. He just walked out of his house as big as life."

Silence again, and then Diego heard a sharp intake of breath on the other end just before Enrique's voice filled the interior once more.

"I was guaranteed he was dead. You have been watching his wife off and on for the last two weeks. And this is the first you have seen of the American swine? Are you sure? There is no question?"

"I am just as surprised as you. I swear on my mother's grave. It is him. He just drove his car past ours and there is no mistake. How do you want us to handle this?"

Jorge met Diego's dark eyes as they waited.

"Watch that house every minute of the day and night. I will be in Boston before you know it. That traitor will get his due."

The phone went dead.

* * * * *

Quinn couldn't drive fast enough going home. The entire time, Calli's face stayed with him. Once he'd parked the car in the garage, he strode quickly into the house, and marched into his office. Rounding the edge of his desk, he sank into his chair as he reached for the work folder he'd studied on Friday night. Flipping it open, his fingers paged through the numerous sheets in a flurry until he found what he was searching for.

He stared down, still finding the facts hard to believe. His stomach lurched when his gaze settled on Raine's name in the middle of the page. He didn't want it to be there...in fact, he'd clung to the slim possibility all the way home that somehow he'd made a mistake.

Raine Lemont: murdered April nineteenth, 2002.

Suspected killer or killers? The Colombian cartel.

Reason? Disappearance of half a million dollars along with the cocaine Raine Lemont was supposed to disperse for the cartel. And nowhere was there a statement that the man had been married.

Angrily, he snapped the folder shut, tossed it to the desk's surface, and slammed his eyes shut. His twin brother had led a secret life as a middleman for a very powerful drug ring—and had tried to dupe them. In the process, he'd lost his life.

His head fell back against the chair as he stared up at the ceiling, again wondering if and how Calli was involved.

Chapter Seven

꧁

Quinn stuffed the papers back inside the manila folder twenty minutes later and headed for the kitchen. His brow furrowed in thought as he dug around inside the fridge, found a beer and slugged down half of it before taking another breath. His gaze fell on the telephone. Glancing at the clock, he knew it probably wasn't a good time because it was Sunday afternoon, but he had to speak with Danny. Finishing the rest of the beer, he crushed the can easily in his hand, tossed it into the garbage and picked up the handset.

Alexa answered the phone on the fourth ring.

"Hello?" her little voice squeaked.

"Hi, Alexa." The familiar turmoil of the Briggs' house roared in the background. "This is Quinn. Is your daddy there?"

"Hi, Uncle Quinn. What's up?"

"I need to talk to your daddy. Is he busy?"

"He's watching football, but he's supposed to be cleaning the garage. My mom's gonna kick his butt pretty soon."

A smile tugged at the corner of Quinn's mouth. "Well, before that happens, why don't you tell him to come to the phone?"

"Okay," the little girl replied. The phone rattled in Quinn's ear as it hit the counter. A moment later he heard Alexa's voice trailing into another room as she hollered for her father.

Quinn plopped onto a stool by the phone and waited. Finally, the phone scuffed against something and Danny's voice came over the line a second later.

"Quinn?"

"Hi, Danny. I know it's Sunday, but what do you say we meet for a beer?"

There was a slight pause on the other end. "Um, sure. Where?"

"The usual. Do you think it'll be okay with Maggie? It sounds like a rec center over there."

Danny chuckled. "It always sounds like a rec center around here. Mag just said she was putting everyone down for an afternoon nap—or at least locking them in their rooms so she could have two minutes of peace and quiet. I should be able to get out of here in ten. Sound good?"

"Thanks, Danny. See you shortly."

Quinn hung up the phone and stared for a moment, wondering why he'd so desperately felt he needed to use the prearranged signal he and Danny had set up years earlier, one they'd used before when caution was needed. His partner would know that Quinn needed to speak to him about something that couldn't be said over the phone just in case the line was tapped. He grabbed his jacket from a chair, and headed out of the house.

* * * * *

Calli curled her feet beneath her as she huddled in the center of her couch. Quinn Morgan had left her home an hour earlier, but still, she shivered with just the thought of him. A quiet groan left her throat as her fingers rubbed her scalp.

The day was as unbelievable as the entire year had been. Since Raine had died, nothing seemed as it should. And now? She not only learned that her dead husband was actually adopted when he was merely days old, but that he had a living twin. A shudder trickled down her spine.

Quinn Morgan. She couldn't quit thinking about him.

The reason Calli shivered was because she still felt the trembling of an unrealistic sexual attraction to the man. For the last hour, she'd been going over the very second her eyes had opened to see him sitting beside her. At first, and of course logically, she'd thought it was Raine. That was why her heart had leapt in her chest, why her breathing had become suddenly strangled, why the blood had flowed instantly hotter through her veins. Even after being shocked to the core when she discovered who he actually was, through the frightening jolt of having a stranger inside her house, and even when he ridiculously asked personal questions that were none of his business, the fact remained that she was inexplicably drawn to the man. The sensual sight of his full lips, glittering, flecked eyes, and the swollen bulge between his legs would not disappear from her thoughts—and along with it the urge to hold him close.

"You're getting them mixed up, Calli…" she murmured to the empty room. "That's why. Quinn Morgan looks so much like Raine that you can't separate the two…"

Her eyes fell on the white business card on the table across from her. Biting her bottom lip, Calli finally rose and reached for it with a shaking hand. She studied his name and then moved on in stunned surprise. Boston Police Department? Raine's brother was a policeman? He must have had the day off, because he definitely wasn't in uniform when he'd snatched her up and brought her back to the couch.

No. No uniform—that was for sure. Calli almost wished he had been clothed for work. It would help to get the picture of his long jeans-clad legs, and the bulging muscles beneath his light jacket out of her mind.

We need to step back and digest the information. That's what he'd stated.

Eventually they'd meet again. Calli knew that in the deepest part of her being. Now that Quinn Morgan had presented himself, she wouldn't be able to rest comfortably.

Forget about it. It's too much.

She spent the next few hours going through monthly bills, a task that should have taken only thirty minutes at most. But more often than not, Calli ended up staring out the window and thinking about Quinn Morgan and Jenny Johnson, two people who had drastically changed her life again in just the space of a few days. She went over the conversations she'd had with both, seeing Jenny's worn features and the strange eyes that always merged into a handsome male face. There were still too many unanswered questions. Her eyes lifted to the curtained window, then darted to the clock.

Jenny.

Raine's real mother might be able to shed light on this crazy situation.

Calli jumped up, raced across the room and up the stairs. She would visit Jenny today. Maybe she could even convince the woman to have supper with her and get her to answer some of the many questions that stuck in her mind.

* * * * *

Quinn's gaze swiveled once more to the large scuffed door of The Tankard—a small unrecognizable bar out in the suburbs of Boston—when it opened and the burly frame of a large man filled the doorframe. This time, it was Danny who finally stepped into the smoky darkness, his eyes alert and searching for his partner. Quinn raised a welcoming hand, then turned to the bartender to order his friend a beer.

Danny ambled to the bar and slung a leg over a stool as he shed his jacket. "Just what I need...a beer on a Sunday afternoon." His eyes swept the interior, unconsciously checking the few patrons. "We sittin' here?"

The bartender set a foaming brew on the sticky bar, grabbed three dollars from Quinn's loose bills and sauntered away.

"Let's get a booth," Quinn replied. Without another word, he grabbed the rest of his money, slung his jacket over a broad shoulder, and with Danny in tow, strolled across the dark room to a private corner.

Once they seated themselves, Danny dug inside the pocket of his T-shirt and pulled out a pack of cigarettes. "What the fuck is going on, Quinn?" A flare from his lighter haloed his face momentarily as he lit his smoke in the dark interior.

Quinn's hand scraped through his hair as he took a sip of his beer. "I really needed to speak to you, Danny. This isn't something that can be done down at the precinct. I don't know why, but my instincts are telling me to approach this cautiously."

Danny drew long on his cigarette, blew the smoke upward in a stream, then leaned forward to take a sip of beer. "You got me listening now."

Quinn's eyes darted quickly around the interior of the bar. "I don't quite know where to start. I've had a hellish few days full of surprises." Quinn took another long draught of his beer, then followed it with a sigh.

"I gotta tell, ya, Quinn. It was one long helluva ride on the way here. It's been awhile since we've had to worry about tapped phone lines."

"Okay, be patient here as I try to get this all laid out for you. There's a brief outline in the report McMartin gave us of a man who was killed by a hit and run last year. His name was Raine Lemont."

"Christ, this has to do with the cartel?" Danny's brow dipped as he reached for his beer.

Quinn nodded. "Fuck… You're not going to believe this. I found out yesterday that Raine Lemont is…was my twin brother."

Liquid spewed from Danny's mouth. He choked and coughed his way to a look of incredulous disbelief. "What?" he croaked out. "What the hell are you talking about? You don't have any brothers or sisters. Who in the hell told you that?"

"The woman who showed up on my doorstep yesterday claiming to be my biological mother."

Danny scooped up a napkin from beneath his glass and wiped off his chin with a shake of his head. "I'm a quick study, Quinn, but I got lost right after you said you've had a hellish few days." He wadded the napkin and tossed it to the table. "So why are we here of all places, having this conversation in secrecy?"

"Just because of a chain of events. I'll get back to the twin brother thing, but first let me ask you something, Danny. Have you ever dreamed about someone who you've never met, never even had a clue that they existed, and then suddenly this person shows up in your life?"

"No..." Danny cocked his head, coughed once more and studied Quinn. "But I have a feeling that you're gonna tell me you have."

Quinn nodded again. "Over the last six months, I've had the...strangest dreams about this dark haired woman..." No way would he give any further details about his reaction to Calli Lemont. Ignoring the sensual vision of his brother's wife, he continued. "These dreams just about drove me crazy because they were so real. The color of her hair, the strange silver eyes when she looked at me...the smell of her perfume...it was all so real—and disturbing."

Danny lounged back and never took his gaze from Quinn's. "Sounds like a bad science fiction movie. Go on. I can't wait to hear the rest."

Quinn sighed. "Okay. So I'm having these dreams, not every night, but enough of them that I'm beginning to wonder what the hell is going on. Then yesterday, someone knocks on my door. When I open it, there's this..." his head shook as he grappled for a way to describe Jenny. "This street person. She announces that she's my biological mother."

"What? It was the woman you think you've been dreaming about? You did ask for fucking proof, didn't you?"

"No, it wasn't the woman that I've been dreaming about. This was someone I've never seen before. Much older. She stood there shivering in this ratty old coat. I asked her in and we had quite a conversation. At first I felt like tossing her back outside because of the ridiculousness of what she had to say. But what the hell, Danny, I just couldn't let her drop a bomb like that and not find out more. I asked for proof because my own parents had never said a word to me about adoption."

"And?"

"She handed it to me. It's all there in black and white in the records. A young pregnant girl who was forced to give up her twin boys at birth. My parents' names were in that damned document. Then she proceeds to tell me about Raine Lemont and that he had died around a year ago. Shit, I'd just read the guy's name in the report that McMartin gave us. And get this. He played violin for the Philharmonic. To think I've seen performances at Sanders Theater where he was a part of the orchestra. Blows me away. The likeness between us is amazing. If I would have had the chance to see him up close, even I think I would have had some questions. I never had a clue, though, up until now."

"You're making the hair stand on the back of my neck," Danny quipped. "What are the odds that you would both play the violin? Hey, maybe the Discovery Channel knows what they're talking about when they say twins have a special connection. Wait a minute. How do you know the two of you resembled one another? Did this woman have a relationship with him and a picture or something?"

Quinn shrugged. "I'm getting to that. Jenny—that's the name of the woman who is my birth mother—also told me that Raine was married. She discovered that when she went to Sanders a few days back to find Raine—for the first time. She met Calli Lemont instead and found out that my brother had been killed in an accident. She gave me the name and address of this woman." He paused. "I went to their home earlier this afternoon."

"Holy Christ." A slow hiss expelled across Danny's lips. "Don't tell me she was the woman in your dreams?" One look at

Quinn's face and Danny knew he'd hit the nail on the head. "You're going to, aren't you? Son of a bitch..."

"I know. It's crazy. There's no rational explanation."

Danny's shook his head in disbelief. "So, keeping in mind that maybe I believe all this... Hey, don't look at me like that. This is the craziest thing I've ever heard. If you supposedly look so much like this Raine Lemont, what was her reaction to you?"

"Fainted dead away after she opened the door. I grabbed her before she hit the ground. I was so fuckin' shocked myself I could hardly think. There she was—alive and breathing—not what I thought was a figment of my imagination. So I carried her inside, laid her on the couch, and waited for her to come to." Quinn struggled against the flash of heat that shot through him when the memory of her soft, warm lips against his, poked at his conscience. With a mental shake of his head, he continued. "Calli Lemont lives in a pretty upscale neighborhood. Old money. New money. It doesn't matter. It's just easy to tell there's lots of it."

Suddenly, Danny's body stiffened perceptively. "I think I just figured out where you're going with this... I think. We already know Raine Lemont is listed as a possible victim of the cartel because he was messing with their profits." He swiped a beefy palm across his jaw. "Geez, Quinn. Of all the things that ran through my mind on the way here, I sure as hell didn't expect a story like this." He eyed his friend closely. "The part about dreaming about Calli is a little bizarre. If I didn't know you, I'd think you were telling me a pretty tall tale."

"I'm telling you the truth. I've been dreaming about Calli Lemont for the last six months. Today I met her." He huddled forward and cupped his beer glass with both hands and watched Danny light another cigarette. "The reason I asked you here is this—something's not clicking, Danny. Neither of us has ever heard the name Raine Lemont before. Because of the cartel riding in on their black horse, every man in the department has been brought in. Suddenly, we're reading about a suspected drug-related murder a year after the fact. Christ, we're DEA detectives. Don't you think that we should have seen something before this? And Calli Lemont's name isn't mentioned anywhere in any report. Why? She's the widow. We're talking about ties to a fuckin' Colombian cartel, for crissakes. There should have been some kind of follow-up or at least something stating that she was brought in for questioning. Nothing. Absolutely nothing. Hell, we wouldn't be having this discussion if it weren't for the fact that Jenny Johnson showed up on my doorstep." Quinn stared at his partner waiting for his declaration to sink in.

A slim line of smoke streamed from between Danny's lips. His eyes narrowed as he stared back. "Are you saying what I think you're saying? That Calli Lemont's name isn't in the report because someone doesn't want it known that Raine had a wife? That someone from the department is playing both sides? That's a hell of an accusation, Quinn. One that you better be only talking to me about."

Quinn snorted. "Why do you think I arranged for us to meet here? You and I have been at this long enough, Danny. Why isn't she listed? Why hasn't anyone been watching the Lemont home for the last year? Hell, that's standard procedure. We're talking hundreds of thousands of dollars and missing drugs. According to the report, the investigation surrounding Raine's death lasted all of three or four days. We never even knew that he was tied into this until a few days back."

Danny continued to smoke silently, but Quinn knew his wheels were turning. When his partner shut up it meant his training had just kicked in full strength.

Expelling the air from his lungs, Danny snubbed out the cigarette into a dirty ashtray. He looked up and pursed his lips just as his eyes widened. "McMartin? You've got to be kidding."

"McMartin or someone as close to the top as he is. What the hell else could it be? Procedure has been tossed to the wind on this one—or at least as far as Raine Lemont is concerned. If this whole crazy thing with my adoption and dreaming about Calli Lemont hadn't happened, we most likely would've missed these subtle clues because someone has gone out of their way to hide them. I'm hoping like hell I'm wrong, but this really bears watching."

Danny scrubbed his jaw again. "I'm feeling a little ill about this. Let's sit tight, though. And whatever you do, don't let anyone know that you've met Calli Lemont."

Quinn tossed down the rest of his beer. "Oh, you can bet I'm not going to. We've got to be careful until we figure out what's coming down."

Danny finished his beer. "Good idea. Hey, I gotta get my ass back home or Maggie will have my balls." He followed Quinn up from the booth and watched his partner zip his jacket. "Are you going to see her again?"

See Calli? Of course he would. *In person*, he reiterated to himself. Now that he'd met the real woman and held her in his arms, the future was sealed. There were too many unanswered questions, too many clashing emotions roiling around inside of him. He'd give her a few days. If Calli Lemont didn't present herself, then Quinn was pushing the issue.

Chapter Eight

৯০

Calli parked in front of the women's shelter and cast a doubtful glance at the dilapidated building. Shabbily clothed women milled about the exterior, some huddled on benches while others spoke to one another within small sporadic groups. Biting her lip, she searched the many faces and suddenly began to wonder if leaving the safety of her car was really a smart thing to do. The shelter was in a poor part of town known for its crime rate and drug raids.

She clutched her purse, fiddled with the strap and thought about all the questions she needed to ask Jenny. And there were so many. The first would be why Raine's real mother had waited so many years to tell anyone about the fact that she'd borne twins so long ago.

Her eyes cast about her surroundings again. *What will it hurt? These women are down on their luck, but it's broad daylight...* She tipped her head and studied the door once more. Jenny most likely was inside. Calli had come this far. *Okay, all you need is just a few answers, and then you can be on your way and out of the area before it's dark...* With a deep breath of determination, her hand found the door latch. *Thirty minutes and that's it. Then you have to be back on the freeway before dark...*

As she rounded the front of her sports car, her gaze darted again to the many disheveled figures sitting about the steps that led to the entrance of the building. Eyes that only a moment earlier seemed blank and uninterested in their surroundings, suddenly widened as they studied what was obviously someone much more elegant than normal visitors to the shelter.

Calli strode boldly across the sidewalk with her stomach in knots. Her heart rate increased when a bedraggled woman rose from the steps, her brooding eyes making Calli again rethink the decision to leave her car.

Calli's step faltered for only a second before she swallowed and forced her gaze away as she picked up her pace. All eyes were upon her. She ignored the sudden silence of the afternoon. If she didn't look to her left or to her right, she'd be inside the building within ten seconds.

She hadn't climbed two stairs before the same woman who had first studied her casually but purposefully blocked her way. Calli was compelled to halt her flight up to the door.

"Excuse me," Calli stated bravely as she met the inflexible gaze.

The woman's eyes silently traveled the length of Calli's body from head to toe. Then she glanced over Calli's shoulder before looking back into her eyes. "What's a lady like you doing down here?" she asked as she stared. "Don't look like you need a place to sleep. Especially with a car like that."

Calli hesitantly glanced back, surprised and distressed to see a number of vagrants milling around her vehicle, looking through the tinted windows and testing the doors to see if they were locked.

What on earth was I thinking?

It was too late, however. She'd come this far. It would only be a few more steps inside to what she hoped would be a safer environment. She swiveled back, tried to hide the trembling of her hands around the expensive leather strap of her purse and struggled against the growing lump of fear in her throat. "Excuse me. I'm looking for someone in particular."

The woman cocked one knee, rubbed her nose and sniffed in an unladylike manner. Her bushy eyebrows bounced slightly over her dull eyes. "Is that so? And who would that be?"

Calli wanted to toss back that it was none of the woman's concern, but didn't dare. "If you'll just let me by, I can get my business taken care of inside."

The woman opened her mouth and let out a cackle. "Feisty one, ain't ya?"

Calli stared at her chipped and yellowed teeth, feeling sicker by the second.

"Your business. My, my, aren't we the hoity-toity one this afternoon? Say," she stated as her dirty fingers came out to rest against the material of Calli's coat sleeve, "pretty nice coat you got there. How about we make a deal? I'll let you in if you loan it to me."

Calli's arm flinched away to shake off the cloying touch and winced as the light breeze carried the tainted odor from the woman's body. Her heart beat frantically and matched the prickles of fear that coursed through her.

"Please, I don't want any trouble. I just need to find someone, and then I'll be on my way." Only a second passed before she was forced to take a step back when the woman swayed closer. She had to get to her car. "In fact, maybe I'll come back another time."

Before she could turn away, the woman's hand shot out to grab the purse strap. "Nice little bag ya got there, too. I bet it's full of primpy little makeup containers and…maybe a wallet?" Her dirty fingers stroked the purse's buckled flap. "I bet you got enough cash in there that you wouldn't miss some of it."

Calli clutched her bag close, extremely frightened now because she wondered if anyone would even come to her aid if she started screaming. Her knees began to shake. It didn't seem to matter to those watching that she was being accosted in plain sight on the steps of the shelter. As her worried silver gaze flicked about, all she could see were the haughty expressions of the shoddy people milling about the entrance. She'd made a terrible mistake by coming here.

Her body jerked when the woman's hand brushed suggestively across her chest. Before she could react further, the woman cackled again.

"How about you and me take a little walk in the alley? I like my women tiny and small. You seem about the right size under there." Her wandering fingers tried to cup a breast that was hidden beneath the coat.

Calli's horror was evident in her widened eyes and the quick breaths of fear she panted out. She slapped at the offending hand and dipped back quickly to break the nauseating contact. She spun to race to her car, but her flight was stopped by another even larger woman behind her.

"What ya got here, Phyllis?" The newest arrival snickered. "Looks like the Queen of England herself. My name's Margaret. You wouldn't by any chance be giving my friend any guff, would you? Cuz you know, it don't pay. When Phyllis wants something, she usually gets it."

"P-please," Calli stuttered as her eyes darted from the newest nemesis to her car, which was still surrounded by curious onlookers. "I... I don't want any trouble. I'll give you some money if you'll just let me leave in peace." She jumped when Phyllis' hand brushed over the surface of her ass from behind. She spun and instinctively backed up to a solid cement pillar that held up one side of the weather-beaten canopy. "Stop that! If you don't leave me alone, I'll scream..." Her heart pounded in her ears and her entire body trembled beneath the luxurious coat. Calli wondered if she'd even be able to get a scream out. She'd never been so terrified in her life. Her stomach lurched when Phyllis licked her lips, barely edging the line of dark mustache hairs just above them.

"Ha! That's a good one if I ever heard one," Phyllis chuckled as she threw back her head. "Like no one screams around here. You know what, Miss Queen of England?" She leaned in closer, her fetid breath swirling past Calli's face. "It's when the screaming stops that it becomes a problem. Me and Margaret here, just want a little fun. And it won't cost you too much money. Come on. Just let us play with you a little, and then you'll give us some money and we'll let you get back to that fancy car of yours. It'd be fun to be with someone like you.

Someone who's probably nice and firm from all the hours spent at your fancy spas…"

Margaret sidled closer to Calli. "You see, mine and Phyllis' 'tendencies' kinda head us in the direction of a woman. Yup, it does. You look surprised. I'd rather be with a woman any day. Easier to please, because I'm one and I know what a woman likes."

There was nowhere for her to run, no respite from the insinuated threat. The two roughly honed women had her escape route blocked. Calli's panicked eyes flew to the many faces that leered at her, waiting to see what would happen next. No one would help her. And no one would even know she was missing if they decided to…

Black spots appeared before her. The situation was like a horrible dream she couldn't wake from. Her brain screamed for help, but her leaden body was frozen to the spot. The nightmare of the immediate future was intensified by the smell of Margaret's putrid breath as the woman nuzzled her soft hair and worked her hand around the back of Calli's neck.

Adrenaline, born from the extreme fear that coursed through Calli, brought her out of the frozen state of panic. She struggled to shove Margaret away, anything to stop the slobbering lips against her cheek and Phyllis' hand, which closed firmly around her arm.

"Margaret! Get your hands off her! Now!"

Calli's knees nearly buckled with pounding relief when both Margaret and Phyllis released their grips. The only reason she was able to stay upright, however, instead of sliding down the cold cement pillar, was because of Margaret's large thighs against her hip.

Calli tried to place the voice, hoping in her heart of hearts that it was one of the employees of the shelter. Margaret's flabby body still blocked her vision. She gasped for air to clear her head and to keep from fainting.

"Aw, get the hell out of here, Jenny. Find your own little piece of fluff. This one is ours," Phyllis muttered.

"If you don't get your dirty hands off her immediately, I'll drag your ass to the nearest precinct and file assault charges myself."

The ominous masculine voice swirled around the inky blackness that threatened to envelop Calli, sending a jolt of ecstasy through her body.

Oh, god, Raine... She flung Margaret's arm from her body. Her tiny form dipped around the woman as she flailed blindly for the safety of his voice. Dark hair and gold-flecked eyes swam before her as she launched herself into the safety of his arms.

"Raine!" she sobbed out against the smooth leather of his jacket and iron-hard chest. Muscular arms encircled her shoulders and held her close. A firm hand comforted her fear by gently brushing her back as she huddled closer to his warmth. His jacket was open and her terrified mind acknowledged the fact that he wrapped it around her to cuddle her even closer. She could hear what she now knew to be Jenny's voice berating her two attackers, but the only thing that mattered was the steady heartbeat against her cheek.

She was safe. Her arms snaked around his large torso and clung firmly to her savior. Before she knew it, one arm securely tightened around her and she was being led back down the steps and across the cracked sidewalk.

"What the hell were you doing down here, Calli?"

That voice...

She pressed away from him slightly, blinked the tears from her eyes and tipped back her head. Her mouth parted, but no words would come.

Quinn kept an arm around her as he dug inside his jacket pocket, dragged out his keys and clicked a button. It only took a moment for him to get the door open before he helped Calli into the front passenger seat of his car.

Her entire body shook badly. "Quinn?" she rasped.

He hunkered down beside the open door, reached up and squeezed her hand. "Who did you think it was?"

Calli blinked and focused on his gentle smile. Once again she was speechless. The likeness to her husband was mind-boggling. Her heart started at the remembered feel of Quinn's firm chest beneath her cheek. She fought past the feeling of the need to leap into his arms and instead concentrated on the fact that somehow he had appeared when she needed him most.

"Calli. What are you doing down here? You took quite a chance. A lot of these women are pretty rough around the edges. You're lucky you weren't mugged."

For some odd reason, his statement almost made her laugh hysterically. She cupped her face momentarily with trembling hands, and then brushed her long hair back, trying to find some semblance of sanity before she broke down completely. "I was mugged. Thank god you appeared. God, Quinn, I was so frightened…and no one would help me." She drew in a deep breath and finally met his eyes—and nearly drowned in their concerned depths. "What are you doing here? Wait. I don't care. I'm just glad you showed up."

"Me, too. Christ, Calli. I pulled up to the curb and almost had heart failure when Jenny shouted out your name. She recognized you immediately. She was out of the car and running before I even had it in park. Then I…" The words died on his lips as his gaze flowed over Calli's features. Features that weren't so set in a hard plane of terror as they had been a few minutes earlier.

He couldn't help himself when he reached out and cupped one soft cheek. His thumb lightly brushed across her skin. What if some strange force hadn't urged him to visit Jenny for the second time that day? What would have happened to Calli? He had followed Danny from the bar intending to head for his house. Instead, he'd turned his vehicle in the opposite direction and had driven back to the women's shelter to invite his biological mother for supper. They had just returned when he'd realized that Calli was shoved tightly against the cement pillar.

He'd died a thousand deaths as he'd raced across the street. That same earlier emotion of always wanting to protect her had roared through his body. Margaret, or whatever the hell her name was, was damn lucky she was still standing upright. Only an extremely tight rein on his anger had checked the urge to pummel the ogre of a woman to the ground.

Calli stared at his lips, which had suddenly become silent. The memory of feeling so safe within his embrace only moments earlier came back to haunt her. Quinn. She'd thought it was Raine at first...

But Raine was dead. Raine only came to her in the dead of the night. Quinn was here now and had plucked her from what would have been a horrible experience—even possibly the loss of her life.

Without thought, she tipped her cheek against the firm safety and comforting warmth of his cupped hand. As his thumb brushed her cheek once more, small tingles rippled through her stomach. She wasn't alone.

Her eyes drifted closed as she breathed deeply to further settle her harried emotions. But in the darkness, the two brothers' faces merged into one and the same.

Her eyes snapped open. She willed herself to pull away from his touch. Her back straightened in an effort to put some distance between them. His bewildered gaze sliced through her shaky emotions, and made her want to reach out and let him know that...

That what? That she had to get away from him before she said something stupid?

"I want to go home." She cast a harried glance to see Jenny striding toward them. "I can't believe she lives here. This place is terrible." Calli clung to the sight of Jenny's wiry little form—anything to distance herself from the tumbled thoughts that Quinn's nearness had set off.

Quinn followed Calli's line of vision. "She has nowhere else to go. Jenny's tough. From the few conversations I've had with her, she can handle herself pretty well."

They waited silently until Quinn's mother stopped beside the car.

The concerned dip of Jenny's brow and the soft glow in her eyes evidenced her distress as she clutched the top of the door. "Mrs. Lemont. Are you all right?"

"Yes…" Calli nodded. "I'm fine now. Thank you so much for coming to my rescue."

The corner of Jenny's mouth turned up. "I don't think it was me that put the fear of god in Margaret and Phyllis. They took one look at Quinn's face and backed right off. I'm just glad he was with me. Those two are troublemakers and love the idea of bullying those around them."

Calli's hand swept away stands of hair that clung to her cheek. "They planned to do more than just bully me. Are you going to be okay, Jenny? Will there be retribution for you coming to my aid?"

Jenny shook her head. "I'll be fine. I haven't survived this long without learning a thing or two. Don't you worry about it. What are you doing down here?"

"I came to speak to you." She peeked a glance at Quinn where he still crouched silently beside her. "Quinn visited and told me about you having two little babies that you gave up. I had to know more. I need to know more about Raine's life and I need to know more about you."

Jenny's cheeks reddened and her mouth pulled into a straight line. "I think right now it's best for you to leave before it gets dark out. Maybe we can meet another time."

It was easy to see by the set of her mouth that Jenny Johnson was not going to say more.

Quinn broke the uncomfortable silence by gently taking Calli's arm and helping her from the seat. "Come on, Calli. I'll walk you to your car and follow you home."

The heat of his tender touch, his gentle smile and his calm demeanor hit her full force. She quickly pulled her arm from his grasp—anything to halt the strange forbidden arousal that moved through her. At the same time, she wondered where it had come from. She was confusing her dead husband and Quinn just because they were so similar. That had to be it. "That's not necessary, Quinn. Just get me to my car without anything happening and I'll be fine."

She turned to Jenny, but was acutely aware of Quinn's male presence at her side. "I'm listed in the phone book, Jenny. Please call me in a few days. I... I just can't come here again, but I don't want to leave it at that. I really would like to visit with you. Please say you'll call and we can meet somewhere."

Raine's mother shuffled beside the car door. Finally, her head nodded. "All right. In a few days. I have to go now." She glanced up at Quinn. "Thank you for supper. I promise to think about what you said. Goodbye." She turned to walk across the street, but Calli rushed forward and laid a hand upon her arm.

"Jenny? Thank you so much for helping me today." She clasped Jenny's hands and pressed her cheek against the older woman's.

Jenny froze for a moment, then let herself enjoy the genuine gesture of thanks. Nodding her head silently, she stepped away. Glancing in both directions, she crossed the street without looking back. As she stepped across the sidewalk with her head held high, the milling crowd parted with a new respect and let her enter the building without comment.

Quinn firmly clasped Calli's elbow, not giving her the chance to shake him off again and led her to her vehicle. As they got closer, the last few voyeurs scuttled away from the shiny doors. His thunderous expression dared anyone to approach the vehicle again as he waited until Calli climbed inside. "Lock your doors and keep them locked. I'll follow you to your house."

"That's not necessary."

Quinn placed a hand on the window's edge and leaned down to stare at her. "You're outvoted on this one, Mrs. Lemont. So just put the key in the ignition and do what you're told. Are you always this stubborn?" He grinned to soften his rebuke.

Calli couldn't help but smile back, the first in a long time. "All right. You win." She admitted silently that nothing would make her feel better than Quinn following her until she was back on the freeway and further from harm's way. The engine purred a second later. "Do you think Jenny will really be okay?"

His gaze moved away from hers as he studied Margaret and Phyllis, smoking beside the building's entrance. "Wait one minute. I want to make sure I'm right behind you when we leave."

Quinn walked purposefully toward the two women. As he came to a halt, they stared up with disinterest.

"Got a problem, big man?" Margaret boldly questioned. She flicked her cigarette and watched it roll to a stop beside his expensive boot.

"I just thought that you should know you'll be in a big heap of trouble if you touch one hair on Jenny Johnson's head."

"You threatenin' me?" Margaret sneered back.

"That's exactly what I'm doing. Consider it your only warning. I'll make your life so miserable that you'll wish you'd never seen my face. I'll have the Boston PD haul both your asses in for assault. And I can easily do it."

Margaret swiveled her neck and elbowed Phyllis. "Like we couldn't use a nap and three squares a day, eh Phyllis?"

"There's no drugs when you're behind bars. Whether it'll be a day, a week or a month, you'll be miserable when you can't get your fix." Quinn smiled arrogantly. That got their attention. "We'll see how tough the two of you are when you're dribbling like a couple of babies and begging for relief from detoxification." It went against Quinn's nature to be so brusque, but Jenny's safety and wellbeing depended on it. "Do we understand each other?"

"Fuck you, mister."

"Do we understand each other?" Quinn reiterated firmly. "I'll be checking daily."

The two women exchanged surly glances. Phyllis turned away and stubbed out her cigarette on the side of the building.

"Yeah, we understand each other." Margaret's brow dipped as she watched him walk away, wondering where Jenny had met her knight in shining armor.

* * * * *

Diego Trejos shifted on the expensive leather seat, amazed at the scene unfolding before him. Raine Lemont's wife looked to be in a bit of trouble as she stood on the steps of an old building that he knew to be a women's shelter. Homeless, no resources whatsoever to speak of, a lot of the women who found refuge within the four walls were nothing more than crackheads and junkies. And a lot of them were his customers. He hadn't dealt directly with them over the last year, but his contacts did. Somehow, they found the money to feed their addictions. They were a piteous lot, outcasts from their families and hungry to steal a quick dollar no matter how it was presented to them. And right now, it looked like Calli Lemont was going to be the main meal.

He grabbed his camera, brought it to his eye and adjusted the telescoping lens until he had a clear view of the terror that contorted her face. As he squinted through the small glass frame, his mind worked furiously to figure out why she would visit what was obviously a place way out of her normal realm. When she'd pulled her little sports car from the garage and he'd followed her out onto the freeway, the shelter was the last place he'd imagined that she would end up.

And where in hell was Raine? Had he sent his wife here for a purpose?

A malevolent smile curled his lip upward. At some point, he would come face-to-face with Lemont. But for now? The only thing Enrique had ordered was that he and Jorge keep a close eye on the house and on the wife. Calli would eventually become the catalyst that would bring El León back to the lair.

"El León," he muttered into the quietness while he studied Calli's frightened posture with cold emotion. The Lion, named because of the man's glittering eyes flecked with gold. Diego had thought the American was his friend, had been pulled in by Raine's claim to be an intricate part of the cartel. Raine, who had worked so hard until he had gained their trust. Then? He'd duped them all. Because of it? He'd been hit. Or so they had all believed until a few hours ago.

A slight gasp left his mouth when things began to heat up on the building's steps. Having the camera's lens was like being in the pocket of what looked to be a possible sexual assault in the clear light of day. Too bad Jorge was sleeping at the safe house. Things were getting interesting.

Diego knew the two—Margaret and Phyllis. Not only tough, but formidable bullies when their systems were loaded with crystal meth. But catch them when they were down and dry, and they'd be on their knees begging for hits.

Diego's cock began to swell when the women's beefy hands wandered across Calli Lemont's breasts and ass. Three women. Shit. He'd love to watch the two fuck Lemont's wife. Maybe this was his lucky day. He had the camera after all—that is if they managed to pull her into a nearby alley. Hell, maybe he'd even give the two ugly broads some free shit if they held her down for him. What the fuck? Who cared? Eventually, she was going to be killed anyway.

Suddenly, the two aggressors backed off…

"What the fuck…"

Diego moved the lens a hair to the right. Jenny Johnson. He knew her, also. A lonely desperate woman who often tried to end her addiction, but was an easy mark a year ago when he and his pushers had held the drugs beneath her nose.

His body tightened. What? The bitch was breaking up Diego's voyeuristic fun by coming to Calli Lemont's aid.

Calli's small form flashed by the circle of his viewing area. Moving the camera again slightly, the air whooshed from his lungs.

Raine Lemont held his wife in a tight embrace, comforting her as she clung crazily to him. Diego had been so intent on enjoying the unwanted overtures that he'd missed the man's arrival.

"That dirty son of a bitch…" It was the only thing Diego uttered as he watched El León lead his wife across the street to sit in a car. Resting one elbow on the steering wheel to steady the camera, Diego zoomed in on the couple and witnessed Raine tenderly cupping his wife's cheek.

The camera's shutter clicked as he took shot after shot. When Jenny Johnson's ratty shape appeared beside the open door, he took pictures of her. Somehow, the three were connected because it was easy to see the familiarity among them. In fact, Diego wondered if the three of them had their own little drug ring going, one that was started with the cartel's money and property. Why else would they be together, especially in this part of town?

He kept the camera trained on the group until Jenny returned to the shelter. Raine soon had his wife settled in her car. Diego finally dropped the expensive camera on the seat and started his own vehicle when Calli pulled away from the curb and Raine swung his car across the lane and followed directly behind her.

* * * * *

The entire ride home, Calli struggled to keep her eyes on the road instead of the rearview mirror. But every time she let her thoughts flow back to the horrific few minutes of that afternoon, her skin crawled with goose bumps and a shiver trickled down her spine. Glancing in the mirror to see Quinn, though, as he drove so resolutely behind her, never more than a car length or two away, immediately settled her nerves. Then, the remembered feel of his strong arms and soothing presence would start her heart rapping.

Her mind sifted through the facts of the day and she couldn't logically dismiss what she now admitted was some sort of unexplained attraction to the man. Did it stem from the fact that Quinn had suddenly appeared when she most needed him? Or was it because she was now finding it difficult to disconnect him from visions of Raine? Their looks and physique were so alike that she had to keep reminding herself they were two separate individuals...

Quinn had treated her gently and carefully after the episode on the steps. He'd refused to let her drive home alone. What was she going to say to him when they arrived at her house? Would he expect her to disappear inside as he went on his way?

The moment of truth approached when she turned into the driveway. Calli reached up and clicked the remote control on the visor, waited for the garage door to completely rise, then drove inside.

Her gaze returned to the rearview mirror. Quinn pulled up behind her. Calli took a deep breath, reached for her purse and opened her door. By the time she stood, he was already out of his car and walking toward the garage. Not knowing what to do, she clutched at her leather bag and waited in the waning light.

His smile made her heart jump erratically. He hesitated by the trunk of her car.

"How are you doing?" he asked.

"I'm fine now. Thank you again. I can't believe what happened in broad daylight...or what could have happened if you and Jenny hadn't shown up. I'm just thankful that you did."

He leaned against her car and crossed his arms. "That's a rough part of town, Calli. If you ever feel the need to speak with

Jenny and can't get hold of her, call me. I'll collect her so you can meet her in safer surroundings."

She tipped her head and stared up at him. "What were you doing with her?"

Quinn shrugged. "I don't know. I guess I just had more questions about the past. She's the only one who can answer them, except for Raine's adoptive parents. You said you didn't want me to approach them, so I won't. Not unless I have your permission." He placed his hands behind him on the trunk and crossed one ankle over the other. "It's been a bizarre couple of days. Everything I thought was real suddenly isn't. It's strange to think that all these years have gone by and I never knew I had a brother."

She felt the same way. Both their lives were irrevocably changed by Jenny's appearance.

She stared up and it hit her that she and Quinn would always be connected and nothing or no one could change that.

Calli didn't want him to leave. The thought of four lonely walls closing in on her was too much after the last few hours.

"Would you like to come in for some coffee? It's the least I can offer after what you did for me today. I'd like to find out more about Jenny and why she's where she is today."

There was nothing that he would like better. "I'd love to. Thanks."

She nodded, walked to the door switch and pressed it. The door lumbered down the rails. With a smile, she headed for the service entrance into the house with Quinn following in her wake.

* * * * *

Diego followed at a distance for the forty-five minutes it took the Lemonts to reach their home. He sat an entire block away, but his high-powered camera put him directly in the yard.

Raine's wife pulled into the driveway first. When the electric garage door opened and she drove in, Raine pulled his car up behind her, shut it off and got out. He strolled just inside the garage.

The camera clicked continually until the door came down, blocking whatever chance Diego had to spy on them.

He pulled away from the curb. Enrique was going to be livid when he discovered the details of the day. His dark eyes darted to the clock on the dash. It was Jorge's turn to sit as watchdog. All Diego desired was a soft mattress and pillow. As he turned the car and headed for the freeway, he wondered how many days would pass before their boss arrived, and along with him, recruits. Only then could surveillance of the Lemonts be carried out twenty-four hours a day. Once on the freeway, he increased his speed and headed for the secluded safe house set up for the head of the cartel.

Indecision rested heavy in his chest as he drove along. What Diego desired was quick retribution. A clean, precise end to a traitor's life. He wanted to knock on the front door of the Lemont home and shoot the first person who answered. The task would be easy because of the gun's silencer. From there, it would only be a few seconds more before the second shot would be ejected. Raine's and his wife's deaths would be sealed forever by his own hand. No matter what, Deigo wanted to be the one to perform the act, therefore raising his status among the cartel. One day, he might be the one to give the orders.

Working for Enrique, however, is what stalled his actions. His employer's plan was to flush out the money and drugs first. They were not going to search blindly any longer. Once things were back in the rightful owner's hands then, and only then, would retribution be carried out.

Chapter Nine

Quinn followed Calli into the kitchen, thinking about the day's strange events. His heartbeat quickened as once again he wondered why Calli had visited the shelter. Was it really to simply speak to Jenny or was there a secondary purpose? Like drug distribution, something she still did to support her lifestyle—the one Raine had created. His brooding gaze moved about the lush kitchen with its expensive appliances. The room, like the entire house, screamed wealth.

If so, why then was she accosted on the steps? There wasn't a junkie wandering around out there willing to ruin their chances of a fix by roughing up a supplier.

No, he had to quit thinking like a cop. Calli's still-pallid features attested to the frightening close call of that afternoon. Innocence before guilt—the American standard.

He watched her as she shrugged off her coat and followed the line of her slender back to the familiar slight curve of her hips and mentally shook his head.

How was it possible that he already knew the joy of holding her body, that he could attest to how his own reacted when she squeezed tightly around his cock as he pounded into her heat?

Quinn rubbed the back of his neck, trying to decide if Calli would think he was entirely out of his mind if he told her he'd known her for nearly six months already.

"Why don't you take off your jacket and grab a chair?"

Calli's voice whipped him back to the present.

"I'll get some coffee on."

His eyes met hers. She stood in the center of the kitchen, hesitantly chewing on her bottom lip as they locked stares.

"I-I just can't believe this whole thing," she murmured quietly.

Christ, what did she mean? Had he spoken his thoughts aloud only seconds earlier?

"Believe what?" He waited.

Her hand swept through the soft hair of her temple before she tore her gaze from his and moved to the coffeepot with a shake of her head.

"Everything. That Jenny Johnson appeared out of nowhere. That she's Raine's real mother... *Was* his real mother. The adoption report. That you're his twin—something I can't disbelieve because you're his exact image." Her hands moved automatically as she scooped grounds into a coffee filter, anything just so she wouldn't have to look at him. "That somehow you and she showed up today when I most needed you..."

He watched a small shudder run through her as she picked up the glass carafe and moved to the sink. Quinn didn't think she even realized the quick physical reaction of extreme fright she'd just experienced, as she filled the pot and poured the water into the coffee well.

"I'm just glad I did. That's a tough lot down there."

When Calli walked purposefully to the table to sit down, he shed his jacket and joined her.

She set her elbows on the surface, clasped her fingers together and settled her round chin atop her raised hands as she stared at him again. "I don't know what I was thinking. The closer I got to the shelter as I drove down there today, the more I realized I had absolutely no business being there, but I couldn't stop myself. Quinn...I need to know more. You were with her. Has she told you anything else?"

"Bits and pieces. What do you want to know?"

Suddenly something that Raine's mother had uttered when they were on the street came to her. "Well, for starters, just before Jenny said goodbye today, she told you she'd think about something you said. Can you say what that was?"

Quinn weaved his fingers together as he leaned on the table. "Have you taken a good look at her?"

"What? That she looks years older than she actually is? I attributed that to the fact she's led a hard life."

"Oh, yeah, that she has. I can't imagine what it must be like to continually be rejected your entire life. Whether it was her parents or the men she was with." He shook his head and stared at his hands. Finally he looked up. "My mother, Calli, is a junkie who will do anything and everything to keep her continual high going." He watched the shock register in Calli's eyes and hoped it was genuine. "I spotted that fact immediately the first time I met her. Spending time with her only confirmed it. I confronted her about her addiction this afternoon. Of course, she denied it at first—they all do. Then she was going to leave the restaurant in a huff. I told her I wouldn't have anything to do with her ever again if she didn't at least listen to what I had to say. One chance. That's all I gave her."

"I take it that she did. The two of you arrived at the shelter together."

Quinn sat back. The aroma of fresh brewing coffee hung in the air. It felt good to sit here with Calli Lemont. Besides Danny, she was the only other person he could discuss his mother with. "It was tough to hold firm. The last thing I want is for her to disappear from my life. But taking a tough stance is the only way to even begin a discussion on getting clean. One thing I've learned in my line of work is if you give an addict an inch, they'll take a mile, so to speak. She finally sat back down. Didn't have too much to say, but at least I had her attention. Do you know, she never gave any indication that what I had to say had even sunk in until she said goodbye at the shelter?"

"How awful, Quinn. I can't even imagine living in that sort of world." Calli rose from the table. "One sees it on the

119

television. Newspapers report about drug addiction daily. I guess I'm guilty of not paying any attention because it's never affected me before." She collected two mugs from a cabinet while she spoke.

Quinn watched her as she poured coffee. Calli was either a great actor or she really had no clue about the darker side of the drug world. He didn't care. He was going on instinct now. She was just too surprised and shocked. What would she say if he mentioned Raine's secret life?

"Are you going to try and get her help? When are you going to see her again?" Calli asked over her shoulder.

"Hopefully, this week sometime. I'd like to get her to consider some sort of treatment or at least counseling that will lead her in that direction."

"Can I help?"

"You? You're not obligated."

"I know that, but she's Raine's mother. And Jenny has this...aura. I don't know how else to explain it. It's as if she's reaching out with one hand and slapping you away with the other. My offer was sincere. I'd like to be involved."

Quinn smiled his acceptance. "Okay. I'll tell you what. How about I set something up and we can both meet with her?"

Calli returned to the table with the first real smile on her face since he'd intervened at the shelter. Her soft expression created an instant need inside Quinn to get closer to her.

"I would like that. I probably need to tell you that I might have made a big mistake the day she came to the theater searching for Raine. I gave Jenny fifty dollars, never realizing that it would go toward supporting her habit. She just looked so...so ragged and in need."

"How were you to know? Be wary, though. Deep down, I suspect Jenny is a wonderful person who knows the difference between right and wrong. Her actions and words are all dictated by her addiction, however. After today, she most likely will be more comfortable about contacting you and requesting money—

especially since you've unknowingly donated to the cause already. She'll give you some flimsy excuse. Don't believe it for a second."

Calli rested the fingertips of one hand against her mouth, closed her eyes and sighed heavily. "I really didn't know," she murmured. "I can't believe how blind I was."

"Well, now you do know. You gave her the money out of kindness and nothing else." Quinn reached out and clasped Calli's free hand to lend support to his words. The touch of her skin sent a surprising spike of arousal straight through his lean belly. Even more surprising was the unexpected glow in her gray eyes the instant his fingers linked with hers.

Calli didn't pull her hand away this time. The slight touch of his thumb brushing across her knuckles was too mesmerizing. She swallowed against the sudden dryness of her throat. Flickers of excitement prickled the honeyed skin of her arms. What was this? What was this strange and exciting…awakening of sorts that she experienced when in his company? Even earlier when consumed with fright, his magnetism had still seized her emotions. She was inexplicably drawn to him.

Guilt burgeoned inside her. Only hours had passed since she'd cried her heart out for Raine. She still loved him with every beat of her heart, but Quinn was real. Quinn was here beside her… Quinn was…

His fingers tightened around hers.

Calli raised her eyes to his. The gold flecks anchored her gaze just before his eyes narrowed faintly. She was suddenly aware of the slight shadow of a beard darkening his square jaw. Her gaze flowed to a miniscule scar just above a firm upper lip, then to the straight line of his nose. The beat of her heart quickened. Suddenly, to simply take a breath was increasingly more difficult. Was he feeling strangled by the same emotion?

"Enough about Jenny. Tell me about you." The words left Quinn's mouth in a lazy, undemanding manner. A playful glimmer appeared in his eyes.

"Me?"

One corner of his mouth curved upward. "Yes, you." He made no attempt to loosen his gentle grip on her hand. "Tell me where the fascinating color of your eyes came from. Tell me why your hair reminds me so much of a smooth piece of chocolate, why your skin makes me think of honey."

She blinked once, then felt a rush of embarrassed heat suffuse her cheeks. "There's not much to tell," she responded slowly. But for some strange reason, she couldn't stop the small grin that tugged at her lips.

"I think there is. Simple questions, Calli. I have to know."

Her eyes lowered to his strong fingers. Quinn wanted to know about her. Simple unobtrusive questions — that deserved uncomplicated answers. She had to understand one thing first. She glanced up. "Why are you holding my hand?"

Quinn shrugged his broad shoulders. "Because it makes me feel good."

She tipped her head in acceptance at his honest reply. Quinn knew what he spoke of. It was nice to hold someone's hand just because it was pleasurable to do so. "My father is of Scandinavian heritage. His hair was blond when he was younger, like so many. But instead of blue eyes like most of his family, his tended toward the color gray. He was drafted during the Vietnam War. I'm sure now that you've already guessed he met my mother there."

Quinn nodded.

"It took a lot of red tape and quite a few years, but he was finally able to gain entrance for her into the States."

"You're a very beautiful and unique combination."

"Thank you."

Quinn's gaze coasted across her high cheekbones, down to her swan-like neck, then back to the silver eyes surrounded by dark lashes. He'd meant every word. Calli was exotic, almost reminding him of a delicate hothouse blossom. Crazy. The similarity struck a chord within him. For the many times he'd held her within his dreams, he'd never compared her to a flower.

"Calli?" His mind raced. What would she say if he told her that now? He wanted that knowledge out in the open. He wanted to understand why she'd haunted him for so long when they'd only recently met. "I need to tell you something. What I'm going to say will most likely sound preposterous, but just hear me out."

A soft smile touched her mouth. "After the last few days, I don't think much would surprise me now."

Quinn hoped that fact remained true. "The first time I knocked on your door, you can't imagine my surprise when it opened and you were standing there."

"I was the one surprised, Quinn. I remember waking up on the couch to see you wavering above me. I can't imagine what you thought when I kissed you. I thought you were Raine—a living, breathing Raine. As impossible as it was..." The rest of what she was about to say withered away to nothing.

"Promise me you won't bolt from the room when I tell you *why* I was shocked."

Her smile cooled slightly, but she continued to hold his hand. "You're giving me goose bumps, Quinn. All right. I promise to stay on my chair."

Quinn took a deep breath. "I was surprised because I had seen you before. In fact, many times."

Calli leaned forward. Her grin widened expectantly. "Really? Where? In a store? At a performance?" She squeezed his fingers, still enjoying the easy reassurance of his touch. "That's so cool. I wish I had seen you because I know I wouldn't have let you get away without telling me who you were. I honestly would have thought you were Raine."

His head wagged slowly. "No, not in a store or at a performance. Please don't think I'm crazy when I say this. For the last six months, I've dreamt about you. Suddenly the other day, you were standing there in flesh and blood, and I couldn't believe my eyes."

Her hand went limp in his grasp. Her smile was gone in an instant. She stared across the table. "I-I don't understand."

"I don't either. When you fainted, I brought you inside and knew that I'd find that little freckle above your lip. When I smoothed the hair from your cheek, I knew how silky your skin would feel beneath my fingers. Why? Because I was already intimately familiar with its texture."

Calli yanked her hand away and tucked it in her lap, wishing heartily for the serene mood of a moment earlier.

Quinn held his breath as he waited for her to say something. Her troubled eyes suddenly glittered with distrust.

She shot off her chair and rounded the opposite side of the table. "I don't know what kind of trick you're playing, but you can leave right now," she tossed over her shoulder.

Quinn was beside her in three bounds. Gently, but firmly, he halted her flight out of the kitchen. "Calli, please. Just listen to what I have to say. It's true. I don't blame you for not believing it. The whole notion is completely ridiculous. But I'm telling you the truth." His fingers tightened around her arm when she tried to jerk it from his grasp. "Please. Just let me explain."

She finally turned to face him, her arm still in his clutches.

His eyes pleaded silently.

"Is this some cruel joke?" God, she should shove him aside, but all she wanted to do was hold him so the lazy grin would return to his lips.

"It's not a joke, Calli." He reached out, slipped his hand into the dark mass of hair at her shoulder and let the strands glide over his fingers. "I knew that day what this would feel like, because I'd experienced it already."

She froze as his hand slipped to cup the back of her head.

"I hadn't realized that I was familiar with the scent of your perfume until it swirled inside my nostrils and reminded me of the many times I..." The words died in his throat.

"What?" she asked breathlessly. "The many times you what, Quinn?"

He didn't want Calli glaring at him with suspicion and doubt clouding her eyes.

"What, Quinn...tell me!"

"The many times I had held you in my arms. The many times I had kissed you and..."

Calli drew in a sharp breath. A split second later, it rushed from her lungs when his head lowered and his mouth whispered across her cheek. Her fingers itched to slap him, but the warm breath against her skin held her captive.

"I know, Calli, what will happen when I press my lips here..." His mouth wavered softly against the velvety skin of her neck. "You have a tender spot that gives away your racing heart..."

It was true. Raine had told her the very same thing so many times in the past. Her heart pounded inside her chest, picking up an even quicker tempo when his tongue flicked against her earlobe just before his lips smoothed a path of languorous kisses to finally rest against her temple.

"Do you believe me?" he whispered. "Think about it, Calli. How can I know all these things about you if they aren't true."

She floated in a shock-induced state. What was Quinn Morgan doing to her? Her heart leapt when he whispered beside her ear once more.

"I don't want you to be frightened of me. I had no control over those dreams. Say the word, Calli, and I promise I'll leave. Right now. Right this very minute."

She battled her emotions, wanting him to stay and wanting him to go. His touch...

"If not, I'm going to kiss you…" He leaned back to look down at her.

She only blinked, hypnotized by the magnetic hold he had on her emotions. He had just offered to do the one thing that had prodded her constantly since they'd first met. Calli didn't step away.

Quinn's satisfied murmur rumbled at the back of his throat when his free arm gently pulled her against him. Calli went willingly. She tipped her head back to stare up. "How…how is it possible, Quinn? How could it have been me? How—" His lips brushed over hers.

"I don't know." Her eyes fluttered shut. "All I know," another soft brush of his lips—slow and sensual—whispered across her cheek, "is that when you kissed me…"

Her mouth slanted as she hesitantly sought his lower lip when he nibbled his way back over her mouth and nuzzled her opposite cheek. A small groan of pleasure escaped when the pressure of his swollen cock rubbed against her belly. He was excruciatingly hard, he was wonderfully warm and alive.

"I realized it was really you," he continued. "The woman who had haunted my dreams for far too long…" Quinn drew her flattened palms up his chest, letting Calli link them at the back of his neck, then he tightened his embrace around her slim waist. He couldn't stop himself. He'd thought about this so many times since first discovering that she wasn't just a figment of his imagination. Without another word, his seeking mouth found hers.

Calli met his demand passionately, reveling in his strength and tenderness. She was powerless against the wanton desire he built with each stroke of his tongue inside her mouth, each fervent moan that echoed inside the kitchen, each surge of his hard cock against her belly.

"Quinn…" she managed between kisses that were becoming harder and more demanding. Sharp bolts of pleasure built inside her womb. Her fingers raced through the thickness of his dark hair and swept across his banded shoulders, as her mound ground against his cock with a will of its own.

Calli was on fire—a fire that had only sizzled a few short seconds ago and now leapt into a building blaze.

Quinn's hands circled her waist. With one effortless movement, he lifted Calli to the marbled countertop, never breaking contact with her hungry mouth. His hands blindly found her knees. He spread them wide, and then instantly cupped her rounded ass and dragged her body against his swollen cock.

She moaned against his mouth as her hands found his clenching buttocks. Moisture dripped between her legs, soaking her panties with each purposeful grind of his covered cock.

"Oh, god...Quinn..." she panted against his lips. Her mind registered one thing—Quinn's hand sketched a path beneath her silky blouse, spanned her waist, feathered up her spine and back, then around her rib cage to seek...

"It was always you, Calli. Always you reaching out for me. We made love so many times..."

She pushed her breast into the palm of his hand. Her nipple pebbled hard when his agile fingers easily undid the clasp of her bra. Instantly, his hot fingertips were back to roll a nipple, then caress the soft underside of a firm breast.

He could fuck her right here on the counter. She didn't care. She simply never wanted the ecstasy to disappear. Nothing mattered except the sizzling passion that sparked between them.

She whimpered when his hand slipped from beneath her blouse, then moaned in anticipation as he worked the buttons open. One...two... Suddenly, his hot breath mixed with the cool air as he dragged the edges away to expose firm petite mounds tipped with coral-colored areolas. His teeth nipped crazily between the hard darts of her nipples.

Calli's flailing hand found the muscled biceps of his right arm and slipped down the flexing length until she found his fingers at one breast. Guiding them to the heated dampness between her legs, she forced his hand against her, knowing full well he could feel her swollen lips as the seam of her pants rubbed against her clit. Her hips jerked against his palm with an urgent request.

Her stomach muscles clenched when his hand slid to her waistband. Furiously he worked the button open.

Quinn couldn't wait. His fingers dipped inside her underwear and slipped across the smooth flatness to the soft down of her pussy. He pressed on when Calli spread her legs further until the tip of his middle finger came in contact with her hot dripping slit and her swollen clit.

"Oh, god, Quinn…"

Their bodies started wildly when the first clanging ring of the phone reverberated across the kitchen, dousing their passion like a cold blast of water.

Quinn's hand jerked out of her pants when Calli scrambled to close her blouse, suddenly embarrassed beyond belief that she was half undressed and panting like she'd run a race. Her gaze dropped to the huge bulge at his crotch. Quinn was more than ready to…

She was off the counter before he even had a chance to help her down. She rounded him quickly, took a deep breath to settle her rocking emotions, and reached for the phone.

"He—" She cleared her throat. "Hello?" God, what was she going to do or say when the phone call was over? "Who?" She tried to concentrate. "No. No, I'm sorry. I'm not interested." She hung the phone back in the cradle. Her chin dropped to her chest as she struggled for air. A telemarketer had just saved her from possibly making a mistake she would be sorry for at a later date. She had simply let her emotions rule cognizant thought. What on Earth had come over her?

She couldn't turn around. Not yet. She closed her blouse one button at a time with shaking fingers and waited for him to say something. What was he doing?

Calli jumped at the touch of Quinn's hand against her shoulder.

"I'm sorry, Calli. Once you started kissing me back…"

She lifted a palm to silence him. The whole episode wasn't just Quinn's fault. Calli had easily slipped into the role of a wanton woman with just a mere touch. Squaring her shoulders, she turned and, once more, drowned in the depth of emotion burning in his gaze. "I'm sorry, too. Quinn, I think it would be better if you left. I'll give some thought to… Just give me a few days."

"I don't want to just walk away, Calli, before saying something. You can believe what I told you or not. There isn't much I can do to convince you that the last six months actually happened to me, but kissing you just now, holding you in my arms was the same. No, I take that back. It was better than a dream, because it was real. I also want you to remember something else. I'm not going to go away—not after what just happened. You felt it, too. Whatever it is that's between us, whatever force has pushed us together, bears some exploration. There's a reason for it. I won't just let it ride, but I will give you a few days."

He stepped back and Calli had the distinct impression that if he hadn't, Quinn would have swept her into his arms again. Once again, the sexual arousal created by his presence in the room intensified.

"Will you call me?" he asked quietly.

She stared at him. Would it matter if she did or not? He'd be back. Of that she was certain. She nodded her head. "Yes. Just give me a little time, Quinn, to digest all this."

She thought he'd say his goodbyes and leave quietly. Instead, Quinn reached out and waited for Calli to place her hand in his. Desiring his touch just for a few moments more, she clasped his strong fingers. He gently tugged until she stood a breath away. Without asking permission, he dipped his head and brushed her swollen lips with his.

"Goodbye, Calli. A few days. That's all. If I don't hear from you, I'll be back."

With that, he squeezed her hand, swiped his jacket off the back of the chair and let himself out.

Chapter Ten

∞

Calli flicked off the bathroom light and entered her lonely bedroom. She ruffled through some magazines, selected one and sank onto the window seat. Less than a minute passed by before she tossed it onto a nearby table with a fair amount of agitation. She'd read the same sentence over and over trying to forget the picture of Quinn Morgan standing in her home that first day she'd met him, but the image was imbedded in her brain—just as was the picture of him sitting across the small kitchen table the night before. Her mind shifted to the memory of his lion-like eyes, which had rendered her insensible when he'd lifted her onto the counter with purpose. The thrill of the passionate and quick sexual encounter still had the power to set her heart racing.

She leapt up and began to pace, furiously working to recapture the heartache that she'd lived with over the last twelve months, but suddenly remembering her life with Raine didn't bring her to her knees as it had in the past. The lonely ache was still there, but the edges of her grief had dulled—something she'd thought would never happen. And it was all because of his twin brother.

Her day had been horrible. She'd gone to Sanders Theater, thinking the long practice would rid her mind of the episode on the counter. She had been so wrong. Even when Maestro James had continually berated her for her many mistakes, she still hadn't been able to forget the feel of Quinn's lips against her breast and his fingers stroking her clit in the tight confines of her clothes.

With a sigh of frustration, she grabbed a brush, sat at her dressing table and attacked the long length of burnished strands that streamed down her back, and finally found the courage to face her dilemma head-on.

No man other than Raine had ever affected her. Not before she'd met him, nor after. Not emotionally or sexually. That was until Mr. Morgan had knocked on her door and given her one of the biggest shocks of her life.

Her hand halted in midair as she stared at herself in the mirror remembering back to the moment she'd awakened from her faint and discovered him kneeling beside her in the living room. At the time, she'd thought it was a miracle. By some act of god, Raine had come back to her. Her love. She'd been so overwhelmed at the sight that she'd latched on to Quinn's neck and drawn his mouth to hers. She had needed to be held so badly, needed to be physically loved, had desperately craved to have the sexual desire that Raine had created years earlier, quenched once more.

Quinn's appearance had changed everything. Calli finally understood one thing about the last year. She had unknowingly fought the revelation, but once it took root, there was no turning away from it and nothing she could do to change it. Subconsciously, she'd been trying to move forward and away from the many grief-stricken weeks.

She straightened on the padded bench. Raine had only returned from his nether world for sex. There was no conversation before or afterward. Just the hot sex for a short time before he was called away by some heavenly power. Could she live with that for the rest of her life? Could she actually exist without any emotional support from the person she loved or the chance to sit cuddled within a man's embrace talking about the little things that happened over the course of the day?

Was that what Raine was trying to relay to her with his silence? And if she could actually believe what Quinn had told her tonight, that he'd dreamed about her, that he had made love to her, was it because of her dead husband? Quinn had stated that some force had brought them together.

A sigh of frustration feathered across her lips.

"I'm sorry, Raine... I never thought I'd ever be able to go on without you. But I don't ache as badly as I did. I'm ashamed... I feel like I'm betraying the perfect love with a perfect man."

A perfect dead man, she corrected.

The brush bounced off the surface of her dressing table when it fell from limp fingers. Calli's forehead dropped into her open palms.

I can't separate one from the other... Raine can never come back. Am I finally admitting that? Is that why Quinn Morgan is haunting my every waking thought? Or am I being pulled in his direction because being in his company is like reliving the past?

Since meeting Quinn, it was as if she'd undergone a metamorphosis. The weepy and continually grieving person that she had been only a short week ago had somehow disappeared.

For some unfathomable reason, when Quinn had said goodbye, she'd shied away from the ivory keys with a strange elusiveness and instead raced to the second level of the house, unwilling to be lost inside the music, and with hopes that Raine would appear. And tonight when she'd arrived home, she'd never even entered the living room. She had not wanted Raine, not when the remembered warmth of Quinn's strong arms from the evening before still heated her desire.

* * * * *

That night Calli tossed and turned in her bed. Quiet feminine whimpers punctuated the dark corners of the master bedroom. In her dreams, she played the piano.

"I'm sorry, Raine. Please, come to me..."

Like a quiet morning mist that rolls across a meadow, his presence built, stronger and stronger. He had answered her call. She spread her arms wide to welcome him. Raine smiled and stepped closer, with his arms reaching out in reply.

But suddenly, it wasn't Raine. It was Quinn Morgan stepping in front of his brother with a dark, brooding look in his eyes as she sat trembling on the piano bench.

"You don't need him anymore, Calli..."

"Yes, it's my Raine... I've been playing so he'd come to me. I want you to go away."

"I can never be completely gone from your mind. Not now. Now when I know what it feels like to have your body wrapped around me."

Calli's heart beat heavily as she strained to see Raine's form where he stood behind his brother, but his image began to fade. His eyes would not meet hers but, instead, stared at his mirror image.

She had to get her husband's attention. If she didn't, Raine might disappear and never return. And it would be because of her infidelity.

"Raine! Tell him to leave! Please...I want you..."

She watched disbelievingly as his ethereal form slithered closer to his brother, Quinn. Separating the two was becoming increasingly difficult as Raine took one more step. His ghostly body disappeared bit by bit as his shape became Quinn's. Two sets of broad shoulders became one. Quinn's face blurred momentarily as the outline of her husband's moved into place. Suddenly, it was only Quinn standing before her, his eyes glittering. The two men were reflections of one another, but Calli understood in the deepest sense that only Quinn remained. One man who was not a ghost. One man who was warm and real, a man she knew existed in the real world because she'd met him.

"He's leaving, Calli, and he won't be coming back. But I'm here. I'll watch over you. I'll keep you from harm. You have to trust me. Raine didn't mean to do the things he did. He didn't mean to put you in danger."

Her silver eyes flashed in question. "Danger? What are you talking about? I'm in no danger..." Her voice cracked as the last word left her lips. Confused tears welled in her eyes. Calli's hands came up and covered her mouth to keep the baffled sob inside.

A gentle hand cupped her cheek. Calli's frightened gaze darted upward in an effort not to react to the aroused emotions streaming through her, knowing that the gentle, loving touch was not from Raine's hand. It was only Quinn now.

"Don't be sad, Calli. It's time to let him go. I promised him that I would always take care of you."

She closed her eyes and tipped her head against the gentle fingers that now lightly threaded their way through her hair. Oh, god, his warm breath against her neck was like the gentle touch of a lover's fingers. She welcomed the wonderful perception of not feeling alone and bereft. Those emotions had clutched at her for so many months...

His hand glided down over her shoulder until it cupped her breast. Another touch—fingers trailing down across her hip, over her flat belly until they teased her sex. The satiny material of her gown wedged between her lips as he stroked her clit, slow and wonderfully masterful caresses that swelled her bud and promised a hot orgasm. Her hips dipped against the pressure. A moan escaped. But the man whose touch was gentle and loving wasn't her husband. Her jaw clenched as she whimpered quietly. She couldn't forget Raine. She would always love him, but Quinn... He would be here when she needed him.

She glanced up to see a shadowed masculine jaw. His lips parted as his mouth lowered to capture hers...

Calli jerked upwards and shot a panicked stare about the darkened room. Brushing tangled strands from her cheek, she tossed the blanket aside in a flurry, scurried to the edge of the bed and fumbled to turn on the lamp.

Squinting against the sudden glare, she waited until her breathing calmed and her heartbeat slowed. A wash of liquid between her legs dampened her thighs. Her fingers flew to her flushed cheeks. It wasn't Raine who haunted her dream tonight.

It was Quinn—and the fact that just before she'd awakened, he was going to kiss her as his fingers played a sensual rhapsody between her legs.

Calli's heart pounded anew as she took flight from the bed and raced from the room. She flicked on the chandelier over the staircase and hurried down the winding stairs. Once in the kitchen, she set about heating water in a teapot, purposely keeping her mind blank. Once that task was finished, she turned for the canister of tea and stopped dead in her tracks when she heard a muffled sound come from the living room.

The hair rose on her neck. She tipped her head, listening intently, not moving a muscle or daring to breathe.

Nothing now. Absolute quiet.

Was she mistaken? Her eyes darted quickly to the security panel situated on the wall by the back door. The red light glowed steadily. Still, she couldn't shake the apprehension that rested in her throat in the form of a solid lump.

"Don't be ridiculous…" she murmured, a bit surprised that she had just whispered. Even so, her words seemed to echo loudly about the room.

She barely breathed. Forcing one foot in front of the other until she reached the arched doorway leading to her living room, she clutched her arms about her. Her eyes immediately fell upon the small lamp she always left glowing in the corner of the large room. Everything looked to be in its place.

Swallowing back the lump, her gaze flowed about the room. She proceeded cautiously past the first chair, her eyes darting constantly to the shadowed corners.

"Raine? Is that you?"

Silence.

She ignored the raised hair on her arms and forced herself to move forward once more.

"Is someone there?"

Did she hear breathing? Her head tipped as she strained to get past the sound of blood pounding in her ears. Calli's hand slid slowly across the smooth wall until it came in contact with a light switch. The room instantly flooded with bright overhead light.

Each breath she inhaled seemed to echo in the room as she passed the baby grand and stopped before the pedestal that held Raine's violin. Her eyes settled on the instrument, then moved to the piano.

Had he been here waiting for her to come to him? As she tentatively reached out to stroke the violin, a floorboard squeaked in the foyer. Her shoulders jerked as she spun in the direction of the sound, every nerve on edge as she stared breathlessly across the room. Without thought, her fingers clutched a small wooden statue. She held it out before her, then darted her eyes back to the edge of the wall that rounded into the entryway, then searched wildly for the portable phone. It was nowhere to be seen. Her eyes glued to the foyer entrance. Something or someone was just around the corner hiding in the muted light.

What should she do? Keep going or run for the kitchen to dial 911?

"Raine?" She blinked against the terror she felt and slid her feet forward, step by step until she was halfway across the large room. "Who's there? I know someone is in this house."

The near silent click of the front door closing was like a blast of sound booming across the room.

Calli clutched the statue tightly and raced forward. She fell against the door with the statue bouncing across the tiled floor. Her fingers scrambled to link the chain. As soon as she managed to slide the rounded bolt into the slot, her gaze dropped to the open bolt lock.

Someone had been in her house. The security system had never gone off when it should have.

A high-pitched shrill came from the kitchen. Mindlessly, she took off and raced through the house to the back door, instantly checking the lock there. It was in place as it had been before going to bed. Whistling steam spouted from the teapot as she shut off the burner. The hissing noise stopped as Calli slumped into a chair trembling, eyes wide and frightened.

* * * * *

Jenny huddled against the cracked brick, clutching her worn coat tightly around her trembling body to shield herself from the swirling wind in the alley. Her head tipped back to rest against the dank wall. She couldn't do it. She'd tried, knowing deep inside that inevitably her demons would once again extract her will to detox. She'd walked most of the night, first by pacing on the sidewalk in front of the shelter. The restlessness, the intense stomach cramps, the anxiety had driven her until somehow she was crouching in pain at her usual pickup locale.

If she could just get through one more night. She needed to get out of the alley. She needed help. But she hurt.

Her eyes drifted shut as a shudder ran through her limbs. It shouldn't be long. The ebony of night had turned to dawn. Soon, one of the pushers would appear beside her like a ghost materializing from nowhere. He or she would have something.

It took great effort to concentrate on the moment, to stay upright and keep her thoughts flowing together. Her eyes snapped open and her gaze was drawn to the puddle of vomit only inches away from her feet. Had she thrown up? Too many days without the stuff. Yes. That was the problem. Just one more time. Just one more little pill or one more sniff or one more injection to get her through the coming hours. Then she'd try again. She had to try again. The dragon slowly exacted her flesh inch by inch. Soon, she would disintegrate to nothingness.

Quinn knew.

Jenny's head lolled against the cement. Her stomach lurched and bile burned the back of her throat. Her only living son understood that she was a user, an addict who needed the sweet euphoric release in order to get through the hellish days of her existence. She'd worked so hard to find her sons. She had to quit for them. No, only Quinn. The other one was dead...

Jenny's fingers slipped into her pocket and fluttered about to locate the rolled fifty-dollar bill. Panic filled her chest. It was gone. She shoved herself from the wall, her eyes wide and terrified as she scanned the ground below her.

She had to have the stuff. If she didn't find the money to pay for it, she'd never get through the next few days. Just one more time. That's all.

Jenny fell to her knees, disregarding the gravel that bit into her flesh and scrambled across the dirty alley with her heart pounding in her ears. Her hands swept crazily in search of the bill. Her own sob of despair echoed against the brick walls surrounding her. What if she couldn't get a fix? The drugs, no matter what form, were her only friends, her only strength to deal with the horridness of her life. She had to find the money.

She reached the alley's dead end where garbage cans piled against one another, overflowing with waste. What if the wind had blown the money there? Yes! That's what had happened. God, she needed more light! Panic overwhelmed her senses as she ruffled through the trash piled on the ground in search of the fifty-dollar bill. Nothing! Nothing! She would never make the day, never make the hour without her fix.

"Hey."

She spun around and her alarmed gaze fell upon a dark shape at the opening of the alley. Outlined by the streetlight, the shape wavered and made her think of the devil himself. She blinked and tried to remember where she was.

"You lookin' to buy?"

Jenny silently reached out, leaned one hand against a garbage can and dragged herself upright.

The dark-cloaked figure walked toward her, the dull thud of his boots ringing in the silence with each step he took until he stopped before her.

"Who… Who are you?" Jenny trembled out. He was unfamiliar, his face mostly hidden by the raised collar and black knit beanie pulled down low over his brow. Not the pusher she'd come to know. "Where's Blackcat?"

"Blackcat couldn't make it. I'm checking for him. Need a fix, Jenny? He said you might."

She watched his hand slither inside his pocket and wondered what he had on him. It should be good if he was here in Blackcat's stead. Blackcat's stuff always made her feel better. Her glassy eyes moved back to his blurred face. She blinked, but the light from the street behind him hid his features. "How do you know my name?"

A quiet chuckle whispered past her.

"Yeah, Blackcat said you'd be here, hungry and craving the stuff. You've missed a few nights."

A sob welled in her throat. She didn't have money. Blackcat would loan it, exacting a promise that she pay the next time, because he knew there would always be a next time. He understood her need. Would the man before her feel the same way? "I… I don't have any money. I had it, but it's gone. Can I pay Blackcat next time?" She wouldn't tell this stranger that there wasn't going to be a next time. She was going to get clean. Just one last hit…then she would get clean.

His stance shifted beneath the heavy coat. "You're hungry for it, aren't you? I can tell. I can hear it in your voice. But you don't have any money… This shit doesn't come free."

Exhaustion rolled through Jenny. Her stomach rolled crazily. She was going to vomit again. "Blackcat knows me. He would give it. Please… I can't do it today. I can't face…"

"Tell me something, Jenny. How do you know Raine?"

Her brow furrowed as she tried to focus on his question. If only her regular supplier had showed. She looked about, confused, and tried to concentrate. "Raine? My son?"

"He's your son." The man's response was not a question, but more a statement. "Does he give you drugs?"

No. No drugs, because he knew she was a junkie. Quinn wouldn't do that because he was a cop. But he was dead. Her brain spun. She was crashing. God, she couldn't go through that. She needed a pill. Just one small hit. Just for today. Wait. Her hand fluttered through her damp hair and clutched at her skull. Raine was dead, not Quinn.

"Please give me something. It's been too many days." Her entire body trembled in the cold.

"But you don't have any money." His hand reached out to stroke the weathered curve of her cheek. "I don't have any pills. Tell me about Calli Lemont. Does she share her money with you?"

Jenny wrapped her arms around her midriff and bent forward slightly. She sucked in deep gulps of air to quell the panic rising. She had to have something. She hurt and she wanted it to go away. What was she going to do? How was she going to make it through the crash? Each time they became worse. Not now. She couldn't go through that now. The devil had asked her something. What? Money…yes.

"Calli gives me money." But she'd lost it. The fifty-dollar bill was gone.

"And then you do what she asks you to? Tell me, is she your boss?"

His quiet words floated past her ear.

God, Jenny needed her fix. "Yes…" Whatever the demon wanted. She would comply because she was going to be sick again any moment now.

"I don't have pills, but I have something else."

"What…" Jenny breathed out.

"You want an injection? Meth...very clean. It'll only take a few minutes to hit your system. Then your pain will disappear."

"But...yes. I want it. But I don't have money. Please give me something."

"Sure, Jenny. But you have to return the favor. Let me fuck you. One hole is like another. A hit for a fuck. You up to a deal like that?"

Her mind spun and eagerly looked forward to the drug's ecstasy swimming through her veins. The intense high would get her moving again, would help her exist through the next few days. A fuck? Who cared? She'd done it before when she didn't have a single dollar in her pocket.

Her head nodded frantically. "Yes... Do what you want. Just give me the stuff."

The demon chuckled again. "You're all alike. All right, Jenny. Take off your coat. Go over there by the garbage can, bend over it and drop your pants. I don't want to look at your ugly face when I'm fucking you. Once you're ready, I'll shoot you up. I've got some good stuff."

Jenny turned and shuffled trancelike to the end of the alley. Soon, soon she'd have the stuff. He could have his fuck if it would provide the relief she craved. Shrugging off her coat, her mind no longer registered the air's dampness as her hands moved to the ripped elastic waistband of her pants. She dragged them and her underwear down past her knees without ever looking back, and then draped herself across a soiled cover of a garbage can. She listened to the footsteps behind her as they came closer. He shuffled behind her and a moment later she heard paper tearing. Out of the corner of her eye, she saw an empty condom packet float to the ground. It wasn't long before his cock cushioned against her bare ass, then the pressure disappeared.

"Spread your legs wider so your cunt is easy to see."

Jenny tried to adjust her stance, but her waistband held her legs prisoner. She kicked off one shoe and slipped her foot through one leg of her pants. Dirty water seeped into her threadbare sock.

Let him look. She didn't care. She only wanted...

"Give me the stuff."

He moved to stand beside her. Turning her head, she watched him slip on rubber gloves first and then pull a syringe from a small case.

"What?" he said when he caught the direction of her gaze. "You didn't think I'd touch or fuck you without protection. You street bitches carry too many diseases. Give me your arm. And keep yourself bent over. Amazing. I'm standing here with my dick hanging out and the only thing you can feast your eyes on is this little needle of happiness."

Jenny ignored him. She reached out her arm, nearly salivating with what she knew would be relief. Her eyes closed as he drew up the baggy sleeve of her sweatshirt.

There was a small prick. A warm feeling traveled up her arm. Soon.

He was behind her again, his fingers spreading her lips. She was hardly aware of his rubber-encased cock sliding into her pussy, or the pain of a dry entry because her limbs suddenly became lighter as the drug flowed through her veins. As he pounded into her, she discounted the metal handle of the dirty lid digging into one breast. Her brain suddenly became clearer, less pain-racked. She would get through another day with the ecstasy in her blood.

Chapter Eleven

🕉

Calli pulled into a parking spot in front of the Sixth Precinct building. She hadn't dialed 911 the evening before. Nothing was taken and her alarm system hadn't gone off. As each minute had passed after she'd thought she heard the click of the door closing, she'd begun to doubt that someone had actually been in her home. Lately, she couldn't think straight. Maybe it was forgetfulness that the door wasn't locked. But she'd still spent a harrowing night sitting at her kitchen table with every light on in the house. She might tell Quinn about the incident depending on how the next hour panned out.

But more importantly, she had something else to say, and something even more significant to carry out. After nearly a year, she was going to take a chance and reach for a new future. Calli was certain that Raine had a hand in her meeting his twin. What other explanation could there be?

As she got out of the car, she convinced herself she was doing the right thing by coming here. Knowing that it wouldn't be much longer before Quinn showed up on her doorstep, she'd made the decision to see him again in a much safer surrounding and on her terms. There would be people around. It was better than the quiet solitude of her home and the chance of him kissing her again. Next time, she might not be so lucky to have the phone ring. Next time, he would have her naked and beneath him. Of that she was certain, and just as certain that she would most likely follow his lead. She didn't want her new beginning to start that way, not one that would be created simply because she couldn't control her sexual urges.

Calli walked through the glass front doors, stopped at the reception desk and asked where she might find Quinn Morgan. Directions were pointed out. With a thank you, she proceeded down the hallway, glancing into every office she passed by. Finally, she spotted a nameplate with Detective Quinn Morgan on it right where the receptionist had told her it would be.

She was excited. Even with all the strange happenings over the past few days and the frightening night behind her, she eagerly looked forward to seeing him again. She peeked around the corner of the doorjamb, spied him at his desk and knocked on the open door.

Quinn glanced up disinterestedly. At the sight of Calli's smiling face, he jumped up and rounded his desk. "Hello! You're the last person I expected to see standing there."

"Hi, Quinn. I hope you don't mind that I'm bothering you at work." He just stood there staring at her with a strange expression. Funny, he wasn't inviting her in. Maybe she'd made a mistake in coming to the precinct.

"No...no it's fine. It's just that I was on my way out in a few minutes." Christ almighty. He really hadn't planned to go anywhere, but he had to get her out of the building before McMartin spotted her—or before the man heard any of their conversation. What had he been thinking to give her his card? There was just too much at stake. "How about a cup of coffee down the street first?"

"Are you sure you can leave?"

"No problem. Just let me grab my jacket."

She instantly felt better. For a moment there, she wasn't so sure he had even wanted to see her. She pushed aside the last of her insecurities. Enough was enough. She'd come here for one reason and she was going to see it through.

He yanked his jacket from a peg on the wall, took her elbow, clicked the lock on his door and slammed the door behind him. They hadn't taken three steps from his office when McMartin rounded the corner at the end of the hall, his head down as he concentrated on an open file in his hands.

Quinn kept his cool and neatly shielded Calli's body with his own as he turned her back. "Hell, I forgot something. Come with me. It won't take too long." He had to get her to Danny's office. If he took the time to fish out his keys and get his door open again, McMartin would be treading on their heels.

Calli did her best to keep up with him. She angled her head and shot him a look. "Do you always walk this fast?"

Quinn slowed his pace, not daring to look behind him. "Sorry. Force of habit." He kept his hand firmly at her elbow, though, and kept her moving. Four more doors to pass and he'd have her out of the hallway.

Danny came strolling through the entrance of an office that seconded as a small lunch area with a bag of potato chips in his hand. Quinn could have hugged him. Even better. "Danny! Hey, I want you to meet someone. This is Calli, the lady I was telling you about."

Danny brushed the salt from his fingers and took her hand. "Nice to meet you."

Quinn's next words were on the same breath as Danny's greeting. "I forgot I had to take care of something with McMartin, who is on his way down the hall. Want to sit with Calli a minute until I get back?"

Danny shot a glance over the top of Calli's head and flashed Quinn a nod with eyes narrowed. "Sure."

Calli was handed off in a second. Suddenly she found herself inside the bleak little lunchroom with a complete stranger and Quinn gone from her side. She smiled hesitantly. "Is it always like this around here?"

Danny grinned, closed the door and offered her a chair as they waited. "Like what?"

Calli shrugged. The corner of her mouth lifted. "I've been whirling in circles since I walked through the front door."

Danny chuckled in response. "I guess I'm so used to it that it seems the norm. Okay, maybe we should reintroduce ourselves. In fact, I don't think that bum, Quinn, really introduced us at all, did he?" He held his hand out again. "I'm Danny Briggs, Quinn's partner."

Calli took his hand. "It's very nice to meet you, Danny Briggs. I'm Calli Lemont."

"And his new sister-in-law."

"He told you?"

He nodded. "Yup. He and I have been together so long that there isn't much we don't share. From what I hear, it's been quite a few days for the two of you."

Calli wondered how much Quinn had told his partner. Hopefully, he wasn't the type to kiss and tell. "Yes, it has been. The shock is finally starting to wear off. It's awfully strange to think that my husband had a twin brother and we never knew it."

"I'll agree with you there. I'm only sorry that Quinn never had a chance to meet him. One thing he always said is that he wished he had an extended family. It was kinda lonely for him growing up with elderly parents. That's why me and my wife do our best to include him in on almost everything we do. He's probably been to more school events than most parents."

"You have children?"

Danny snorted with glee. "Sure do. Me and my Maggie are on our way to creating our own soccer team. Three girls and one boy. Another on the way."

Calli laughed aloud, enjoying Quinn's friend immensely.

"He's a great guy, Calli, and a great partner. I wouldn't want anyone else at my back."

* * * * *

When Quinn turned, his heart sank. Chief McMartin eyed him closely as he walked down the hall. To keep this superior away from the lunch door, he strode toward the man, hoping like hell that he'd never met or seen Calli. He had to go on the assumption that the man was somehow involved in a cover-up. It was pure instinct, but something that couldn't be discounted.

"Hi, John," Quinn said as he stopped in the center of the hallway. "I was just about to come to your office."

McMartin studied him. "Didn't look like it. Who's the little lady?"

Shit!

"Just someone who got turned around in the hallway. She needed a cup of coffee so Danny's helping her out."

His superior shrugged his shoulders and started to walk around Quinn. "Nice little number. Think I'll take a better look."

"Hey," Quinn shot out. "Think you have time to take a look at the vacation schedule first?" As inane a stall tactic as that was, it was the only thing Quinn could think of to stop the man from heading to the lunchroom. He knew Danny would keep Calli busy and out of sight until he got back. Whether instinct served him or not, he still didn't want his boss to meet her. Quinn knew too much about the man as far as women went. John McMartin was one of the biggest womanizers he knew, would crawl between the legs of anything that smelled like a woman, and Calli was just too delectable a treat to dangle in front of him.

* * * * *

When Calli's car turned into the parking lot of one of Boston's precinct buildings, Jorge drove right on by, stunned beyond belief. He was a brave man and usually laughed in the face of danger, but to endanger the cartel's presence with outright foolishness by following her in would be a huge mistake. If he jeopardized the details being carefully laid out at the moment, Enrique would end his life without thought.

He slid into an open spot further down the block, slammed the car into park and spun in the seat to watch the infidel's wife walk across the parking lot. His dark, brooding eyes followed her slim form across the sidewalk until she disappeared through the doors.

What was going on? Precinct Six housed the Boston DEA office. His fingers drummed the seat beside him as his mind raced. He and Diego had thought that if she was going to alert the police because of her late-night visit, she would have carried out that task already. In fact, they were surprised that she hadn't done it immediately.

His eyes fell to the satellite phone case. He flipped open the cover and dialed the number to the safe house and hit the speaker button. He wasn't going to make any decisions on his own. It didn't pay. The last time someone had tried that, they had ended up with their throat sliced and their tongue nailed to their forehead.

Someone answered after the first ring.

"What?"

"She just entered Precinct Six."

"Where are you?"

"I am parked down the street. I did not think it prudent to wave a red flag and follow behind her." His dark gaze lifted to the rearview mirror.

"Then stay there until she comes out."

"That will not be possible." Jorge hissed out. A patrol car pulled up behind him. He watched the policeman point with a stern look on his face. Jorge turned slightly to see a No Parking sign. "There is a fucking cop behind me motioning me to move. Son of a bitch." He engaged the car and pulled out onto the road. His eyes darted from the mirror to the road in front of him and back, keeping a close eye on the cruiser that had also pulled into the line of traffic behind him. "What the fuck do you want me to do?"

"Are you still being followed?"

"Yes."

A frustrated sigh sounded in the car from the speaker. "Make sure you lose him, then return here. The boss should be here shortly. There is nothing you can do now. Hopefully, our mole will discover the reason for her visit."

Jorge flipped the case shut when Diego hung up. As he approached the freeway exit, the policeman pulled off to the side, waited for traffic to clear and swung the cruiser back in the direction of the precinct house.

A lazy smile widened across the Colombian's face. "Stupid pig."

* * * * *

Quinn left McMartin's office, his patience just about at its end. His superior had kept him nearly thirty minutes, asking him questions about where his vacation plans were leading. Then suddenly, the man had shifted the conversation back to the woman. His interest was disturbing—especially when Quinn had stated earlier that she was just someone who had taken a wrong turn.

As he neared the now-open door to the lunchroom, Danny's laugh belted out into the hallway and a feminine giggle followed. When his large frame filled the doorway, both Calli and Danny looked up.

"Sounds like the two of you are getting along fine." His gaze shifted to Calli. "Sorry about being so long. It couldn't be helped."

She waved a hand airily and wiped at the corner of one eye. "No problem. Danny explained that it happens a lot. You left me in good company, though. He's been entertaining me with stories about his kids."

Quinn sauntered into the room, slightly envious of the way Calli reached out and playfully punched his partner's arm. "Yeah, Danny's a real comic."

"Hey," Danny quipped with a nonchalant shrug. "You're the one who took off. It was nice being the center of attention for once."

Quinn rolled his eyes and shook his head. "Don't believe a word that comes out of his mouth, Calli. He's always the center of attention. Speaking of that, the Chief wants to discuss your vacation plans with you."

"But…I'm all signed up for my weeks already."

Quinn met his gaze, hoping that Danny would pick up on the silent message he was trying to get across without seeming too obvious. He knew the second that Danny understood by the way his partner's eyes widened for a split second. A small nod of his head followed. Good. He'd keep McMartin busy and in his office until he spirited Calli out of the building.

"Guess I better go get things straightened out then." Danny turned and smiled at his one-person audience. "It was really nice meeting you, Calli. Hope you weren't too bored. I was serious about the dinner invite."

"Well, I was serious about accepting. I'd love to meet your wife and family."

"Good. We'll set something up and let you know." He swung his gaze to Quinn and elbowed him as he headed out of the room. "Maybe if you're good, you'll get an invitation, too."

Quinn just shook his head and waited for the man to leave. "He's such an idiot at times."

"But a good friend. It was very easy to recognize the respect he has for you." She set her hand on her hip and tipped her head. "Now, what about that cup of coffee you offered me?" Her smile widened. It had been a year since she'd felt this sound of spirit. Whether it was because of Quinn's presence, Danny's friendly joking or a combination of both, she didn't care. It was just good to feel excited about something.

Quinn was amazed at the change in Calli's attitude. The former times he'd come in contact with her were always when she had been under an extreme amount of stress. The glimpse into the real person behind the exquisite exterior and her bright smile had his heart rapping against his rib cage. He had actually expected a rather solemn meeting. When he'd last left her, her features had been drawn and tight with anger. Distrust had shone in her eyes even though she'd let him kiss her goodbye.

Not so now. With a light heart, they left the room and headed for the back door where his car was parked.

They spoke of inconsequential things during the short three-block ride to a little restaurant in a nearby strip mall. Once they were inside, they found a quiet booth and ordered their coffee.

As the waitress headed off for the kitchen, Calli crossed her arms and studied Quinn. She wasn't going to beat around the bush. She wouldn't put herself through another day like the day before.

"I've been giving a lot of thought to what happened in my kitchen the last time we were together."

That statement shocked the hell out of Quinn. He figured he would have to be the one to bring it up — even if she became upset again. He was twenty-nine years old and way past an age to play games. Their lives were indelibly entwined by the other's connection to a man named Raine Lemont. That one common denominator would always be there, unable to be broken or forgotten.

Quinn planned on the future being much more than just that. He'd made that decision the day he'd left her rumpled and shaken. In fact, if he was honest, he had to admit the decision had been made long before he'd even met the real woman behind his dreams.

"You're awfully quiet," Calli continued.

Quinn reached out and took her hand. "I was just thinking about a great response that would knock your socks off."

"Well?"

"I couldn't think of anything."

Calli's head fell back in a full-blown laugh. Quinn was stunned at how the sight of her slender neck and elated expression set his blood on fire. Whoever or whatever had brought them together, he'd be infinitely thankful for the rest of his life. He couldn't believe it. She sat there laughing at him and all he wanted to do was kiss her senseless.

Finally, she wiped her eyes when the waitress set two cups of coffee on the table and left them alone again.

"Quinn. I'm sorry to laugh. It's just that…that it's been so long since I actually enjoyed the sunshine and looked forward to the next day."

"I guess my ego will be fine then. I can't believe the change in your whole demeanor. What brought that on?"

She squeezed his fingers. "I'm going to be completely honest here. I've thought of nothing else but what happened on the counter the last time we were together. Don't look so surprised. You said you were going to give me a few days to think about everything. I'm not going to pretend that it didn't happen. We're adults. I think we can both handle it. You also quite purposely stated that you would be back if you didn't hear from me. Well, I'm here now, and I've also thought about the fact that you stated you knew me long before we actually met. That you dreamed about me. Well, I had a dream also."

The smile left Quinn's face. "And?"

"You and Raine were both there. Even though you two are nearly identical, I could still tell the difference. You told me that you would take care of me. That Raine would never be back." Her thumb brushed across his knuckles as she organized her thoughts. "Exploration. You said this bizarre situation we've found ourselves in bears exploration. That's what I want to do, Quinn. I'm drawn to you. And not because of a kiss or the fact that you look so much like your brother. It's because something's there that I can't let go. I've so desperately wanted to move on with my life, but I had no direction. Until you. I'm not talking about some torrid affair either. I'm talking about taking it slow and exploring the future. A few nights back, you said you were holding my hand just because if felt good to do so. I'm feeling that now. There isn't any other place I'd rather be than sitting here holding your hand. And you know what else I think?"

His happy grin accompanied the slight wag of his head. "No. So tell me."

"I think you feel the same. No, I don't just think it. I know it."

Quinn couldn't stop the grin that spread across his face. "So you want to take it slow."

Her silver eyes twinkled. "Okay. I'll be completely honest. Would you think me wanton if I said, no, I don't? But I'm not letting that side rule me in this matter, because there's more to think of besides just you and me. I most definitely want to be involved in Jenny's recovery. We're like three lost people floating in a rubber raft in the middle of the ocean. I want to believe that Raine had a hand in bringing us all together. Because of it, I say we contact Jenny immediately and do whatever it takes to get her on the road to wellness. In the meantime, you and I learn about each other. Our likes. Our dislikes. What do you think?"

His head shook slowly. "You amaze me, Calli Lemont. I expected resistance from you. But I wasn't giving up the good fight until I had nothing left. Yes, I feel the same. Whether it was Raine or simply fate, I'm not going to question. I'm just glad that I'm sitting here," his smile widened wonderfully, "holding your hand, knowing that I'll have the same chance come tomorrow. You've got yourself a deal."

It was enough for now. Quinn would say nothing about Raine and his copious ties to the cartel. Not yet. Not until he was certain that Calli had fallen completely in love with him. Plus, he wanted her as far from danger as possible the next few weeks. The less she knew, the more assured he was that she would be safe. "I probably should get back to work. What about you?"

"I took the day off. Playing hooky from practice."

"Do you have a cell phone?" he asked.

She nodded.

"Give me the number. I'll try to contact Jenny today. If you want to help, then we're starting immediately. I'll see if she can meet with us tonight. I can get a bunch of brochures from the State Social Services Department. Would my place be okay?"

"That would be nice. I'd like to see where you live."

Quinn was already writing down his home address on a napkin. "Hey, supper is included in this conversation. How does steak and potatoes sound?"

Calli's face split into a smile. "Sounds wonderful." Life was suddenly a little more breathtaking than of a week earlier. All because of the sexy man sitting across from her.

"So what are you going to do the rest of the day?"

"I think I'm going to treat myself to a wild shopping binge. I haven't done that in a long time. I plan to pick up some goodies for Jenny, too. She won't get money from me anymore, but at least she'll have clean clothes and a few personal items that I'm sure she needs. Oh, I was going to do one more thing, but then I'd have to go home and wait for a rep from my security service. But I'm downtown, so as long as I am, I don't feel like backtracking. I'd rather go shopping."

"What's that all about?"

"I had a rather strange night. After I had dreamed of you and Raine, I woke up and decided to have a cup of tea. When I was in the kitchen, I was certain I heard something or someone in the other room."

Quinn's attention honed in automatically.

"When I checked the front door it was open."

"Calli..."

"No, don't worry. Everything was fine. I have a security system. It was on, but never went off. The more I think about it, the more I think I imagined the noise. I've been so upset over the last few days that I'm willing to bet the door not being locked was my own forgetfulness."

"It wouldn't hurt to have it checked."

She shrugged. "I know. But not today. I have better things to do—like have a handsome man cook supper for me. Guess we should be going."

Quinn tossed a few bills on the table, stood and waited for Calli. After he helped her with her coat, they headed out to the car. As he opened the door and she was ready to get in, his hand caught her arm.

They locked gazes, both feeling the rush of a heady attraction and sexual awareness of one another.

"I can't do it in the parking lot back at the precinct, but I can kiss you here. *May* I kiss you?"

A smile ghosted her lips, the only indication that she wouldn't object. She watched his mouth move closer, relishing the feel of how his hand caressed the small of her back, his thumb brushing gently in tiny circles. Her eyes drifted shut just as his lips touched hers. His kiss wasn't demanding, but more a firm branding of her mouth. Quinn had just silently stated that he would be ready whenever she was.

"Thank you," he murmured quietly beside her cheek. "Ready to go?"

Chapter Twelve

ം

Calli glanced around at her surroundings as she drove down the quiet avenue. Quinn lived in a cozy little neighborhood in an older part of town. Every house was decorated with snug covered porches. Children played in their front yards and people laughed over fences with their neighbors. A far cry from her own neighborhood, she mused. Hers was modern and screamed financial success to anyone who drove by and saw the contemporary lines and fancy cars in the driveways.

Her excitement mounted as she counted out house numbers and finally pulled into Quinn's driveway. Once she shut the car off, she hopped out, reached in to gather up the many bags she had for Jenny, and then slammed the door shut with her hip. When she turned, her heart beat crazily at the sight of Quinn standing in the open doorway.

"Hi! Finally made it," she called out as he crossed his porch and hurried down the steps.

"Good thing. The steaks are ready to go. Here let me help you with all that." Quinn emptied her arms and juggled the bags. "What is all this stuff?"

Calli had the grace to blush slightly. "I sort of lost control. It's all for Jenny. She's here, isn't she?"

"In the kitchen. Hey, just so you know. She's rather uncomfortable. I don't know when she used last, because she's jumpy, nervous and pale."

The smile left Calli's mouth. "God, Quinn. We've got to make this work for her."

By this time they were on the porch.

"I've already told her what we have planned. You just need to keep reinforcing that we're here to help her. Calli?"

She stopped just before entering the house and glanced back.

"Come here." Quinn juggled the packages again and took a step closer. Without another word or permission, his mouth lowered and he pressed a warm kiss against her raised lips. Finally, he broke the contact. The flecks of gold darkened in his eyes as he stared down. "I've been waiting all day to do that. You didn't mind, did you?"

Calli stood on her tiptoes and kissed his mouth once more. "No. I was hoping you would."

Quinn leaned in and breathed in the sent of her perfume. "Good. As much as I'd like to do it again, I suppose we should go inside. We did say we were going to take it slow. I'm beginning to regret that pact I made with you."

Calli giggled at the look of remorse on his face. "No regrets, Quinn. We'll live. Let's make Jenny our first priority."

"I suppose you're right. Want to grab the door?"

Calli opened it, stepped back and held the door as Quinn jostled the packages inside. She followed, glancing about the quaint, but male décor and immediately loved how the house made her feel warm and welcomed. She hurried after Quinn, through a more formal dining room and then into the kitchen. Jenny sat at a small table with her hands gripping a mug of coffee.

"Hi, Jenny. It's so nice to see you again." Calli helped Quinn with his load of bags and smiled at Raine's mother. "I hope you don't mind, but I went shopping today. Want to pick through the bags and see what I got for you?"

"For me?" Jenny's confusion showed in her eyes.

"For you."

Her lips parted in surprise. "I… I don't need anything."

"Neither do I, but I still go shopping anyway." Calli sank into an adjacent chair, reached out and took the woman's hand. "Quinn told me that you two have already had a discussion about getting clean." Immediate wariness glowed in Jenny's eyes just before she ducked her head in embarrassment. Squeezing her hand, Calli glanced up at Quinn where he stood quietly beside the oven. He smiled encouragingly and nodded his head for her to continue. As hard as it was, she dragged her gaze away and turned back to the other woman. "Don't be embarrassed. Just be happy that it's out in the open. We'll take this one day at a time and both Quinn and I will be here whenever you need us. Let's think of the clothes and items in the bag as a way to celebrate a new beginning. We understand that it'll be difficult, but you can beat this. Jenny? Are you all right?"

Raine's mother finally lifted her chin from her chest. A shudder ran through her as she struggled against the tears on her cheeks. No one had ever been this kind to her. No one had ever cared enough. Not until these two strangers became a presence in her life. Her head wagged as she caught her bottom lip with her teeth, then took a deep breath. "Why? Why are you being so kind to me?"

"Because we're connected. Because suddenly we've become a family, a family of strangers maybe, but Quinn and I plan to change that."

Calli glanced up when he crossed the room, then sat in a chair across from her. His eyes rested on his mother.

"You're my mother, Jenny. You had the courage to find me, so there isn't a chance in hell that I'd let you walk away and continue the life you have right now. It's going to be hard, but I'll be with you every step—" His eyes bored into Calli's, and then a grin tugged at his mouth. "*We'll* be with you every step of the way."

Jenny pulled her hand from Calli's gentle grip and covered her face. "I don't know if I can do it. I've tried...and..." A small sob sounded between her fingers. What would they think if they knew the lengths she'd gone to just to get high?

"Let's just get through tonight," Calli responded through slightly blurred vision. Jenny Johnson broke her heart. Quinn knew better what the woman had gone through, but she was bound and determined to learn more about drug addiction. Calli also suspected that she would be shocked beyond belief as more of Jenny's story unfolded. "How about we let your handsome son cook supper for us while we look at all the goodies in the bags? How does that sound?"

Jenny finally nodded as she wiped the dampness from her cheeks. Quinn patted his mother's shoulder encouragingly and left the table.

The next half hour, Calli did her best to ignore the fact that Jenny was jumpy and jittery. The effects of the woman's addiction hit her as they sat and emptied the bags. One minute, Raine's mother would be trying her best to enjoy the gifts and the next she'd be twitching and eyeing the clock. It was going to be a long haul.

Supper was also a trial. Jenny ate little and only shoved her food about the plate with a fork gripped within a shaking hand. The many brochures on drug addiction lay untouched on the counter. Both Calli and Quinn knew they couldn't push her too far, but they stayed positive and upbeat even in the face of Jenny's hidden obstinacy.

Quinn didn't want to take his mother back to the shelter. More than once, he brought up the fact that she was welcome to stay in his home, but Jenny would have nothing to do with the notion. Quinn suspected it was because it put her further away from the pushers she depended upon. Finally, he gave up. She was an adult and he couldn't force her to stay. Just the fact that he and Calli were able to open up a running dialogue so soon was more than he could have hoped for.

Once the meal was over, Calli was bound and determined to get Jenny cleaned up. With a bit of convincing, she finally managed to talk Jenny into a shower, telling her she might as well wear some of her new clothes back to the shelter. Once the two had picked out a new outfit and gathered up toiletries,

Quinn showed his mother the upstairs bathroom, hoping like hell when he left her that she wouldn't steal something that could be sold later for payment of whatever she could get high on.

He came back downstairs once Jenny had locked the door and found Calli finishing up the dishes. "You didn't have to do those."

"There wasn't much." She turned and leaned her hip against the counter's edge as she wiped her hands dry, slightly ill at ease because Jenny's presence was no longer a buffer between them. She would simply keep talking, or risk throwing herself into his arms. Her brain flitted back to the many thoughts of the day she'd had while running from store to store. She hadn't been able to get him out of her mind. Suddenly, she'd been like a teenager, setting plots within her head—ones where she always ended up within his embrace. And with each pretend scenario, she'd gotten hotter and hotter. But, she'd set the rules and would have to live by them. It was difficult to look at him while struggling to keep the hunger from showing in her eyes.

Quinn ruffled his hand through his hair and flexed his neck muscles with a sigh. "For a while there, I thought she was going to bolt."

"This is going to be hard, isn't it? One minute I think we're getting to her and then suddenly she gets that look on her face. As supper progressed, I think I finally began to understand how terrible the grip of dependence really is." He just stood there, saying nothing, so she continued to rattle on. "The very first thing I'm going to do when I get home tonight is read some of those pamphlets you brought. I think I'll even go online and…" Her words drifted to nothing as he strode across the kitchen, his eyes locked on her with sudden determination glowing brightly.

He never asked permission, never discussed with her the fact that at the moment he wasn't interested in Jenny. He wanted her in his arms and, with his mother safely tucked in the tub on the second floor, he wasn't about to waste one second.

She squealed when he scooped her into his arms and headed out the back door. Once Quinn had nudged the door closed with his hip, he tightened his hold, angled his head and met her lips with a ferociousness that surprised even him.

Calli moaned low and wrapped her arms about his neck. Her pleasure heightened when Quinn let her body glide slowly down the front of his own. His erection was hard against her belly when the kiss deepened further.

"Oh, god, Quinn...we were going to take this slow," she murmured between licks against his tongue.

"I know. But I had to kiss you..."

Their heavy breathing resounded around the small porch as he backed her against the outer wall of the house.

Calli was pinned. Quinn's cock ground against her as he cupped her cheeks and demanded more from her mouth. Jenny was forgotten as his tongue swept the inside of the sweet cavern.

She answered by winding her thigh around his. Anything to pull him closer, to feel the heat of his skin. It was difficult to breathe, difficult to stay focused when all she wanted were his lips against her breasts and his probing cock between her legs. Except for the night when he'd lifted her onto the counter, Calli had always fought her deep sexual attraction to Quinn. Joyfully, she let her desire take precedence. It was an exhilarating experience to feel the boundaries she'd set crumble away.

Quinn slid his hand over her hips, grasped her firm ass and lifted her higher. With her back propped against the house and her legs wrapped around his hips, the position put her pussy firmly against his throbbing cock. He was wild to have her, wild to bury himself deeply into her cunt. His hips began to thrust as their tongues danced and her hands swept the breadth of his shoulders.

"Christ, I want you, Calli..." His whisper against her swollen mouth was shallow and breathy.

"We can't," she moaned. "Jenny... Slow...we said slow..."

Quinn's hips jerked faster against her spread crotch.

"Oh, god, Quinn," she rasped out. "I want…"

Still pinned against the house, Calli suddenly discovered her feet were back on the porch. Quinn tore at the snap of her jeans, his fingers fumbling to yank down the zipper that stood in the way.

She knew where he was going. She needed it. She didn't care where they were or if anyone would catch them with his hand down her pants. Her own hand slipped down his chest and flailed until she cupped the hard bulge behind his zipper. She planned to free his cock, but when Quinn's fingers slid carelessly between the flat of her belly and the waistband of her bikini underwear in search of her clit, her knees nearly buckled.

"Hurry! Oh, god I'm going to…"

His lips silenced her the same moment his hand clamped her mound tightly within the confines of her pants. Her gasp echoed against his mouth when he drove two fingers into her cunt and ground the heel of his hand back and forth until the base of one finger split her dripping lips and found refuge against her clit.

Calli's orgasm exploded. His finger stroked upward, time after time, coaxing her entire body into a frenzied shudder. Her breasts ached, her stomach clenched and her womb throbbed in response as the pulses squeezed around his fingers. She was delirious with the ecstasy pounding through her belly.

Quinn grabbed her flailing hand and dragged it to his cock.

Her mind registered the fact that somehow he'd freed his hard length and she hadn't even been aware because of her shuddering orgasm. They licked at one another's lips crazily as she wrapped her fingers around the warm, hard thickness and began to milk it, long drawn-out pulls meant to entice him to come.

The fingers inside her quickly found the same rhythm as her hand. He refused to stop the wondrous and unexpected encounter.

Calli's hips swelled against the pressure. She gripped his cock tighter, loving how it throbbed wildly, frantically kissing him as she jerked her hand. Her lips searched crazily for his mouth when he broke the contact to press kisses across her cheek.

His breath was harsh beside her ear... A tight growl from the back of his throat intensified with each magical stroke of her hand. His hips rocked to the rhythm she'd set.

Milky cum filled her palm and soaked her fingers just as another orgasm racked through her belly. She squeezed around his fingers, her body sucking at them, her surging hips a silent plea for his fingers to bury themselves deeper. They shuddered against one another, each supporting the other until the stream of cum ended and their surging hips slowed.

Calli's arms dangled to her sides. Her head fell weakly against the wall behind her, eyes closed, as she panted wildly. Quinn's hand rested against the side of the house as he tipped his head and settled his cheek against her perspiring brow, his rasping breath filling his lungs. When he slipped his hand out of her pants, his finger trailed a path across her sensitive clit, making her jump uncontrollably.

His mouth dipped to gently caress her swollen lips as he tucked his cock inside his pants. Silently, he pulled up her zipper, then let his hand rest on the slight curve of her hip. He took another deep breath.

"Is this slow enough for you?"

A muffled, but delighted giggle bubbled around him. Calli took one more deep gulp of air before she answered. "Um...yeah. Although, I did think about asking you to pick up the pace a little."

His snort erupted in the quiet, but he became instantly sober as he gazed down into her shining eyes. "I didn't plan for this to happen. I'm not sorry it did, though."

She reached up and brushed a wavy lock from his forehead. She wasn't sorry either. Even now, her heart quickened just looking at him. She eagerly looked forward to the hours spent within his company. When Quinn stepped away, it hit her how much she missed his warmth shielding her from the cool air of the night.

He grabbed a stack of napkins from the patio table and returned to take her hand and wipe the semen from her palm. She should be totally embarrassed at the gesture, but the security of having him close overrode that emotion.

"We better get inside before Jenny comes down. I've got to go change before my appearance gives us away." He used the same napkin to swipe the wetness from the front of his jeans.

"Kiss me again."

His head came up with the whispered words from Calli's mouth. He tossed the napkins away, slid his hands around her waist and pulled her close. His mouth lowered again to capture hers. Calli clung to his shoulders, wishing the moment would last forever.

His kiss ended when he dragged his lips softly across her cheek and guided her head to his chest. They held one another in the quiet.

"I can't believe I found you," Quinn stated softly. "I have to tell you something, Calli. When I dreamed about you all those months, it wasn't just your face that came to me. I've made love to you many times already. Always...always I made love to you."

She blinked, but remained stock-still with her head against his chest and tightened her hold around him.

"I don't want to frighten you, I don't want to pressure you. But I think before we even met I fell in love."

"Quinn...I—"

"Shhh. You don't have to say it back. I don't expect you to. You've only known me for a very short time. But I'm not going to go away. I'm not going to let you get away if I can help it. Does that frighten you?"

She smiled in the shadow of his embrace. Frightened? Calli didn't think she'd ever be frightened again. "I'm fine, Quinn. I'm not sorry tonight happened. I wanted it to happen. But this has all come about so fast. I need to step back—just for a bit and regain my balance."

"That's good enough for me. I won't pressure. Just know that if you need anything, all you have to do is call. As much as I'd love to stand here all night hugging you, we better get moving. I imagine Jenny will want to get back to the shelter. Do you want to ride with us?"

His arm encircled her shoulders as they walked back into the kitchen.

Try as she might, a shiver ran through her at just the thought of being near the women's shelter. "Uh-uh. I should really get home myself. I've got practice in the morning."

"Let's plan on dinner tomorrow night. If you don't mind, I'm going to try and have Jenny join us. The more we can keep her close, the quicker it'll be until she agrees to treatment."

"Absolutely. One thing you'll learn about me, Quinn Morgan, is that once I sink my teeth into something, I stick with it. Jenny needs to come first. When all is said and done, I'm going to hold you to a romantic dinner for two. Then we'll see where the evening takes us."

Her unspoken promise hung in the air. Quinn hugged her one more time before he left for his bedroom, his heart happy and his world right.

* * * * *

His world was right until he received a phone call the following afternoon. He reached across his desk on the third ring. His eyes glanced up at the clock above the door hoping it was Jenny returning his call. He'd tried all day to get hold of her, leaving messages and his phone number. She hadn't called back. Quinn hoped like hell it wasn't because she was high on drugs somewhere.

"Detective Morgan here." One moment he lounged in his chair, the next he shot forward, his body tense and wound like a spring. Fear trickled down his spine.

"When?" His eyes closed as he ran his hand through his thick hair and listened to the voice on the other end of the line. "I'm leaving now."

He slammed the phone down, jumped out of his chair and grabbed his coat. The call was from Mercy Hospital. Two policemen had found a woman lying in an alley, beaten and unconscious. They'd called an ambulance, waited until the screeching of the siren heralded their arrival and then began questioning people in the neighborhood. They'd finally been directed to the women's shelter to discover that the woman's name was Jenny Johnson. It wasn't until she'd finally awakened in a pain-filled haze saying Quinn's name that they were able to make a connection and contact him.

He flew out of his office and raced to Danny's. A second later, he shoved the door open.

Danny sat behind his desk pecking away on his keyboard and frowning at the computer monitor. He jumped in his chair when the door banged against the wall.

"Jesus Christ, Quinn. What the hell's going on? You scared the hell out of me."

"Mercy Hospital just called. They found Jenny in an alley, beaten and half dead."

"What?" Danny exclaimed, and then leapt up. "Christ, do you know anything else?"

"No, but I'm heading down there now. I'm going to miss the conference meeting at four. I don't even know if I'll be here tomorrow."

"Hey, do you want me to come with you? Just say the word."

"Isn't Lexi's play tonight?"

"Oh, fuck. That slipped my mind. Hey, Maggie will understand if I'm not there, especially in light of what happened. If you want me to come, I will."

Quinn was rattled. Maybe he should take Danny up on his offer. While he sat with his mother, his partner could start nosing around immediately. The longer it took to put coherent facts together, the harder it would be to find the assholes who were responsible. "All right. Maybe you should come. Once we find out exactly what happened, I just might need you to start our own private investigation."

"All right. You take off. I'll be right behind you." Danny snatched the phone from the cradle. "Just let me call Maggie. Christ, what next?" he mumbled as Quinn spun out of the office.

* * * * *

Quinn stood at the intensive care desk on the fourth floor of Mercy Hospital listening to the attending doctor's evaluation. Jenny was lucky to be alive. When she'd arrived, her vital signs had barely registered on the monitors. They had done a tox screen and more than one drug showed up in her system. Whether it was traces from recent use within the last day, no one knew for sure, but the man was not looking forward to the imminent crash that detoxification would bring on. Especially when she hovered on the edge from the horrible beating she'd received. Jenny's life would slip from one hell to another when her body began the process of withdrawal. The doctor used all the terms that Quinn was already familiar with—significant physiological changes, nausea, increased blood pressure, increased heart rate, or even seizures. She could easily end up in a withdrawal crisis, which included the chances of a stroke or even a coma. Jenny was in dire straights.

The elevator doors opened and Danny hurried down the hall just as the physician prepared Quinn for what he would find in the sterile hospital room.

Together, they walked in, the only noise being the many monitors beeping regularly, ready to alert the hospital staff if Jenny's organs began to shut down. Both men were ill-prepared for what greeted them. Quinn's stomach roiled at the sight of Jenny's small, bruised body lying beneath the stark white blanket. The air hissed from his lungs. A second later he felt Danny give his shoulder a squeeze of encouragement, although his friend had just had the same reaction.

Silently, Quinn took a chair beside the bed. Careful not to disturb the tubes, he clasped Jenny's thin hand and simply stared. He was aware of Danny standing at the bottom of the bed. He looked up and wondered if his face mirrored his friend's pale features.

"Jesus..." Danny mumbled quietly. "I don't even know her and this makes me sick as hell. Who would do something like this?"

Quinn's eyes moved back to his mother's face. One side of it was so swollen and discolored that it took a second to get past the shock and realize it was really her. Cuts and abrasions crisscrossed her forehead. Two fingers on her opposite hand were splinted to protect the broken bones. He closed his eyes for a second and took a deep breath. From what the doctor said, most of her torso was the same color as her face. She'd been kicked and punched and had almost died because of it. She still could.

"It's connected to the drugs." Quinn's voice was barely audible.

Danny leaned closer. "What?"

"Drugs. That's what's at the bottom of this. Whether directly related or not, it leads back to drugs. Look at her. At the wrong place at the wrong time. She was probably looking to buy. She was at my house last night, agitated...nervous. I tried to talk her into staying, but she wouldn't have any of it. If she lives through this, I'm not giving her a chance to say no again. I'm getting her the hell out of that shelter if it's the last thing I do. Then I'm going after the devil who did this."

"Quinn?"

He spun in the chair. Calli stood in the doorway looking frightened and concerned. He'd called her from his cell before he'd even gotten to the parking lot at work. She'd said she would get to the hospital as soon as possible. He watched her fingertips press against her lips as she moved closer to the bed, her eyes filled with horror.

"Oh, no...Jenny..." Calli blinked back her tears. "My god." She glanced around, smiled wanly at Danny and then brought her gaze back to Quinn's. "How bad is it?"

Quinn shook his head and rose. He reached out and gave Calli a quick hug. "The next twenty-four hours are going to be rough. The doctors can tell us more once she gets through tomorrow. It's up to her right now."

Jenny moaned as she struggled to open her eyes.

Quinn was immediately at her side. "Jenny. It's me, Quinn. It's all right. You're safe now."

Another whimpering groan whispered through Jenny's opened lips. One eye slitted open. Her gaze darted about the room. She groaned louder and weakly clasped Quinn's offered hand. Her lips moved soundlessly.

"Don't try to talk, Jenny. Just rest. You need to rest so you can get better. I'm going to be here with you."

Her eye closed, but she continued to cling silently to his fingers.

"Quinn?" Danny interjected. "As long as Calli's here to sit with you, where do you want me to start? You name it, and it's done."

Quinn swept his hand across his brow trying to think. It was difficult at best. "Maybe the women's shelter. There are two women I want you to talk to. I don't know their last names, but they're big and brawny. Names are Phyllis and Margaret. Start there. They might have something to do with this because I threatened them. If you find them, haul their asses in. I want to talk to both of them in the morning." He felt more than saw the shudder that ran through Calli's body when he mentioned the two lesbians. "I'm pretty sure they might have had a hand in this. Watch for the pushers and pin their ears against the wall. Put a message out that you want some answers. A beating like this doesn't happen without word spreading. I can't go with you. I just can't leave quite yet."

"All right. I'm out of here. Call me if anything changes."

Quinn reached out his hand and clasped Danny's. "Thank you."

Danny clapped his shoulder and grinned encouragement. "I'll be in touch as soon as I find anything out." His eyes moved to Calli's and he shook his head. "I figured the next time we met it would be over my dinner table." He shrugged then, at a loss for words. "Well, you two take care." He turned and hurried from the room, his shoulders squared and his features resolute.

Quinn and Calli stayed at the hospital until midnight, talking quietly and watching for any sign that Jenny was responding to their pleas for her to come round. Finally, the nurses convinced them there was nothing they could do. She was in the best place possible and if she awakened, a call would be put through immediately to Quinn. Against his better judgment and with Calli's urging, they finally headed for the elevator.

Quinn walked Calli to her car and waited for her to get in. Once she was behind the wheel, he leaned down and kissed her upturned mouth. "Thank you for coming today—and for sitting all evening with me."

"Are you going to be okay, Quinn? You look terrible."

His shoulders lifted with a weary sigh. "I can't believe this. What an ironic twist. We just found one another and now she might be gone from my life for good. If she lives through this, I'm getting her out of that damn shelter, even if I have to move her in with me. They'll start treatment here in the hospital if she ever wakes up. Because of it, maybe I'll get her to listen to reason." He rubbed the back of his neck. "God, I'm tired." He straightened and leaned on the open door. "I'll follow you home."

"No you won't. You're beat, Quinn. Just go home. I've got an early practice. I'll call you as soon as I get a break. Hopefully Danny will discover something or at least find Phyllis and Margaret and you'll have news. If something... If something happens tonight to Jenny, will you call right away?"

"Of course. Are you sure you don't want me to follow you?"

"Go home, Quinn. I'm a big girl. Try to get some sleep tonight."

The engine started. He simply smiled at her, shut the car door and stood watching until she drove out of the parking lot and picked up speed on the frontage road. He waited until her taillights disappeared before shaking himself out of his stupor. Digging in his pocket for his keys, he let them dangle in his hand as he glanced up at the well-lit building. Deciding to go back up for a while more before heading home, he turned and headed back toward the main door.

Quinn never gave a second glance at the gray Lincoln Continental leaving the parking lot. The vehicle turned south and headed in the same direction that Calli had.

Chapter Thirteen

🕉

Calli's eyes snapped open to the darkness of her bedroom. Someone or something evil shared the night.

She wasn't alone. It was there...

Primitive instinct born from fear such as she'd never experienced, urged her to lie completely still until she located the intruder's position.

It wasn't Raine. She knew that with every fiber of her being. Instead, she suffered the unknown in the innermost level of sanity. The dark and threatening presence in the room exuded a chilling, bone-shaking terror that caused waves of panic to course through her limbs, to firmly root her sudden fear even deeper. Calli swallowed against the blood pounding within her head and silently strained to discover the whereabouts of the unseen menace. It was out there, curled in the dark, waiting to strike — waiting for its next victim.

A quiet thump to her right.

She counted out imaginary steps behind her closed lids — long paces she would need to rush across the room one step ahead of the danger. How many would it take to discover freedom on the other side of her bedroom door?

Another muffled sound. A board squeaked beneath the thick carpet beside her bed.

Run!

She sprung up as a hand clamped evilly over her mouth, strangling her scream behind its gripping force. Her wide eyes flew to the shadowy figure looming above her. She struck out with a blinding blow to the side of his head, but his strength was too much. Her attacker's heavy body slammed atop her as she was shoved back to the surface of the bed. His hand secured itself tightly over her lips. The scent of heavily musked cologne swirled about the room, clogging her throat with the taste of it as she desperately sucked air into her lungs through the slitted masculine fingers covering her mouth. His wide palm swiveled to cover her nostrils. The painful grip compressed her tender lips, pressing them harshly against her teeth. The metallic taste of blood flowed across her tongue.

Her weak screams continued in the form of muffled whimpers as her fingers plucked frantically at the hand. She needed air. She swung out again as shards of light exploded inside her head. She struggled to escape, but the hand of death was unforgiving. She couldn't fight the danger. Her arms weakened, her head spun crazily. The bursting pinpoints of illumination behind her closed eyes funneled to a dim glow. She would suffocate and never know her killer...

Calli's eyes fluttered open to a shadowy figure wavering only inches from her face, then slowly they rolled back in her head to near unconsciousness. She fought the darkness as its strength overtook her and she began to lose the battle.

Hazy light suddenly spilled from the corner of her room.

"Let her go before she passes out."

The Spanish-accented words filtered across the room to her spinning senses.

The hand disappeared along with the weighted terror that had pinned her to the mattress.

Blessed air. Calli gasped, drawing in the sweet life that filled her lungs. Lifting a weak, trembling hand, she swept her tangled tresses from her face and was forced to face her terror.

He stood above her, his dark features shadowed by the light behind him. Even in the haze, she could see slicked-back hair, a square chin set with irritation and a holstered gun at his side.

She clumsily scrambled backward, grabbed the mussed blanket and yanked it to her heaving breasts as she continued to gasp for air. Her frightened gaze moved across the room to another man who sat in a chair beside the glowing lamp. A thin mustache curved above his full lips. His dark eyes glittered menacingly when he reached into his pocket, pulled out a long cigar and bit the end. Uncaringly, he spit the tip onto the carpet and used his foot to grind it into the clean fibers.

Calli stared silently, choked with fear, as he ran the tobacco-wrapped length beneath his nose. A moment passed before he slid it across his lips. A lighter flared and haloed his dark-skinned face. The tight, angular shape of his jaw blurred against the flaming light. Yes, this was the devil himself.

"Hello, Calli Lemont."

Her heart jumped as her fingers curled around the edge of the blanket. The accent again. Spanish. Lilting and husky and cognizant of who she was. Her fear trembled through her body.

Two men. In her room…

"Who—" She swallowed to clear her tight throat. "What do you want?" Her frightened gaze bounced between the two men as she cringed against the brass headboard.

"Ah, *bello mujer* has a voice," Diego snarled just before he drew on the cigar. The end sizzled and snapped in the quiet. A puff of smoke billowed slowly across the room.

Calli winced as its sweet scent floated in the air around her.

"Do not be frightened. Or…" His head tilted to the side. An evil grin curled his lip. "Maybe you should be."

"How…how did you get into the house?" The pain of fear rested heavily in her chest.

Diego's lips thinned an instant before they curved upward again. "Easily. We opened the door and walked in."

The security system? What had happened? "Impossible," she stated bravely. "I have—"

"Quiet!"

Calli's body jerked at the sound of his scathing command.

"You will discover your answers at another time. For now? My friend will bind your eyes and we will take a short ride."

The other man immediately clamped his hand around her upper arm and dragged her resisting body from beneath the blanket.

"No! Please!" The satin of her nightgown tangled around her calves as she fought. Once she regained her balance and was on her feet, she struck out in an effort to escape.

"Halt your struggle," the man spewed from the chair. "There is nothing you can do. You will come with us and you will behave."

"Never," Calli ground out and tried to jerk her arm free. For her effort, she received a stinging slap that snapped her head back. Her knees gave out and she crumpled to the carpet, clutching her face. Blood bubbled at the corner of her mouth.

The man in the chair rose and crossed to stand beside her huddled body. "That was a warning. Persist in this way, and it will be worse." He crouched down to stare at her closely.

Calli pushed herself to a sitting position, blinking back her frightened tears as she flinched away. She waited silently, knowing she needed to be smart. They hadn't killed her yet. They wanted something. She battled a sob at the thought of what it could be.

"What will it be, *bello mujer*?" His hand reached out slowly and a brown knuckle washed across the skin of her upper arm.

Calli froze with fear, praying that he would remove his hand.

"*Si. Bello mujer.* Beautiful woman. My greatest wish is to dally, but someone waits to speak with you. Just let it be known that the result of my dalliance would not leave you feeling well."

Calli jerked away and wrapped her arms across her chest. She didn't even want to think about what would happen if she didn't go quietly with them. She had no choice. There were two of them who could easily overpower her if they chose. Escape would come if she just watched for her chance. She prayed that it would.

"You have not answered me." The soft cadence of his voice belied the intent in his gleaming eyes. He reached out and none-too-gently clasped her chin, forcing her to look at him. "Will you be good and do as you are told?"

She nodded her head slowly, too frightened to respond aloud. Leaving with them was the worst possible circumstance. Her stinging cheek and bleeding lip throbbed, but were bearable. What would she endure if she continued to fight them? What would she endure hours into the night if she did not?

His biting fingers left her chin. Diego's mood changed in an instant as he gently took her arm and helped her to her feet. "My friend here is going to cover your eyes."

"Please! I'll do what you say. That's not necessary..." she pleaded.

One thick brow rose over his eye. "You will fight this?"

She had no choice. She was helpless to do anything. Another sob thickened her throat, but she swallowed it away. "May...may I get dressed?" She knew they could see the outline of her body beneath the gossamer material. She wouldn't make it easy for them.

His gaze swept her petite length. A hand reached out in her direction. She quit breathing as his finger drifted along the edge of lace resting against her cleavage.

"As much as I would love to feast my eyes on you, I will grant you this request. Do it quickly."

It took extreme effort to get her trembling legs to move to the walk-in closet. The man's breath warmed her neck as he followed closely. The smell of cigar tainted the air around her as she flicked on the light. His menacing presence filled the small space.

Calli was barely able to pull a sweatshirt from the shelf. It took three tries to shake it out and get it over her head. Afraid to look into the eyes of her abductor, she turned to face him anyway and slipped into a pair of washed-out jeans, struggling the entire time to hide the bare skin of her legs. With shaking hands, she tucked her nightgown past the waistband and drew the zipper up. Finally she met his appreciative gaze. Once again, she curled her arms around her body and waited.

Diego pursed his lips as he stared. Finally, he stepped back and held out an arm, silently ordering her to leave the closet.

Calli shuffled past him and hesitated in the middle of the room. The other man had a cloth blindfold in his hand. It took great strength of will to stand quietly as he placed it over her eyes. Her heart pounded harder when everything went black. He moved behind her as he tied it tightly, pulling strands of long hair into the knot without any thought to her comfort. She drew in a deep, shuddering breath before nausea completely overtook her.

A firm hand wrapped around her arm again. Another rested against her spine and she was urged forward. Behind the darkness of the blindfold, Calli pictured her upper hallway, and then the steps as she was led to the main floor. Once at the bottom, she was hauled across the living room and through the front doorway. The chill of the late March evening washed over her. Something small and sharp poked at her cold bare feet as she moved down the sidewalk. A dog barked somewhere in the distance. The buzz of the streetlight intensified as she neared the end of the walk. The hand on her arm pulled enough to make her stop. A moment later, door hinges squeaked and she was guided onto a cool leather seat. The smell of cigar permeated the interior.

"Slide over."

Calli put out her hand and felt across the width of what she thought was the backseat and slid to the middle. Her stomach lurched when the weight of one of the men settled beside her and the door slammed shut. Terror screamed silently inside her head because there was nothing she could do. Nowhere to escape. Another car door opened and the vehicle trembled when the other man sank to the front seat. Another slam of a door as it closed.

"Sit back and enjoy the ride, *bello mujer*."

The car vibrated around her as it pulled from the curb.

* * * * *

Calli sat silently in her dark prison and tried to keep track of the time. At first, she'd concentrated on turns, trying to keep them straight in her mind, but was soon lost. She'd estimated that forty-five minutes had passed before the car turned sharply to the left, braked to pass over a small bump, and then came to a stop. Her head tipped to listen closely when a muffled grinding sound reached her ears. It sounded like a gate opening. They were bringing her somewhere private and behind a locked gate? She winced with frightened tears. Soon she would find out what they wanted…and maybe look into the face of death.

The man beside her had been utterly silent the entire trip. The driver had made a phone call, but she hadn't been able to hear clearly. Only quiet, muffled words intended only for the receiver of the call. The taste of blood in her mouth and her aching jaw were reminders enough to remain silent.

The car stopped. Her knees began to shake again. The door beside her opened.

"Get out."

Calli lifted a hand to find something to brace it against so she could do as ordered. Her fingers were immediately clasped within larger ones, and she was pulled from the backseat. Gravel bit into the tender flesh of her bare feet as she was led forward and up cement steps. She didn't know if she shook from the all-consuming grip of fear or from the cold wind blowing at her back.

Warmth blasted her cheeks and a door slammed behind her. She was yanked onward into the depths of what must be a large home or building, because many turns were made. Tiled floor now. She could feel the cool, smooth texture beneath her feet and hear the sharp sounds of the men's heels.

Suddenly the cool tile switched to thick carpet beneath her feet. A dozen or so paces and she was forced into a chair. Adrenaline shot through her blood when she felt hands at the back of her head. Someone untied the knot. Wincing when strands of hair were pulled, she waited breathlessly, frightened beyond belief.

She squinted against the bright light. It took a moment to adjust to the change. She clutched the arms of the chair as her gaze darted about her surroundings. The same two who had secreted themselves in her bedroom were in the room. Her gaze moved to an older man reclining comfortably in a massive black chair less than three feet away. Graying temples and streaks of the same color across the top of his head were highlighted in the lamplight. Dark eyes bored into hers. His expensive suit was black and he looked like the devil himself.

"Mrs. Lemont. How nice of you to join our little party tonight. I am Enrique." He studied her bruised face. "It seems that you might have shown a small bit of resistance to being invited out in the middle of the night. I hope Diego and Jorge were not too rough with you."

Her fingers curled tighter. Names. Three of them.

"I-I don't know why I'm here." It was a nightmare Calli felt she would never wake from.

"You are here because I have some questions for you." He accepted a snifter of amber liquid from the cigar smoker and took a sip. "You are married to Raine Lemont?"

She cast a questioning gaze and struggled to keep her wits about her. "I was at one time. He's no longer alive."

Enrique snorted. "Let me be clear on the rules we will follow tonight. There will be no mistruths. Your life depends upon it."

Despair swept through her. She most likely would never get out of this house alive, but she had to at least try. "What do you want?"

"I want you to tell me where Raine is. Why wasn't he in your bed tonight?"

She swallowed to wet her throat. "I told you. He's dead. He died in a car accident almost a year ago. Why Raine? How do you know him?"

"Raine and I were... Let me just say we had a business relationship."

Calli's mind raced. She didn't have a clue what he was talking about. She knew everything about her husband. They were musicians, people who enjoyed the fine arts. That had been their business.

She huddled instinctively into the chair when Enrique leaned forward.

"Has Raine ever acknowledged me?"

Her head wagged slowly. "I don't know what you're talking about. Please. Why am I here?"

"Why were you at Precinct Six?"

The same eerie notion of being followed that she'd experienced recently, slammed through her chest. She'd been right. It hadn't been her imagination. Calli remained motionless, but her brain worked overtime to try and follow the conversation.

"I went to see a friend. That's all."

"Is Raine seeking help because he knew we were coming to the States?"

Calli swallowed her frustration. "I told you, Raine was—"

"Raine was *not* killed in that accident, so let us move on to the truth!" Enrique shot out. "It will behoove you to begin speaking truthfully. We know he is alive. Diego and Jorge have seen him. He cannot hide any longer behind the skirts of his wife!" He slammed his drink against the surface of an ornate table beside him. Amber liquid splashed across the shiny surface. "Show her the pictures. Now!" Enrique's eyes narrowed as he waited for Jorge to round the back of his chair.

Calli watched fearfully as the man opened the drawer of an oak desk, pulled out a manila envelope and crossed back to her. Raine...alive? Impossible. Good god, she'd watched them close the casket! The envelope landed on her lap. Jorge stepped back.

"Go ahead," Enrique ordered.

With shaking hands, Calli opened it and slid out a number of photos.

The breath caught in her throat as she stared down.

Quinn Morgan's face stared back. She knew it was him because they were pictures from the horrible day at the shelter. Quinn hunkered down before her as she sat on the edge of his car seat. His hand cupped her cheek. Quinn standing with Jenny. Quinn leaning against the trunk of her car that same day after he had followed her home.

Raine's identical twin brother.

These men thought Quinn was Raine.

Think! My god, what am I going to do? Calli scrambled to put her thoughts together. Somehow, she had to escape and warn Quinn. But what did Raine have to do with all of this?

She mentally shook herself. She had to play along. Calli suddenly understood that it might be her only chance to survive, get back to her home and figure out what to do next. It might be the only chance for Quinn to survive.

Her head came up. She struggled mightily to appear composed. It was a horrible trial when her stomach lurched steadily with nausea. "So...you know Raine is still alive. Yes. He is." Ideas tumbled through her head as she fought to stay focused.

"Where was he tonight?"

"He...he's out of town. I'm hoping he'll be back tomorrow, but I'm not sure."

"Straight answers, Mrs. Lemont. I want straight answers. Do you actually expect me to believe that when you both were observed in a hospital parking lot?"

They had been there tonight? "I-I'm sorry. I'm upset. Yes…yes we were visiting a sick friend tonight. I went home, and then Raine was going out of town. I don't know when he'll be back."

Enrique snorted derisively. "Now, you are his wife and you tell me you have no idea when your husband will arrive home?"

"It's true! Raine disappears at times. What is this all about? I don't know anything else."

Enrique's features tightened. She could easily tell that he didn't believe her for one second. She had to keep going.

"I-I love my husband more than anything else in this world. It doesn't matter to me. Someday he will tell me why. For now? I don't care. I think he's in some kind of trouble and is just trying to protect me by his refusal to answer my questions." Terrified that her charade would blow up in her face, she plunged on. "I just don't want you to hurt him. I still don't understand why you are looking for him." She needed to discover Raine's past ties.

Enrique continued to stare. His dark brooding gaze contemplated the exquisite face before him. Finally, his jaw softened slightly and he settled back in the chair.

Calli's heart pounded. She prayed that she wouldn't make a mistake.

"At one time, I trusted him. He was an integral part of this organization. He was paid well for his contributions. That was until he became greedy."

Calli didn't move a muscle as she waited. In the mere space of a few seconds, a thousand thoughts and smiling images of Raine rushed through her mind. She pushed them away, however, because one fact reared up inside her. She fought against it, but it took hold and blossomed. Raine couldn't have been the man she had thought him to be. He'd had secrets—ones he'd kept from her, and she was about to discover what they were.

"Your husband was one of my main connections on the East Coast. Raine distributed my drugs, collected the money, and...assured himself of becoming rich far beyond what inheritance and the Boston Philharmonic could ever do for him."

Calli gasped loudly and couldn't stop her hand from flailing up to cover her mouth. Shock-induced trembling overtook her. Drugs?

She'd believed everything he'd ever told her about their financial security. He'd made wise investments. That's what he'd said. It took her a moment to catch her breath. Everything was a lie. His love, the life he had promised her...everything. In this one moment of realizing Raine's silent betrayal, she didn't care whether these men took her life or not. It was because of men like them and her husband that people died...that innocent people like Jenny Johnson lay in a hospital on the precipice of death. Why good men like Quinn Morgan risked their lives to rid the world of these silent killers.

Quinn! She couldn't give up. If she did, these men would kill him.

She blinked back her tears of remorse and slowly raised her eyes to Enrique's bold gaze. They locked stares.

"Did you ki— Did you try to kill Raine a year ago?"

"Of course," Enrique replied arrogantly. "He crossed me. But, somehow he managed to dodge the bullet in a manner of speaking. How he did it, I do not care. I know that he is alive and that is what matters to me at the moment. That and the fact that he has quite a bit of my money hidden—money that he pilfered. I want it back. He may also have an entire shipment of cocaine hidden somewhere. You will be the way I will retrieve what is mine."

"Me?"

"Stand up."

Calli's heart leapt in her chest. "Please. I had nothing to do with this."

"I said stand. Now," he ground out.

Jorge, at least she thought it was Jorge, stepped menacingly in her direction. It spurred Calli to get to her feet as quickly as possible.

"Step closer," Enrique ordered.

Breathing deeply to ease her fear once more, Calli took a hesitant step, then another, until she stood directly before him. Her body shook horribly. She locked her knees in order to stay upright.

"Closer." Enrique's knees spread in silent invitation.

Calli stepped between them, knowing she had no choice but to obey.

A shiny knife appeared in his hand.

She wanted to look away, but terror kept her gaze rooted on the gleaming blade. She watched in a dreamlike state as the tip of the blade came up and rested against her covered belly. They weren't going to let her leave. No one would ever know what had happened to her.

Enrique's free hand came up and he curled his fist in the heavy folds of her sweatshirt. With a quick flick of the knife, he slashed upward, slicing the bulky material open. The blade rested over the quick pulse at the base of her neck a split second later.

Calli's mouth went dry. Her eyes drifted shut as she waited for death.

"Look at me." The blade's pressure increased.

"Please. I don't want to die..." Calli's words fizzled to a small sob as she brought her pleading gaze to his. She had been wrong. She did not want her life to end. Not this way.

"I do not take kindly to people who conspire to take what is mine." He spread the edges of the tattered material to the side, exposing the soft silkiness of her nightgown. Slowly, his free hand settled against her belly. When the woman in his clutches flinched, he pressured the blade tighter against her throat.

"I would not move if I were you." His hand traveled over her midriff and up across her ribs. His fingers spread across one breast. They clung to the firm roundness as he rose from the chair to tower over her.

Squeezing her breast harder, Enrique let the flat side of the blade slide ominously against her skin as he moved to stand behind her.

Unbidden tears flowed down Calli's cheeks. She was helpless to stop them as Enrique squared the blade back against her jugular, fondled her breast once more, then let his hand drift to the snap of her jeans.

A whimpering sob escaped Calli. This is how it was going to end. He'd take what he wanted and cut her to pieces. His erection prodded the line of her buttocks. There was no doubt as to what would happen.

The snap was undone. Enrique's fingers teased the soft skin of her navel through the satin, and then slowly drew the nightgown out of her jeans until the edges draped over his hand.

Nausea rolled through Calli's stomach as his fingers moved to the elastic band of her panties.

Moist lips pressed hotly against the skin below her ear, then nuzzled her earlobe. She felt the chilling breath of his words mix with the blade's cold steel before he spoke.

"What is mine…is mine. If I decide to give it away, that is my choice. Your husband's greed has put you in a rather perilous situation."

So frozen with fear, Calli couldn't reply. She couldn't think.

"I am the power, Calli Lemont. You will remember that." One lone finger dipped inside her panties and found haven in the soft swirls of her pubic hair. "If I so chose, I could lay you on the floor and fuck you. Diego and Jorge could fuck you. Look at them."

Calli had no choice but to blink away her tears and stare into their leering gazes. The cold blade still held her in its grip.

Diego reached down and massaged the bulge at his crotch. Never taking his eyes from her, he directed his words to the man with the knife. "Let me fuck her, Enrique. I will make her scream with pleasure. That is my promise." His lip curled up. "When I am done, you can spread her cheeks and fuck her in the ass."

Enrique's breath was instantly hotter against her skin. "Would you like that, Calli Lemont? Would you like to feel my cock spreading your body wide?"

She squeezed her eyes shut and struggled to stay absolutely still against the metal blade. Her heart pounded when his fingers swirled once more through her pubic hair, then slid up to rest against the bare skin of her stomach.

"By the grace of everything that is holy, however, I have decided that when it happens and *if* it happens, your husband will watch. It will be an enjoyable little show."

Calli's body sagged, but was held in place by Enrique's steel-banded arm around her waist. She fought unconsciousness and gasped for air.

"I want you to remember something," Enrique whispered. "You will never be alone. Dark eyes will always rest upon your head. You cannot escape. We will not play any more games. When you speak within your home, I will hear you. Your doors cannot be locked against my power. Did you wonder how Diego and Jorge entered so easily?"

She simply shook within his unwanted embrace.

"Do you remember the days after Raine's counterfeit funeral? We were in your home, searching for my money. Then... Well, Jorge is quite the master of many talents. You left your home for many days. Before you returned, he easily installed a small bypass switch, Calli. That is all it takes. Only a few nights back, you so bravely asked if someone was in your home. You surprised my friend, Jorge, by waking in the night. It is a good thing he finished his work. Wherever you speak in your home, we will be listening now. So, remember. You will never been alone again." His hand drifted up to cup a breast once more. "I do not know where Raine hid for so long, but *El León* has been discovered. You will wait for him to return to his lioness. If he calls you, he will not know about this night. Remember, someone will always be listening. Once he is back in your loving arms, you will tell him that we will all meet again soon. If he runs, you will pay the price." His finger slipped back to her underwear. He dipped inside again and played his finger against her smooth skin. He dragged his hand lower and clamped his large palm tightly over her mound. "We will all have our chance to visit you here. I have been known to fuck a woman to death. Do you understand now?"

Calli nodded her head when the pressure of the blade lessened.

"That is good." Enrique pulled the knife from her throat, flashed it before her face and gave it to Diego. With a kiss against her neck, he pulled his hand away from her body.

Jorge stepped forward and handed the blindfold to Enrique, who in turn tied it tightly around Calli's eyes.

"Return her to her home."

Chapter Fourteen

ഇ

Calli's hand shook as she wiped the endless, flowing tears from her cheeks. Every light in the house shone brightly as she waited for sunlight to break across the city's skyline. The shadows frightened her to death as she huddled on the couch, knowing that a locked door meant nothing anymore. All because of Enrique.

No, because of Raine...

She clawed at the thick quilt to wrap it more snugly around her body in an attempt to find warmth.

When Diego and Jorge had whisked the blindfold from her eyes and laughed uproariously as she'd stumbled to get out of the backseat, she'd fallen to her knees on the hard sidewalk as the car had driven off. Calli couldn't even remember now how long she had lain in the cold, shivering from both fear and relief that she hadn't been killed. Finally, her fear and quaking limbs had forced her to the warmth of the house.

She had to get to Quinn. But how? They were watching her. Dark eyes. They were listening to her every conversation. Maybe they even had a camera in the house.

Her gray eyes moved about the room. She couldn't even look for one, because of Enrique's pledge for retribution if she even dared to make a mistake.

Calli drew in a deep breath. She would never give him and his hired band of thugs another chance. She wouldn't make a mistake because she wouldn't be here. No matter what it took, she would leave when the sun crossed the horizon and never return.

Her gaze lifted to the portrait hanging above her piano. It was another time and a life that had slipped between her fingers to be lost forever. She had been so naïve and trusting. When Raine was alive, she had always felt that nothing in the world could ever go wrong. She had loved him so much…

A new bout of tears poured down her face.

Her marriage had been such a sham. Raine wasn't the wonderful man she'd thought he had been and she had naïvely cried out her grief over the past year for nothing but lies and deceit.

Anger budded inside her chest, overtaking the fear bit by bit until Calli thought she would scream aloud with its force. He was a bastard. He'd made such a mockery of her love for him. He'd put her in danger without a care. The quilt fell from her shoulders as she searched wildly for something… Her anger built, demanding to be let loose. She didn't care if eyes watched her within her house. Let them. Let them laugh and plan her demise, because if she couldn't come up with an escape, Enrique would end her life.

She raced to the gilded stand that held Raine's most prized possession, her eyes wild, her lungs filling with the air she sucked in with huge gulping swallows. Because of his dishonesty, his lies, his deceit, he'd put her in harm's way. He had to have known what could happen by crossing the cartel and striking off on his own with their profits.

She yanked open a drawer of a small table, scooped out a key and ignored her shaking hands as she worked it into the lock of the iron cage. It clicked and she swung open the door. Grabbing the bow, she easily snapped it in two over her raised knee. The blood rushed inside her head as she yanked his precious violin from its perch, sending the stand crashing backward.

Spinning crazily, her eyes darted about the room as a huge sob escaped her.

"Are you watching?" she screamed out. "I didn't know! I didn't know what a horrible person he was! I didn't know anything! You can have him and you can all go to hell!"

The dam burst inside her as she charged across the room, gripped the neck of the violin and swung it against the portrait. The force of the blow vibrated painfully through her hands. Glass shattered in a thousand directions, but Calli didn't care. The red haze of betrayal pushed her onward.

She firmed her grip, darted her gaze one last time at Raine's smiling face and swung with all her might.

* * * * *

Enrique tipped his head when he heard Calli scream out from inside her home. He reached over to turn up the speaker, chuckling as he listened to her tirade. She didn't care if she was being watched? That was good. It meant that she thought there was a camera within the home. Raine's wife would give him what he wanted. And that was her traitorous husband and the money owed. And, when he had what he desired most? Then he would take a little more. Calli was too delectable to simply kill her and be done with it. First, he would sample her delights, then end her life. Foolish woman. He hoped she did not think that leading *El León* to his day of death would be a means of exoneration for her. Calli Lemont was privy to too many details.

He jumped slightly at the sound of shattering glass then smiled. "Hmmm, the lioness is far more untamed than I first thought." He would enjoy the chase and the sexual act of subduing her hot blood.

There was one more crash, then utter silence. He cocked his head and waited. Nothing. It seemed her temper tantrum was complete.

His dark eyes met Diego's. "It has been a long night. I do not think she will give us any trouble. I am going to my bed. Find someone to monitor this speaker and sleep yourself."

* * * * *

Calli sank to her knees and stared incredulously at the floor, her chest heaving from the physical exertion of only moments earlier. Her wide eyes swung upward to stare at the torn and ripped portrait, then back to the floor once more.

One-thousand-dollar bills, too numerous to count, were scattered across the thick carpet. She raised her eyes in wonder at the thick layer of money littering the top of the piano, then moved back to the shattered violin in a heap at her feet.

She had slammed the instrument against the portrait so hard the second time that the violin had splintered into pieces — and released the secret of where Raine had hidden some of his money. Her eyes swept upward again to the torn portrait where loose bills hung on the ripped edges of the canvas. How many more were hidden where she couldn't see them behind the frame? How many had been stuffed inside the violin? All the time, his ill-gotten gains were right beneath her nose.

She slapped her hand across her mouth to stifle the horrified scream that threatened to burst out. Tears blurred her eyes. Memories. Recollections of the many times she'd begged him to play in the months before he died pounded at her building terror. Raine had always refused, always stated that the instrument was too fragile, too special because of her carved likeness when all this time, he'd used it to hide his stolen riches. He had held her in his arms, telling her that if he had to play with something so delicate, than the choice was her petite body. He had pressed warm kisses to her neck as he quickly built her passion, making her forget everything but the fire that threatened to consume her.

Fool!

He had worked her body to a heated fervor to simply hide his deception.

She spun on her buttocks, frantically searching for a camera. It didn't matter anymore. What if Enrique had witnessed what had happened? Then he already knew about the money.

What if he hadn't? Surely, someone had listened to her outburst. But had they actually seen the end result? Her eyes swung to the many windows whose heavily brocaded curtains shuttered prying eyes from viewing the interior of the house.

She would have to hope they hadn't.

Suddenly, her mind cleared and she knew what she would do. At least make an attempt. Grabbing a basket that held various magazines, she quietly dumped them onto the floor and began scooping bills. The amount of money was staggering. Drug money. Her fingers burned as she hurried to gather them all. Carefully, she removed the portrait from the wall, amazed that Raine had added another piece of canvas to the backing to hide money between the two layers. She swallowed back the bile in her throat as she reached inside and added to the basket.

It was drug money that the cartel would never see again.

The wicker basket was overflowing by the time she finished. Tens of thousands of dollars. Calli hurried up the stairs and into her room wondering if more cash was hidden inside the house. She skidded to a stop and spun in a circle, her eyes wide and her chest heaving. Taking a deep breath, she set the basket down and calmly walked to the bathroom and turned on the shower to help drown out any noise. Returning to the master suite, she turned on the television for extra sound as she glanced at the clock on her bed stand. Five minutes after six. Her eyes moved to the window. The skyline had taken on the orange hue of coming daylight.

Clutching the basket, she headed for her closet. Once inside, she set it down and carefully pulled the door closed. Her hands felt along the wall until she found the switch. The small space immediately glowed with soft light. Thank god she had a step stool to help her reach the highest shelves. She situated it at the back and climbed up. Her hands found the small door that led to the attic. Carefully and quietly, she slid it to the side, hurried back down to the basket and tucked it within her grasp.

She was breathing hard by the time she'd stuffed the basket into the ceiling. With determination and hope swelling inside, however, she let herself out of the closet and hurried to shut off the shower, still hoping against hope that there were no hidden cameras in her room. The television was shut off next.

The quiet in the room was eerie, but Calli wanted the ears that listened to think she had finally gone to sleep. A wave of weariness washed over her when she glanced at the bed. She couldn't rest now.

Don't think about it. Concentrate on how you will escape this nightmare. Concentrate on Quinn. She had to discover a way to get to him without being followed. As frightened as she had been, she would not hand him over on a silver platter to the cartel. Not his life and not hers.

She paced quietly, her mind spinning with different avenues of escape. They would follow her if she left the house. *Think!* She had to leave. She had to get to Quinn because she couldn't call him. The phones in the house were out of the question. If she went outside to use her cell, they would shoot her dead without a thought.

Suddenly, she froze. Her eyes settled on the closet door. Her mind spun in a thousand directions as she chewed her bottom lip. Calli prayed that her plan would work.

* * * * *

The appointed hour arrived. Calli had changed and was now wishing that she had actually used the shower, but there wasn't anything she could do about it. She rose from her kitchen table and checked one more time to assure herself that her cell phone was in her large purse along with a few other items she would need later.

Already, perspiration ran in small rivulets down her spine. She wasn't sure if it was extreme hysteria and nervousness that caused her to feel so warm or the heavy layer of clothes she wore. No matter. If she could escape, she could easily put up with the discomfort now.

Her gaze scanned the kitchen. So far, so good. If the cartel had a hidden camera, they would have blown down her doors already to get to the money. Ignoring her trembling hands, she squared her shoulders, slipped on a pair of sunglasses, opened the service door and walked into the garage.

Once inside her car, she hit the automatic locks. She almost broke out with panic-stricken laughter. What would a few tiny locks protect her from if someone decided to shoot her? At least, though, a locked car might buy her some time if she needed it.

"All right...this is it," she whispered aloud. Taking a deep breath, she reached up and hit the automatic garage door opener. Immediately, the heavy door squeaked and began to rise, allowing the sunshine to filter in.

She started the car, backed out of the garage and immediately searched up and down the block for any surveillance. They were there. An unknown car parked two houses away. It had to be one of Enrique's henchmen. Her hands trembled against the steering wheel as she wondered if it was the car used for her kidnapping.

Don't think about it. You can do this...

She hit the remote control button again, glanced at the garage door to make certain it closed and continued backing down the drive.

As she pulled out onto the street, the gray Lincoln pulled out, also. Just knowing who might be sitting behind the wheel sent a shiver of apprehension through her, but Calli shook it off. If ever she needed to be sharp, now was the time. Her life and Quinn's depended on it. There would be plenty of time to fall apart if only she lived through the next two hours.

She drove to the same strip mall Quinn had taken her to a lifetime ago. It was situated only three blocks away from Precinct Six. Her "tail" dogged her vehicle, never more than a few car lengths away. They stayed close as she drove around and finally found a parking spot closer to the first shop on the end. Her wary eyes lifted to the rearview mirror. She watched them pull up into the empty spot behind her.

"Please, Lord," she whispered aloud. "Don't let this be the day that Quinn decides to do some shopping." She had no choice. She'd specifically chosen midmorning just for the fact that he should be at work and not eating breakfast or lunch. Maybe right at this moment he was grilling Phyllis and Margaret, trying to discover who had tried to take Jenny's life. She took a deep breath and glanced around. If her plan was to work, she had to be as close to his workplace as possible—and pray that a silent bullet wouldn't shatter her skull.

Calli's fingers curled around the steering wheel as she breathed deeply for the second time. "Okay, this is it. It's do or die." Her stomach lurched when she realized what she'd just uttered. She didn't want to die.

She got out, ignored the faces in the tinted windshield behind her and headed for a sewing store. Once inside, she plucked the first bolt of material at the end of one aisle and hurried to the counter.

"I'll take one yard, please."

She waited impatiently as the older woman took her time, talking the normal drivel about the weather, summer on the way and a planned vacation. The woman stared when Callie rudely grabbed her material and sales slip and headed for the front counter.

Once it was paid for, out the door she went and nearly collided with a dark-haired man who hovered just outside the entrance. He wasn't Jorge or Diego, but his dark skin and unsmiling mouth sent a chill through her.

"Oh, excuse me." Calli forced the inane smile to her lips even though her knees shook. He could so easily grab her and toss her into their car. She hurried to her vehicle. The man followed, then turned and leaned against a truck when he realized Calli was just dropping off her purchase. He scared the hell out of her with his presence. This was going to be more difficult than expected, but she wasn't giving in.

Each time Calli entered one of the small shops lined in a row, and then exited, her nausea increased. It took four stores and a weaving path back and forth to her car to drop off packages before the dark haired man finally crawled back inside the surveillance vehicle to watch her entrance and exits as she headed out again. At least he wouldn't be peeking through the door or following her through the shops. She needed to make her move soon.

Calli gave thanks that she'd picked a mall that had quite a number of small shops or the morning could have been a horrible waste. For good measure, she ducked into a pet store, quickly purchased a brush and made one last trip to her car. Her watchers still waited behind the tinted glass.

Struggling to maintain her nerve, she headed back across the asphalt and entered a clothing shop. Grabbing three pairs of pants off the first rack she came to, she ducked inside a changing room and pulled her cell phone from the side pocket of her purse.

Twice she had to scroll through the pre-programmed numbers in her cell because her hands shook so badly, a delayed reaction to the seriousness of her situation.

"Please…" she whispered. "Be there…"

Someone picked up on the fourth ring.

"Detective Briggs."

Calli opened her mouth, but nothing came out.

"Detective Briggs. Can I help you?"

"Danny?" she managed to croak out. "This is Calli Lemont. Just listen. I can't talk long. Quinn's life depends on it. So does mine. You can't tell him about this until later. You can't bring him with you, do you understand? You have to come and pick me up at the Thunderbird Mall."

"Calli? What the hell is going on?"

"Please no questions. Someone is following me. If you don't give me this chance, I might not live to see another day." Her voice cracked, but she forged on. "I'll be wearing a bright red wig. Short and only covering my ears. A striped skirt and big platform shoes. Please Danny. Get over here now. Park your car by Jerry's Pet Store. Oh, shit. I don't even know what color your car is!" She was starting to panic.

"It's blue. Christ…" his voice trailed off for a moment. "I'll be there within five minutes. I'll watch for you."

Tears of relief welled in Calli's eyes as she gripped the phone. "Thank you, Danny. Remember, don't let Quinn come with you or he could be hurt. I'm being watched."

"Five minutes…" was all she heard before the line went dead.

Hurriedly, she slipped off her coat. Next, she wiggled her pants down her legs to reveal a striped skirt she'd worn to a past Halloween party and a pair of yellow tights. Her hands flew as she yanked out a pair of brand-new platform shoes wedged inside her baggy purse. Slipping them on, her shaking hands dug to the bottom of her bag. A short, flaming red wig was tossed onto the bench as she quickly pulled her hair up and wrapped a tie around the long length to keep it in place.

Her hands flew as she dug out a bottle of matte finish makeup, and then scrambled to catch the container as it flipped from her shaking fingers. It hit the floor and shattered. The creamy liquid splattered across the lower edge of the mirror. Without thought, she dipped her fingers into the mess at her feet and scrubbed the light-colored makeup across her skin, changing the hue of her cheeks and chin. She layered the bruise at her lip so the discoloration was covered. There was nothing she could do about the slight swelling. Donning the wig and a pair of gaudy red sunglasses, she studied her appearance as rivulets of perspiration streamed down her back.

Calli looked like a teenager out to piss off her parents by wearing the adolescent attire. She checked her watch and swore softly because she wasn't sure if she should leave the safety of the dressing room yet or not. But, she had to get going because she wasn't sure how long Enrique's men would let her wander inside the shop without checking on her.

Please, Danny... she prayed silently. *Please be out there...*

Fear and panic bubbled through her chest, but she had to keep going. Buckling now would be her undoing. She was too close to freedom. Biting her lip to keep from breaking down into a sobbing mess, Calli checked her appearance one more time, slipped the cell into a front pocket of her jeans jacket and left her belongings on the bench along with the empty purse.

She peeked out, hoping the sales clerk wouldn't see her until she was closer to the door. The woman was busily folding shirts at a display with her back to the dressing room entrance. All she needed was some woman hollering out into the parking lot that she'd forgotten her purse.

Holding her breath, she ducked behind a rack and wobbled as fast as she could atop the platform shoes while keeping her head down. Each time she moved past another aisle, she peeked at the woman, then hurried to get to the door.

The woman brushed her hands together and started to turn. When she spotted the young girl, she glanced with surprise at the door. "Hello there? Did you just come in?"

Calli's heart pounded in her ears as she straightened. "Sure did! You didn't hear the bell?" Her eyes darted to the glass door. She didn't see Enrique's man hovering anywhere.

The woman shuffled closer, mild suspicion dawning in her eyes. "No I didn't. Is there anything I can help you with?"

Calli grasped the first thing that came to her mind. "I'm looking for a jeans jacket just like this one. It's for...a friend's birthday. Do you have anything? I've only got a few secs. My mom is waiting for me in the car."

The sales clerk swept the length of Calli's body. "Not in this shop. We're geared more toward an older clientele." Her eyes swung in the direction of the dressing room as if she suddenly remembered one such client hadn't come out yet.

"Hey, no prob," Calli replied to garner her attention. She had to get moving. "Well, okay, maybe I'll try another mall.

Better get going or my mom will really be mad. See ya!" She turned, praying that Danny was waiting somewhere close.

She stepped into the sunshine, refusing to let herself glance in the direction of the cartel's vehicle. They had to be watching the door closely waiting for her to appear.

She turned and almost ran into the chest of a large, dark-skinned man. Calli's ears buzzed with the force of her pumping blood. "Oh, 'scuse me, mister. Nice day, hey?" She shoved her hands into the pockets of her jeans jacket.

He didn't move. She couldn't see his eyes behind his dark glasses. It took every ounce of courage she had left not to bolt around him as she waited.

Finally, he moved to the side to let her pass.

Calli almost fell to her knees. Instead, she focused on the blue car waiting only seconds away. She tipped her head and strolled in Danny's direction using every bit of resistance she had to not break out into an all-out run.

Not far now. *Please...*

The front passenger door popped open.

Two more steps.

She waved at Danny with a huge smile for anyone who might be watching, ducked into the car and slammed the door.

The car immediately backed up out of the spot and slowly drove out of the parking lot. As it turned onto the busy frontage road and picked up speed toward the freeway ramp, Calli turned back and spotted the salesperson race out of her shop. The woman glanced up and down the sidewalk.

She turned to Danny to say thank you and, instead, burst out crying as her hands cupped her face. She rocked in the seat, hardly able to maintain her upright position.

A gentle hand squeezed her shoulder. Danny shot her a quick glance before his eyes returned to the rearview mirror. "What kind of car am I looking for?"

"A...a..." she hiccupped another sob and struggled to answer. Just a few minutes more. She needed to hold her emotions together. "It's a dark gray L-Lincoln." She yanked the red wig from her head and tossed it to the seat. "Just take me somewhere to hide. Does... Did you tell Quinn?"

"Not yet. Just take a few minutes to compose yourself. As soon as you're ready, tell me what the hell is going on. It's okay, Calli. I don't see anyone following us."

It didn't matter. She still slid lower in the seat. Waves of exhaustion rolled through her. It wasn't over yet, but at least she'd live to see another day.

Chapter Fifteen

 හ

Quinn was just about to leave his office and head for the hospital when his phone rang. With an exasperated sigh, he tossed his jacket on a chair and reached across his desk, hoping against hope it wasn't Mercy calling with bad news. He'd had enough bad news. True to his word, Danny had managed a few trumped-up charges against Phyllis and Margaret and had delivered them to the holding cell about four o'clock that morning. They'd spent the morning with Phyllis and Margaret, and hadn't gotten any information whatsoever.

"Morgan, here."

"Quinn? This is Danny."

"I was just going to walk down the hall and let you know I'm going to the hospital."

"I'm not down the hall. I'm at home."

Quinn let out a snort. "Home? When the hell did you leave? What's up?"

"Well, I left to grab an early lunch because I wanted to get working on some paperwork. Once I got outside, my stomach started acting up. By the time I got on the freeway, I had to pull over to throw up. I haven't even had a chance to let anyone know I was gone. Must have been the cheap beers you bought me last night."

Beers? What the hell? *Shit!* He tensed.

"I tell ya," Danny continued, "it's the last time I meet you in some out-of-the-way joint that doesn't have decent beer. I probably have food poisoning or something. Oh, and next time, you can bring your own girlfriend home. Maggie was ready to kill me last night when I got in. So, hey, tell McMartin I'm taking a sick day. And that's all he needs to know."

The hair at the back of Quinn's neck stood on end. Something big was coming down. Danny had been the picture of health less than two hours earlier. Tired maybe from his long night, but healthy nonetheless. His partner's signal came through loud and clear. No details, just in case someone listened in on their conversation.

"So, you need any chicken soup?"

"Nah, can't stand the stuff. Maggie's got some Vietnamese cuisine in hiding somewhere. If I feel better, I'll have that."

Calli! The air rushed from Quinn's lungs as he sank to a chair. He was positive she was involved somehow. How? He didn't have a clue. Before he could say anything else, Danny butted in again.

"Say, Quinn. I think you've been working too hard. You should probably think about taking a few vacation days. Well, my stomach's starting to roll again. I should really let you go if you were just leaving."

"Ah...yeah, good idea. Hope you'll be feeling better soon."

"Oh, Maggie says to plan on dinner sometime—like real soon."

Quinn eyes squeezed closed. He was sure Danny wanted him at the house as soon as possible. "Tell Maggie I can't wait. Why do you think I paid for those beers last night? Not because I like you. Because I was hoping for an invitation. Talk to you real soon."

The phone clicked on the other end and nothing but a busy signal crackled between them. Quinn jumped off the chair, grabbed his jacket and headed out. Fuck McMartin. He was getting his ass to the Briggs' as quickly as he could.

* * * * *

Quinn drove to the first fast-food place he could think of. As a young woman leaned out the pickup window and handed him his change, his brooding eyes surveyed the parking lot, then flicked to his rearview mirror. Nothing looked out of the ordinary. He tossed the takeout bag onto the seat and pulled into traffic. Eating was the last thing he wanted to do, but he didn't dare head for Danny's until he knew he wasn't being followed. As hard as it was to do, he took an exit off the freeway, and then pulled back on. His gaze continually darted to the mirror. Once more, he left the freeway, drove a few blocks, then returned. Finally certain that he wasn't being tailed, he made a beeline for Danny's house.

As he pulled into the driveway, the Briggs' garage door came up. Danny stood just inside with a dour expression and motioned for Quinn to pull forward. As soon as he did, the door came back down.

Slamming the car into park, he jumped out and rounded the hood to join Danny who now stood beside the service door into the house.

"What the hell is going on?"

"I've got Calli. She called me at work this morning. She's upstairs with Maggie. They're back, Quinn. The cartel's head is in town. Enrique Palacios."

Quinn caught himself from stumbling. His heart sank. Just that one name pointed the finger of accusation at Calli. She must have been involved in the operation—especially if she had names. How else would she know? He didn't want to believe it. No. He had to hear it from her lips first. "I don't know what she's told you, but I refuse to believe she's involved in drug running. She cares too much about Jenny and what she's going through."

"Christ, she's not involved. Those bastards yanked her out of her bed last night."

His ruddy cheeks paled. "What about the fucking security system she's got?"

"When she had it installed, it was only a week after Raine was killed. Someone who worked for the cartel installed a bypass switch. Enrique's henchmen hauled her out in the middle of the night to their safe house. They told her everything about her husband's involvement. And delivered an eventual death sentence because of it."

Quinn winced and struggled against the queasiness in the pit of his stomach. "Why did she call you, Danny?"

"They think Raine Lemont is alive. They saw *you*, Quinn. They think you're *him*. She put an elaborate scheme together to get the hell out of the house and warn you. They've been tailing her... She's pretty damn courageous. Led them on a wild goose chase and beat them at their own game."

"She shouldn't have taken the chance. Christ, she could have been killed."

"Oh, no. They won't kill her yet. She's their trump card. They had planned to use her to bring you in. Threatened her..." He shook his head. "I don't know what else they did but she could hardly talk about it. Hell. Just go upstairs and let her tell you everything. She's pretty shaken. Enrique himself vowed to kill her if she didn't bring you...crissakes, I mean her husband to them. I've got a few more things to do, and we'll have you ready to go. You've got to get the two of you out of town."

Quinn was already racing through the door, his mind flying in a thousand directions. He reached the top of the stairs just as Maggie stepped through an open doorway with Danny Jr. slung across her hip. She met him halfway down the hallway.

"She's calmer now, Quinn. Be gentle. I don't know if Danny had a chance to say anything, but you're leaving shortly so don't be too long. Both of you have to get out of the city. I'm going to pack you a bag of clothes since you and Danny are about the same size. I'll try and find something for Calli, also."

Quinn leaned down and gave her slender shoulders a quick hug. "Thanks, Mag. I don't know what I'd do without the two of you."

Maggie just squeezed his arm. "Just stay safe." She headed down the hall.

Quinn hurried into the bedroom. Calli sat huddled in a chair. When she looked up, the sight of her swollen lip and her tearstained cheeks were like a punch in the gut.

Calli flew from her seat and flung herself into his waiting arms.

"Oh, god, Quinn. They want to kill you…" she sobbed.

"Shhh…" he said gently while rubbing her back. Appalled by the way she trembled in his hold, Quinn led her to the edge of the bed and settled down beside her. Calli clung to him. "I'm here, Calli. I'm not going to let anything happen to you. Now, tell me what happened last night."

"I-I woke up and there were two men in my room. They blindfolded me and took me somewhere in their car." She glanced up tearfully. "Danny told me that you know about Raine and his connection to the cartel. I didn't know about Raine, Quinn. Not until last night. They told me all about him. It's horrible. How could I not know?"

His hand lightly brushed the length of her upper arm. "He hid it well. That's not your fault."

"They killed him. Enrique…the man they brought me to, had pictures of you and me together. That day at the shelter, at my house when you followed me home… They think Raine somehow outsmarted them and that he's alive. When I finally realized what was going on, I admitted that it was true—that Raine never died in the car accident. They've been watching the house. Danny says we have to get away. He's sending us to a cabin somewhere."

"Slow down and take a deep breath, Calli."

"But they're out there. They—"

"Quinn?" Danny leaned against the doorjamb. "You two have to get moving. These guys are too smart. They already have to know that Calli has slipped through their fingers. Every contact they have in the city will be on the lookout for you."

Quinn held Calli's hand as he met his friend's concerned eyes. "I know. What do you have planned?"

"Maggie's dad, Rocco, is here. He's driving you to Portsmouth. From there, you'll take a rented car and go inland. We didn't want to put you in a hotel where there'll be a paper trail, so you're using Rocco's cousin's place. I've got everything written down and food packed."

"How are we going to make contact?"

Danny held out a cell phone. "Rocco's phone. Whatever you do, don't use yours or Calli's. These guys have fingers all over. I'll call you from a pay phone or have Maggie call you. Even if those bastards figure it out, it'll still take them a few days to do it. By then, we can have a new plan in the works. Come on. You've got a six-hour drive in front of you."

Calli was speechless—and feeling safer by the minute. Her life was in Quinn's hands now. She had someone to share her fear with. He would keep her safe.

* * * * *

Calli's slender body was hidden beneath a baggy sweatshirt and even baggier pair of Maggie's windpants. She sat perched on the edge of a threadbare couch and watched Quinn set a fire in the brick fireplace to take the chill out of the air. They'd already hauled in the boxes of food that Maggie had so quickly thrown together. The entire time, she'd continually watched over her shoulder for the faces of the Colombian devils to appear. To top things off, by the time they'd gotten everything in the cabin, a thunderstorm loomed on the dark horizon.

Her eyes shifted to a window. It was pitch black outside except for shafts of lightning streaking the sky. Her eyes drooped with exhaustion. Wearily, she combed her hair with her fingers and thought back to the long day.

After Rocco had bid them farewell in Portsmouth, she'd spent the next three hours answering question after question that Quinn continually shot at her in regard to her kidnapping.

She'd finally become hysterical and he'd backed off with an apology. The rest of the ride was silent as each mulled over the events that had led them to run for their lives.

As her eyes moved to the wide expanse of his shoulders, she wondered when he would start up again. She was too tired to answer any more questions and too tired to worry about the future. Other than slipping off and on into a troubled sleep on the ride north, she'd been awake for nearly thirty-six hours and she could feel her emotions crashing. Sagging back on the couch, her head fell to the cushion behind her and she closed her eyes. When Enrique's evil eyes appeared in her mind, she pushed his vision away, refusing to let it overtake the little bit of reserve she had left.

"Calli?"

Her eyes fluttered open, but she didn't say anything. She only stared at Quinn with round solemn eyes.

He settled beside her and guided her body beside his. She tipped her head against his chest with a sigh.

"Are you hungry?"

"No," she mumbled. "I just want to sleep." She shifted slightly. "You're not going to ask me any more questions, are you?"

He smiled against her soft hair. "No."

"Can I ask you one?"

"Go ahead."

"Do you think they'll find us here?"

He thought about it for a moment. There was always the chance. They'd done what they could. Depending on what Danny had to say the next time they spoke, he'd wait until then to reevaluate their safety.

"Quinn?"

He rubbed her arm comfortingly. "We'll be okay. Danny will let us know when we have to move. Why don't you go to bed?"

"I'm fine right here."

A grin tugged at his mouth. "Well, I'm not. If you continue to cuddle, I'm going to fall asleep." *Or find you naked beneath me...*

He made a quick decision, slid her onto his lap and scooped her into his arms as he stood.

"What are you doing?" she asked sleepily.

"I'm going to tuck you into bed, then come back out here."

Her hand came up to rest against one shadowed cheek. "Stay with me in there."

Quinn fought the urge to give in. There was nothing more he wanted to do than to climb into a bed, yet... "I'd love to, but I need to stay awake. Once it's daylight, you can watch out the window and I can sleep a few hours. Calli, these guys are dangerous. We have to continually be on guard. If I climbed into a bed with you now..."

His eyes drifted to her mouth. No, he couldn't. He tightened his hold and headed for the bedroom. Once there, he set Calli on her feet, noting how she swayed slightly with exhaustion.

Just looking at her and then glancing at the bed, he instantly became hard. No, now was not the time. When they actually made love—not a quick groping to find immediate release—he wanted her tuned to his every desire—not exhausted and living on the edge of danger. He yanked back the quilt and she never said a word. She simply crawled in and burrowed into a pillow as he covered her up and tucked the edge of the comforter beneath her chin. Sinking to one knee, he reached out to smooth the hair from her cheek.

Calli's heavy-lidded eyes stared up. "Thank you."

He grinned and lowered his mouth to kiss her. Just one kiss. That was all. His mouth captured her soft lips. It took every ounce of reserve to pull back. "You're welcome. What you did today was very brave." His mouth pulled into a serious straight line. "If something had happened to you, I would have been beside myself." His voice lowered as his thumb brushed across her bottom lip. "I love you, Calli. When this is all over, I'm going to prove how much."

A smile spirited across her mouth. "I love you, too. This isn't how I imagined I would tell you, though. I figured it would be when you pulled me into your arms and romanced your way to my heart. Then we would make love…" She yawned and fought to keep her eyes open.

He pressed a kiss against her forehead and allowed himself the luxury of sniffing her hair for a quick second. "We will make love…when the time is right." Quinn wasn't sure Calli heard him. Her breathing changed and her lips parted in slumber. He tucked the comforter across her shoulder and rose to head back to the outer room.

* * * * *

Calli jerked awake when a blast of thunder shook the cabin. Her frantic eyes darted about the unfamiliar surroundings until she remembered where she was. Even though a candle sputtered atop a worn wooden dresser, she scurried to flick on a nearby lamp. Nothing. Quinn must have lit the candle because the power was out. Thunder boomed again at the same time that lightning ripped across the sky. She sent a wary glance to the dark corners of the room and swallowed her fright. Her gaze settled on the partially closed door. Quinn and the safety of his arms were just on the other side.

The shadows closed in. Her heart pounded at a frenetic pace.

Calli scrambled from the mussed blankets.

She stepped into the living room to see Quinn's profile outlined by the fire's light. He stared blankly across the room as if in deep thought. A board squeaked beneath her bare foot, drawing his attention. Her heart pounded crazily when his breath whistled across his teeth as he glanced up and saw Calli's slim figure.

"Calli? Is everything all right?"

Instead of responding, she silently walked toward him.

"Did the storm wake you?"

She stood before him. His fingers curled into tight fists in an effort to not reach out and drag her down beside him. Not a second had passed through the long hours of the night that he hadn't thought about her and the fact that once life returned to normal they would make hot, passionate love. He would bury himself inside her body until she begged him to stop. He would never let Calli go, no matter what.

"Do you mind if I sit here with you for awhile?"

Quinn patted the cushion beside him. "Sure. I'd love the company."

She sank down wearily and sent Quinn a wan smile when he dragged a blanket from the back of the couch and handed it to her, not knowing that it wasn't only her comfort that precipitated the gesture.

Quinn wanted her covered up so his eyes couldn't feast greedily on her slight form. "So you don't catch a chill."

She tucked the blanket beneath her chin and hugged her knees to her chest when another loud crash of thunder rumbled directly above the cabin. "God, I hate storms."

He already knew that by her drawn features and wide eyes that darted about. "Well, then we'll sit out here together until it blows over." Quinn leaned back into the couch and watched the fire's reflection shimmer across the floor. How in hell was he going to keep up this charade of being the protector when his only desire was to have her beneath him?

Calli's mind began to race as she thought about everything that had led her and Quinn to be here, hiding from desperate men who had no qualms or concerns about killing either of them. Men to whom her husband had, at one time, been connected.

The force of Raine's betrayal crashed inside her head. The terror of the future had yet to unfold and the uncertainty of how it all would come down caused her throat to tighten. The events of the last days all combined into a tempest as fierce as the storm that raged overhead. Calli had tried so hard to keep her emotions together.

She slapped a hand over her mouth, embarrassed by the sudden tears… When had she become such a sniveling weakling? Up to this point, she'd managed to stay tenacious in her effort to escape.

Hearing the quiet hiccup of despair come from her throat, Quinn turned his head to witness her sudden tears. "Calli?"

Her head wagged silently as she sucked in deep breaths to regain a hold on her swirling emotions.

"You want to talk about it?"

Calli's face dropped to her raised knees. A sudden, hoarse sob echoed in the room. Quinn waited patiently by her side, stunned by the complete despair he witnessed as the sob turned into one wretched moan after another. Without thought, he lifted his arm, wrapped it around her heaving shoulders, and pressed her head against his shoulder.

Calli came willingly as her frazzled mind searched for some small beacon of solace that would make the horrible pain of her past life and present terror disappear. She was only vaguely aware of the strong, warm hand that stroked the outline of her arm beneath the woolen blanket as she sobbed against his broad chest.

Quinn's free arm reached out to coax her tighter into his embrace, and his fingers caressed the soft hair at her temple. Resting his cheek against the top of Calli's head, he closed his eyes and kissed her chocolate-colored tresses. "You cry as long as you want. I'll be ready to listen when you're done."

Her cold fingers curled into the material of his cotton shirt, holding him close, numbly absorbing the warmth of his big body and the sheltering comfort he provided. An entire year had passed since Raine had died. And the entire time she'd grieved his loss…and for what? To discover that he wasn't the man she had thought he was? And then there was Quinn , a man who appeared when she most needed him—a man she'd fallen in love with over the course of a few days. With each reassuring caress of his gentle hands, Calli wept harder.

Quinn held her shivering body in the dim light, with the sudden understanding that there was no other place on Earth he would rather be. Calli's immediate emotional dependence affected him like nothing ever had. It felt so right to hold her and share her pain.

Minutes passed as the storm continued to rage. How much time, he wasn't quite sure but finally her sobs slowed to small hiccups. Her body ceased to tremble except for random small shudders with what he suspected was a full-fledged reaction to the past horrific hours.

Calli kept her head pressed close to his chest, not yet ready to face the world, letting Quinn silently share her pain. Another tender kiss that was pressed against her hair filled her body with warmth. Her lids fluttered shut. She would remember every warm breath against her cheek and the sound of his heart beating beneath her ear in the trying days to come. Quinn was a sanctuary against the threatening world.

Finally, her tears ebbed. He said he would listen when she was ready and Calli needed to talk. Swiping at her cheeks, she snuggled closer and stared at the fire. His hand continued to brush softly across her upper arm, cloaked by the warm blanket.

"Tell me, Calli. Tell me how you're feeling." The soft plea whispered past her ear.

She rubbed her cheek against his shirt, trusting him, thankful for the fact that somehow he had come into her life. "How could I have been such a fool? How could I have grieved so horribly for what I thought was the love of my life when that life with Raine was such a sham? He was so wonderful, so loving. But there was a side that I never realized. How could I have not known that he lived another life that I was completely unaware of?" She hesitated and shook her head in bewilderment. Thoughts of the cartel and the ominous future swirled in her mind. What if they found her and Quinn? What then? She had to tell him.

"I've tried so hard to forget what happened between us the other day. I can't...even though I feel guilt and remorse. But since the day I met you, you're the only thing I can think of. I had a dream, Quinn. I dreamt that you said you would always protect me." Her head lolled against his chest. "That one statement in the dream has now become reality. Somehow we found one another. I've rolled it over and over in my head. Was it Raine, in a final act of seeking forgiveness, who brought us together?"

She breathed in the light scent of cologne that clung to his shirt, finding great comfort in the fact that the smell was familiar and she had not even realized it. How could she explain her emotions when she could not put the details together?

"I remember a time when I laughed and looked forward to the following day with such anticipation. Then those emotions just slipped away with his murder. That was until you arrived at my door."

Quinn wondered at her sudden silence, but remained quiet as his heart became lighter by the minute. He would let Calli continue when she was ready.

"I was numb to everything," she finally whispered, "until you. Until that day, I would look into the mirror and," she shuddered with a quiet sob, "wonder if I was going insane. Why?" Her hand rested over his heart. "I haven't told you this. Raine came to me more than once after he died. He never spoke, he never stayed long. But when he did, he made sweet wonderful love to me. You said you knew what it was like to hold me, to kiss me—even before we met. It's so hard to understand, Quinn, but do you think it was really you those times? That somehow Raine really did cross some invisible line to make up for his deceit and protect me from those awful men? I want that to be true. I don't want to live the rest of my life resenting him."

Quinn's breath hitched at the memory of her naked body and the many times he'd held her in his misty dreams. The hair raised on the back of his neck as he imagined a force so powerful that it could bring two people together. Was that how the connection worked between twins? A unique bond that was able to traverse both time and space to relay a message? If so, he would always be thankful because that link had brought him to the woman now in his arms.

Quinn used a finger to tip her chin up. "I don't understand all of this either. When did your dreams start?"

She shrugged. "Maybe six or seven months ago."

"Jesus..." he whispered and closed his eyes for a moment. Was it possible? "That's when I started dreaming of you."

She straightened in his hold and met the many questions in his eyes. "Did you really make love to me?"

He nodded and gently cupped one cheek. "Maybe you're right. Maybe it was Raine. We'll never really know how we were led to find one another, but now that we have? Once we get through this—and we will get through this—I will never walk away from you. I told you earlier, Calli, I love you. That's not going to change."

Her lips parted at his statement. Light, gray eyes met shimmers of gold.

Quinn lowered his mouth before thinking further on it, and pressed his warm lips against hers.

Calli's eyelids wavered shut as she relished the warm softness of his lips against her mouth. She did not respond, but rather marveled at the reverence in his kiss. Breaking the contact of their mouths, she stared into his gentle gaze. In their depths she saw a rare honesty, never encountered before. But, at one time, she had thought that Raine was an honest man, too...

Calli waited for the fear to build, for her mind to scream some sort of denial. Raine had taken advantage of her many times and she had never guessed his true deception. But Quinn was a different man from his twin. She would trust him or she would never find peace in her life again. With him, she'd never have to be frightened and alone.

Her fingers trembled as she lightly touched the coarse stubble that darkened his cheek and jaw. Strangely, the fear of the future evaporated on a cloud of building love. Nothing was more important at that moment than feeling the safety of this man's tender embrace or the intense heat that built in her blood.

Their mouths were only a breath apart. It was Quinn who slanted his head and drew her body tightly beside his and pressed his lips to hers. It was Quinn who threw out the lifeline.

He fought an internal battle as they embraced. He wanted to feel the softness of her skin beneath his fingers. He yearned to rediscover the dips and valleys of her body, to memorize the sweet scent that clung to her hair... She'd been through too much over the last few days, however. When he finally made wonderful hot love to her, there would be no more problems in their future. There would be nothing but joy between them.

He finally drew back and tucked an errant tress behind her ear, amazed that his hand shook slightly. "Are you ready to go back to bed or do you want to sit for awhile more? The storm shouldn't last much longer."

She stared up at him in wonder. "Why did you kiss me?"

A gentle smile widened across his face. "Because I think you're one beautiful lady. Because I haven't been able to get you off my mind since the day we met. Because I couldn't help myself."

Her fingers skimmed his cheek once more. "Then kiss me again."

"Calli..."

"Kiss me. Tell me that I'm beautiful," she breathed. "It's been so long since someone said that. I...I can't face another night alone." Her fingers curled around the bunched material of his shirt as she tipped her chin upward. "Love me, Quinn. Keep me safe if only for the night."

He searched her gaze. The dim light of the fire turned her eyes to the color of soft pewter. He's seen that strange wonderful color before. Her lips trembled as she waited. He didn't simply want this minute or just this night. He desired a lifetime.

Chapter Sixteen

∞

Quinn lowered his mouth. The initial kiss was tentative, another light touching of lips—exploring, wondering—but it quickly grew passionate as Calli's breathless whisper of his name demanded more. Her arms clung to him tightly now, capturing his innate strength and transforming it into her own long-dormant passion.

Her desire heated his blood as she shifted her body and straddled his lap, her eyes dark and determined, her gaze steely, yet loving at the same time. Her tongue flicked at his mouth as she cupped his face. Holding Calli, feeling her body pressed intimately against his swollen cock made Quinn's heart pound wildly. The rush of heat in his body was more than a simple physical excitement, though. Because of her, he'd finally discovered true and perfect happiness.

One last thread of conscience forced Quinn to draw his lips away from hers. They had both spoken of love. He was certain of his emotion. What if Calli had said the things she had because of the past twenty-four hours? "Are you sure, Calli? I don't want you to be sorry in the morning. I'm willing to wait."

Her mind searched for a reason why this night should not happen and couldn't find one. For the first time since she'd been left alone a year earlier, Calli's heart opened wide to the fact that she could love again. Quinn was the man. Quinn was the person she never wanted to leave her life.

She unfastened the top three buttons of his shirt, slowly slipped a hand inside the opening, and rested her palm over his beating heart. Her silent, steady gaze met his.

"I'm not, Quinn. I'm not willing to wait. The fact is, we have no choice because fate is fate. I don't want loving you to be a dream any longer." Her eyes burned into his as she continued to unbutton his shirt. Spreading the material wide, her hands fluttered across his lightly furred chest, exploring the wide expanse in wonder.

Quinn reached up, but she stayed his hand. A tiny grin tugged at her full lips when she crossed her arms, gathered the hem of her sweatshirt, and slowly pulled it over her head.

Even in the flickering light of the fire, his hungry eyes darkened as his gaze skittered across her bare chest. Pouting, erect nipples waited to be suckled. She reached out to draw his mouth closer as her head fell back and her eyes closed. A quiet moan left her when his lips closed over one hard bud. His tongue swirled around the sweet, erect thickness. His teeth nibbled lightly, then he drew the hard dart into his mouth, sucking deeply.

Spirals of heat shot from her nipple to her womb. Her pussy clenched, her stomach muscles tightened, and still he sucked as his hands scorched a path across her bare midriff in search of a softly mounded breast to knead.

Her fingers wove through his dark hair as she dragged his mouth to her opposite breast. It was the same. That slow burn that immediately flamed hot to make her cunt drip with anticipation. Her crotch surged against his covered erection with a will of its own.

Quinn's hands encircled her waist as he slipped to his back and pulled her willing body with him. Stretched full-length on top of him now, Calli dipped her head to initiate another kiss as his hands ran a slow path down the trim line of her back in search of her firm buttocks. His fingers kneaded the roundness, then followed the line of her ass. A growl rumbled in the back of his throat as her soft moan urged him on.

His tongue sought the warmth of her mouth. Calli was there to meet him, to draw him in as she straddled him and surged against his aching cock.

A shiver ran through her when his fingers sought the hot space between her legs.

"Calli…"

"Don't stop…Quinn. I want this…I need this. Don't leave me alone in the dark…"

His body supported their weight as he guided them over the edge of the couch to the floor. Muscular limbs entangled with lithe ones as they continued to kiss passionately. Thunder resounded across the night, shaking the ground and rattling the windowpanes, but neither heeded the flash of lightning that immediately followed as their hearts pounded crazily in unison. One love. A night filled with passion—it was their only desire.

Quinn groped to find a breast when Calli rolled to her back, barely able to suppress his physical power as he squeezed it and groaned against her lips.

Her fingers worked frantically to unbutton his jeans and yank down his zipper. She needed his touch. Her only desire was to feel his hard shaft in the palm of her hand. His cock sprang forward when she freed it, throbbing and glistening with pre-cum. Her grip clamped around him, stroking him. God, she wanted him buried inside her.

Quinn refused to relinquish her mouth as he quickly shed his pants and underwear at the same time. Kicking them away, he yanked the windpants down her legs, and then dragged her panties past her ankles. With one liquid motion, she was completely naked and feeling the wiry hair that dusted his muscular thighs against her skin.

"Hurry!" Calli breathed as she clung to him and kissed his chest. "I'm on fire, Quinn!"

"No," he panted as he pinned her to the floor and straddled her body. His fierce gaze devoured her. His chest heaved with the deep breaths he sucked in. "I want to taste you in my mouth, Calli. I want your scent in my nostrils. I want you to come time after time until you're weak with exhaustion. I'm going to fuck you until you beg me to stop. So many ways…"

"Never…I never want you to stop…" Her heart thudded madly as she stared up at him, her hungry desire blazed in her eyes. Her hands skidded across the muscles of his chest. Hot cream dripped from her body. She would never let him stop. "Then fuck me, Quinn. Fuck me all the ways you desire. Then fuck me again."

It was crazy. It was insane, but unstoppable.

"I want to watch you come. I've dreamed it too many times. I've shared you too many times with a ghost. Tonight you are completely mine." His hands covered hers and took them in a firm grip. Using his knees, he nudged her thighs wide. His eyes shuttered darkly as he dragged her fingers down the length of his firm torso, over his throbbing cock and to the dark vee between her legs. His gaze flitted from hers for only a second as he took both of her hands and forced them against her cunt and began to drag her fingers through her slippery wetness.

A gasp shot from Calli as she was forced to touch herself. Her eyes closed, but every nerve was tuned to the fact that her clit began to tighten.

"Look at me, Calli…" Quinn wanted to witness those first shudders in the silver depths of her eyes.

"I…" Her eyes fluttered open, glazed and hot with desire.

He guided one of her hands to her clit, heating the swollen nub with friction as he made her rub herself. He took her other hand, gripped two fingers and guided them into her hot tunnel, joining them with one of his own, filling her with ecstasy.

His breath rasped above her as her hips began to surge against the pressure of her hands. "Come for me, Calli. Make yourself come… You're ready. You're hot and dripping."

"Oh, god!" The hot, soft walls of her pussy clenched around the fingers inside her. Her knees came up as she fought to spread her legs wider. Her hips bounced, faster and faster.

She jerked beneath him as the orgasm hit her. Shards of light exploded behind her tightly squeezed eyelids. A scream of release clogged inside her throat. She could barely breathe.

Quinn grasped her hand more firmly and worked her fingers in and out of her burning sheath mercilessly as her body shuddered around them. He flattened her soaked fingers over her engorged clit and ground against it time after time, drawing the orgasm on, sending her body into spasms as she gasped and struggled for air. Her head rolled wildly from side to side when he leaned over and clamped his teeth around her nipple and forced another finger into her pussy.

His thick cock throbbed for release at the sight of Calli within the throes of a passionate and breathtaking orgasm. So much the same, yet different from all the times he'd worked her body into a heated frenzy during the hazy vestiges of a dream, because this was real. The heat of her wetness against his hand, her writhing body, her guttural moans of sexual pleasure almost made him come. He ached to come. Not yet, though. There was so much more waiting for them over the course of the night.

Her limbs quaked, her muscles clenched tightly, her breasts burned as she rode the wave of Quinn's passionate bondage. She continued to gasp as the pulses slowed, feeling faint and disorientated. Her blood roared through her veins as her knees weakly fell open. Quinn slowed the sensual assault until her body only jerked sporadically beneath him.

She was barely aware when he let go of her hands and slid up her slender length until her breast flattened against his chest. His panting lips met hers, licking at them, coaxing her to meet his tongue. Her limpid eyes opened to the smoky gold flecks simmering above her. A smile touched his mouth just before his tongue ran across her teeth once, then probed until she met it with flicking darts of her own.

"I love you, Calli," he mumbled between licks. "Forever."

Eagerly, she met the thrusts of his tongue with a ferociousness that surprised them both.

"I love you, too, Quinn. Oh, how I love you," she murmured. "Fuck me again. Fuck me forever…"

A rush of air left her when he whisked her body from the floor, lifted her against his naked chest and headed for the small bedroom. She pressed kisses against his throat and skimmed her hand through the dusted sprinkles of his chest hair, her body still tingling from the massive orgasm. Her swollen pussy lips clenched, knowing it wouldn't be long before Quinn found haven within her heat once more. And then? Another earth-shattering orgasm that would take her to the edge of reason?

The abating storm rumbled as he laid her on the bed, rolled down beside her and once more pulled her body atop his. Reaching down, he gently pressured her legs open, then ran the tips of his fingers across the smooth velvet of her inner thighs until he came to her swollen lips. Tauntingly, he traced a path along their outer edges until she squirmed above him, her body dipping in search of, always dipping in hopes that his long, thick finger would slip inside.

"Don't tease me, Quinn," she pleaded while wriggling atop him.

The teasing touch of his hand immediately disappeared as he cupped her face. Silently, he kissed her, his mouth worshipful and loving.

She broke the contact a moment later and lifted her head to stare hungrily into his eyes. His tousled hair was dark against the stark whiteness of the pillow, even in the candlelight. "What you did to me..." Her stomach flipped as she remembered the way her pussy had throbbed around her fingers. "It was unexplainable, unbelievably erotic and I loved it."

A smile curved his lips upward as his hand wiggled between them until his fingers rested against the downy hair between her legs. God, he loved her. "I'm not through with this night, Calli. I've only begun."

An impish smile reached her eyes as she began to snake her body in slow brushes down the length of him. The look of wicked promise that burned in her eyes stayed with him as he closed his own and drew in a ragged breath.

Calli's lips rained kisses along his lean belly, her hands stroked his cock and her mouth dipped lower and lower.

A flush of heat suffused his lower body when her tongue flicked against the tip of his cock. He lay spread-eagled with her petite form between his legs. His ass surged from the mattress when she clasped his erection with both hands and began to lick the length. The air rushed from his lungs when her mouth closed over him and she sucked his cock forcefully. Shivers raced across the skin of his legs and arms. It was a heated yet tender assault, one so different from the wild, shattering experience of their first sexual encounter in the cabin's small living room.

Her tongue licked gently at the swollen crown of his penis, darting out, tasting him time after time. Quinn's soft grunt echoed around her as she worked her way down his shaft, and then back up to flit her tongue against his slit.

She softly stroked his balls with one hand and began to pull at his cock, long slow glides that knotted his belly. Quinn opened his tight fists and threaded his fingers through the silky tresses that tickled across his skin. His hips began to follow her rhythmic motion as her mouth repeatedly slid the length of his cock, sucking first at the tip, then swirling her pink tongue around it. Heat churned in his stomach when her hand clamped tighter around his thickness, building his arousal hotter with each burning second. He shuddered when she began to nibble the side of his cock, nipping lightly but hard enough to make him waver on the edge of delightful pain. Her thumb brushed across the moist, velvety tip of his cock, the action in stark contrast to her tantalizing bites.

He was going to come. His rock-hard cock throbbed, but Quinn wasn't through with her yet. More roughly than he intended, he wrapped his fingers in the long strands of chocolate and forced her body up over his. In one fluid movement, he had her back pressed firmly to the mattress. His mouth plummeted to capture her swollen lips, which now sought his—lips that demanded he share his body with hers, lips that the taste of his cock lingered on.

Masculine fingers trailed over the curve of one feminine hip and then moved on to explore the wet heat surrounded by trim thighs. Calli groaned against his mouth, her fingers scraping across the skin of his broad shoulders, her thrusts against his hand feral and untamed. The gentle temptress of a moment earlier disappeared as passion exploded between them once more.

Two thick fingers drove into her hot cave. The force of his entry pinned her hips to the bed. He ground his thumb against her clit, circling it hotly as their tongues danced against one another. In and out, faster and faster. He couldn't shove them in deep enough. He wanted to fuck her with his cock, but wasn't willing to yet chance the many orgasms he'd promised. If he fucked her now, he would explode.

Calli tugged at his shoulders, gasping breathlessly each time he shoved his fingers into her hot cunt. She writhed against his palm, finding herself lost in the heat of his masterful attack, knowing that he wouldn't stop until he was assured she had come. And then? He would make her come again.

Her body rode his fingers, her hips surged upward against the pressure as she squeezed and tried to suck him deeper. Quinn bit at her breast until she writhed uncontrollably and began to shudder around him. Her body pulsed and he drove his fingers deep as she careened through another massive orgasm.

Before the spike of heat sizzled to completion, Quinn's demanding lips raked across the tender skin of her belly as he burned a path lower. Rising to his knees, he yanked her legs apart.

Calli's eyes burned into his. She still panted through the last traces of the sexual explosion he'd created, but that didn't stop her. She licked her lips tauntingly with a glistening tongue.

Quinn nearly came on the spot, but he never took his hooded gaze from hers.

His hands slid across the skin of her upper thighs, forcing her legs as wide as possible, and then kept going until he spread her swollen pussy lips to expose her shiny, engorged clit.

Calli continued to run her tongue suggestively across her lips despite how her stomach flipped in excitement. "Do it again, Quinn," she breathed bravely. "Make me come. Make me scream…"

Her breathless dare turned to a staggering gasp when his head lowered between her legs.

Quinn was wild. His heart hammered in his chest, his cock ached for release, but she'd tossed out her dare and he would happily see it through. His fingers pulled her lips wide, and he dragged his tongue the entire slick length of her pussy. Her body surged. Another wanton gasp. Her musky feminine scent swirled inside his head, setting him on fire.

He clamped his teeth on her clit and began to suck. Calli's moan echoed around him. He tortured her and relished how her hips thrust the swelling bud against his mouth. Slipping two fingers into her, he followed her tempo. Flattening his tongue against her, he lapped at her dripping slit, forced his fingers hard up into her and gave no quarter.

The skin on her arms goose bumped in contrast to the blazing inferno that built in her blood. She held her breath as he took her further into the heat, higher and higher, demanding that she come. The flames instantly licked hotter against her womb, and Calli groaned aloud as she grabbed his head. Suddenly, passionately, one tremor after another shook her to her soul.

The pressure of his fingers was quickly replaced by his cock as he pounded into her shuddering body. His fierce, short jerks shook the bed they lay on. Her cunt stretched wide around his thick shaft, sucking at him with each orgasmic pulse. She strained to meet his slamming thrusts, gasping for breath as his strokes kept her coming. Their bodies glistened with a sheen of perspiration.

Quinn exploded inside her. Liquid heat filled her cavity as he grabbed her buttocks and slammed deep one final time. His cock emptied, throbbed with each spasm of ejaculation as she wrapped her legs tightly around his waist and clung feverishly to him.

Their lips crashed against one another. They couldn't get enough. They couldn't think of the future, only of the intense moment they were experiencing as they shuddered with hands racing across bare, dampened skin. Heavy rasping breaths filled the darkness between passionate kisses. Thunder rumbled in the distance. Their tongues continued a sensual dance.

Finally, hearts began to slow. Calli's legs fell limply to the mattress. Quinn rolled from her sweat-slicked body, gathered her close, and sucked in huge gulps of air. They lay stunned to discover what they had just shared. Spine-tingling sex and a voracious desire they'd never experienced before. Once Quinn's limbs quit trembling, he rolled to his side and smoothed the dampened strands from her cheeks with a shaking hand.

Calli reached up and pulled his mouth down to share one final kiss. Their lips mingled as her fingers trailed across his shadowed cheek. Finally, she allowed him to pull away as she drank in the sight of his heavy-lidded eyes.

"I love you, Quinn. I love you so much. I needed you so badly. Never...never has it been like that."

"Loving you, Calli, was the one thing missing from my life." His gaze whispered across her flushed cheeks. Even after all the dreams, nothing would ever compare to this first time he had loved the real woman. It amazed him once more that they had found one another. Happiness and contentment softened her gaze for the first time since they'd met. He wanted the moment to continue. His biggest wish was that time would stop, allowing them to bask forever in one another's arms.

And as hard as he tried in that moment to drown in the silvery depths of her loving eyes, thoughts of the impending future returned. He had to keep her safe. He had to assure that they would have a long future together.

Guilt nipped at his conscience at having forgotten the evil that lurked around them. Christ, his gun was even in the next room rather than close by if he needed it. Calli's allure, however, had rendered him incapable of anything but his desire to be lost inside her body. She nuzzled into the crook of his neck and sighed, opening up the opportunity for him to bring up their current situation. The voice of reason returned.

"Why don't you sleep for a few more hours? I'm going back to the living room."

"What? Why? I don't want you to leave. Stay with me and get some sleep."

His hand brushed her bare arm as a frustrated sigh left his lips. "I can't, Calli. We took enough of a chance as it is. You sleep and I'll take my turn when you wake up."

She lay with her head on his shoulder, the realization that her happiness of a moment earlier was suddenly gone. Being in Quinn's arms and responding to his sexual demands had made her forget for a time that the cartel was out there in the dark, hunting them down. A shiver crawled through her. The last thing she wanted was to be alone, but Quinn was right. She needed to sleep in order to stay awake when he rested. Rising to an elbow beside him, she lowered her mouth and brushed her lips to his. "I don't want you to go, but I'm going to listen to everything you tell me. I promise to sleep. Do you think you'll be able to stay awake?"

He tucked her hair behind her ear with a smile. "It's only a few more hours until daylight. I'll be fine. In fact, I'll stay awake by getting a good hot breakfast ready for you. How does that sound?"

She stared at his handsome features that were suddenly drawn with concern. It would be nice to pretend that the two of them were on vacation with no worries, but that's not how it was. A quick streak of pain flashed in her eyes before she managed to hide it.

"What do you think our chances are?"

"Calli…" He didn't want to discuss anything, not when what he really needed to do was get back to the living room where his gun would be close by. But he didn't want to frighten her at the same time by telling her just that.

"I want a straight answer, Quinn."

"We've just got to stay smart and keep a close watch on things. I have complete faith in Danny. We've got a lot of feelers out there, moles who can discover cartel whereabouts and plans because they're on the street all the time. Danny will alert us if we need to move quickly."

"You still haven't answered the bottom line."

"We'll be fine. We just can't let down our guard — like we're doing at the moment. I've got to get up, Calli. You get some sleep, okay?"

He rose from the bed. Her eyes followed the line of his back to the narrow width of his naked hips. When he turned, her gaze settled on his soft cock before meeting his eyes. Quinn bent over and tucked the blanket over her shoulder and gave her a lingering kiss. "I love you. Don't worry — just sleep."

Her fingers drifted to his jaw. "I love you, too, Quinn."

The corner of his mouth turned up when he squeezed her hand and then turned and headed for other room.

Chapter Seventeen

๛

Calli rolled over when the sound of a cell phone ringing in another room brought her out of a dead sleep. She sat up, tilted her head and listened to Quinn's muffled voice. Her eyes cast about, noting that the sweatshirt and pants she'd worn the day before were slung over the back of a chair. Quinn must have brought them in while she was sleeping. Her cheeks heated as she thought of the moment he'd stripped her partially nude body. Somehow in the midst of rolling to the floor and clamoring to kiss, he'd gotten them both undressed.

Her hand drifted through her hair to work out the tangles. If they could just get through the next few weeks, life with him would be something to look forward to. It was wonderful to be in love—especially with a man like Quinn.

She leapt up and shrugged on the soiled sweatshirt with a frown. It was even more distasteful to slip on the pants. Calli needed a shower. Her stomach growled as the smell of bacon wafted through the partially opened door. She also needed to eat—and to find a bathroom. She hadn't used any of the facilities since they'd arrived the night before.

She walked into the cozy living room. A small fire still burned in the fireplace to take the chill out of the air. Her gaze was drawn to the couch and then to the floor. A rush of sexual anticipation washed through her. Tonight they would make love again. Maybe even this afternoon. Her nipples hardened beneath the shirt and her stomach clenched with desire. They were running for their lives and all she wanted was Quinn pounding into her.

Mentally shaking herself, her eyes settled on a closed door. She hurried to it, opened it up and almost shouted with glee when she spied a toilet and a small shower stall. The room was in dire need of repair, but she didn't care. She would have the chance to bathe.

A few minutes later, she exited the bathroom and went in search of Quinn. He stood leaning against the counter, his face solemn. His hair was mussed, there were bags beneath his eyes, and his shoulders slumped wearily. Her gaze settled on the cased pistol strapped over his shoulder.

When he saw her, his face lit up. Holding out one arm, he motioned her across the room until she was cuddled beside him.

"Say that one more time." Quinn listened closely and suddenly burst out laughing. "Leave it to you to take a shitty situation and turn it into a comedy." He listened again as his eyes swept over Calli. Even as he listened to Danny, his mind pictured her naked and spread beneath him. "She's right here. Sure. Hey, before I hand over the phone, I just wanted to say thanks for everything. When are you going to call again if things remain quiet?" There was a silent pause. "Sounds good. Thanks for checking on Jenny. I can't tell you how much I appreciate you keeping an eye on her. Tell her that I'll be back as soon as I can. Okay. Here she is." He handed the phone to Calli.

He turned to the stove, his mind working furiously as he listened to Calli's light giggle. Danny was a good one to make her laugh. They didn't talk long and by the time he was cracking eggs into a pan, she'd said goodbye. He rounded his mouth, blew the air from his lungs and pasted a smile on his face.

"I'm so happy to hear that Jenny has regained consciousness." Calli sidled up to Quinn and was welcomed into his arms.

He gave her a quick kiss and a hug that quickly turned into a passionate embrace. Immediately, the air sizzled around them. Memories of the night flitted about them.

A full minute passed before the eggs in the pan snapped, drawing the two forlornly apart.

Quinn cupped her chin and shook his head. "It's amazing how you make me lose my train of thought."

Calli couldn't respond. She simply ran a trembling hand through her tangled hair.

When Quinn grabbed two plates and a spatula, she inhaled deeply to clear her whirling brain. Not knowing what to say after his breathless good morning, she jumped to the subject at hand. "What a relief to know that Jenny is on the road to recovery."

"I know. I've been so worried about her. The doctors say though, that the next few days will be rough as she goes through detox."

"It's a start, Quinn. When this is all over, we'll be there to support her. Danny didn't say anything about the cartel, so I didn't ask. But I'm asking you."

With a shrug, he answered. "It's still quiet. If we don't hear from him, then we can relax a bit." He cocked his head to the side and looked at her as he leaned a slim hip against the counter. "*Just* a bit. I wouldn't put anything past the cartel. From what Danny hears, they're spitting tacks because you managed to slip through their fingers. He'll call again tomorrow to check in. Hey, ready to eat?"

He moved about the tiny kitchen, buttering toast and retrieving the sizzling bacon from a pan. Calli stared at his back while he kept up a line of inane chatter. She instinctively knew he was keeping something from her. When he turned to hand her a filled plate, she took it and also his dish and set them on the counter.

"What? Aren't you hungry?"

She crossed her arms over her chest. "What aren't you telling me?"

"I don't know what you're talking about."

"Come on, Quinn. You said you wanted to keep me safe. How can you do that when I don't know all the details and might make a mistake that could cost both of us our lives?"

He pursed his lips, closed his eyes for a second and then heaved a defeated sigh. "All right. Danny and I have suspected something for quite awhile. When Raine died, neither of us was on the case. We had no idea that Raine was involved with the cartel until the DEA discovered they were heading out of the jungles in Colombia and back to the streets of Boston to recoup losses from the year before. Most of which is the money and drugs that Raine stole." He watched her face when he mentioned his brother's name again. Calli didn't even realize that she gritted her teeth. Her jaw tightened, but she remained silent.

"We might not have even discovered the holes in this case if it weren't for your appearance. Without getting into the many reasons, it seems there is a spy for the cartel down at the precinct. Someone higher up. All fingers are pointing to my supervisor, John McMartin."

The implications raced through Calli's mind. No one could be trusted. The cartel had managed to pull in assistance from all avenues.

"Do you remember the day you came to my office and I hustled you down the hall?"

She nodded.

"I did that because John came around the corner. I didn't want him to see you. For some reason, Calli, regular procedure wasn't followed when Raine was murdered. He was a known member of the cartel, but the investigation into his death lasted all of a week. The reports I received a while back don't even list Raine as being married. They should have. You should've had surveillance on you twenty-four hours a day. We're talking a homicide tied to a drug cartel for crissakes. That day when I saw John, I knew I had to hide you because I didn't want him knowing you were my sister-in-law. I suspect you weren't being tailed by anyone from the department over the last year because the cartel is running the show on this one and didn't want to draw an ounce of attention after the hit. Once they came back, they took matters into their own hands."

Calli grimaced behind her hands as she wearily scrubbed her face. It seemed at every turn the plot thickened. Raine had left her a horrible legacy and had never thought about future consequences where she, or all the other innocents whose lives would be ruined because of them, were concerned.

Quinn's fingers wrapped gently around her arm and he drew her into his embrace. She went willingly. "So now you know why I'm upset. Danny and I weren't too sure who was the mole, but he's more and more certain every day that we're right about John." He sighed against her hair. "I've known and worked for the man for years. I just can't believe that he would be greedy enough to fall into this mess."

He hugged her and pressed a kiss against her forehead. "Let's eat. You know, we need to be alert, but Danny thinks we've got another day or so before we will even have to think of moving on. Let's just have breakfast and try to enjoy the afternoon. Who knows where we're going to be tomorrow."

"I don't think so. I mean enjoy the day. We're not doing that until you get some rest."

"I'm not even tired."

"Have you looked at yourself in the mirror? You're exhausted."

He chuckled and pulled her to his chest. "That's your fault. You gave me a run for my money last night."

Calli had the grace to blush, but it didn't stop her next words. "Well, then you'd better get some rest, because I expect a repeat performance." Even before the words left her mouth, she felt his cock harden where it pressed against her belly. "I'm not arguing with you. And that's the truth, because I have a feeling you might win. However, the deal was that I got to sleep last night. You're going to eat and then get in that bed—alone. I'll keep an eye on things." She reached up and played with the hair trailing along the back of his neck. "Please, Quinn. You look beat."

A wave of weariness washed through him. She was right. He wouldn't be any good if he was exhausted and they had to get out fast. "All right. You win."

"Good! Then let's eat. My stomach is growling."

* * * * *

Calli used the tip of her toe to keep the swing moving at a slow, lazy pace. The warm rays of the sun heated her cheeks as her gaze moved about the yard. She watched two ducks swimming in the small lake and smiled at their antics. The contentment and serenity she felt would make it so easy to pretend that the afternoon was just like any other normal day. But the fact that one of Quinn's guns lay beside her on the wooden slats for protection against the unknown, belied the quiet bliss.

Her head tipped back to capture more of the sun's heat. Closing her eyes, she pictured Quinn lying in the bed just inside. She'd gone and checked on him on hour earlier and still, he slept soundlessly. Deciding to simply enjoy the sight of his naked chest, she'd sat quietly for a bit, trying not to let the sight of his handsome face and one bare leg peeking out from beneath the quilt get to her, because they combined to send her mind in a totally different direction.

Sex with Quinn was torture in itself. Last night still had her heart rapping, and she eagerly looked forward to the next encounter. It was wonderful to be in the first exquisite throes of love again, to experience that all-consuming rapture that stole her breath away. He was a commanding lover, gentle one moment, then unbridled the next as he manipulated her body.

She let out a long breath of air thinking about how she had dared him to fuck her and how he'd surprised her beyond belief with one orgasm after another. God, she wished he would wake up.

Calli rose from the swing, delicately picked up the gun and headed inside. Crossing the living room, she poked her head inside the bedroom and noticed that Quinn was now sprawled on his belly. Maybe he was ready to awaken and she wanted to be ready the moment he did. She wasn't waiting a moment longer to get clean.

She turned as her eyes settled on the duffle bag that Maggie had quickly packed and set in the corner of the living room. She ruffled around inside, found a clean sweatsuit, soap, shampoo and even some scented lotion. With one last quick glance at the bedroom door, she hurried to the bathroom and dumped her load onto the counter, careful to place the gun close to the shower. Flipping the water on, she stripped and tossed her clothes outside the door wondering if there was a way to get them washed. Steam began to billow over the top of the cheap plastic shower curtain, a heavenly lure that quickly coaxed her into the confined space.

She stepped into the stall and moaned audibly as the water pelted her tender skin. Ducking her head beneath the spray brought on another long sigh. The dirty corners of the shower made no difference, nor did the rusting fixtures. The hot water and a chance to get clean was paradise itself. Tipping her head back, she let the water stream over her body, enjoying the sensation for a minute or two. Finally, she reached for the shampoo and scrubbed her hair until her scalp tingled. Next came the bar of soap. She didn't have a washcloth, but at the moment didn't care. She scrunched her body into a corner away from most of the spray and quickly lathered her limbs and torso.

Her heart leapt when a hand grabbed the edge of the curtain and moved it to the side. The gun! The soap dropped from her hand.

"Want your back scrubbed?"

She sank against the back of the stall as her heart slowed with relief. "Quinn, you scared me." Was she finding it difficult to catch her breath, however, because of panic or was it the sight of Quinn's hard, naked body as he crowded beneath the pelting water? She didn't have time to wonder because he was pulling her into the spray with him.

"Did you plan this?" he asked while nuzzling her neck and squeezing her bare ass. "If you did, I couldn't be happier to find you naked. Although, if I would've found you dressed, you'd probably be naked by this time anyway. I woke up and all I wanted was you."

"Quinn..." she sighed happily while wrapping her arms around his neck.

His hard cock bumped against her belly. His lips suckled her earlobe. "I'm going to fuck you, Calli. It was the last thing I thought about before falling to sleep. I dreamt about it. And once I'm done? I'm going to fuck you again."

She pulled his mouth to hers, forever inscribing the moment in her mind. The way he massaged her ass, slippery with soap, the touch of his lips as water trailed in rivulets down their cheeks, the feel of his hard cock prodding against her stomach and the growl of approval from the back of his throat. All of it. She would never forget.

A rush of pleasure immediately followed when he turned her away from him, then pulled her back against his chest. His hands instantly sought the roundness of her wet breasts, squeezing, rolling her erect nipples with the tips of his fingers as he settled his cock against the line of her ass.

"I don't think I'll ever get enough of you," he whispered beside her ear.

"Quinn...I love you." She dipped back and ground her ass against the rigid line of his erection. Desire blazed—instant, hot and yearning. Her hands covered his at her breasts. A slow pulse inside her began to throb. He would take her how he would. She didn't care. As long as he kept the heat going.

His hands drifted from beneath hers and slipped a path over her ribs, down across her flat belly and lower. Threading through the wet curls between her legs was enough for Calli to spread her stance even though her knees were weak. She braced herself against his chest and tried not to jerk when he spread her lips wide. Her clit throbbed. Rivulets of hot water funneled down her stomach and over the swollen nub, sensitizing it further.

The tip of his middle finger began to swirl around her clit, teasing, flicking, making her hips dip forward in anticipation. Both hands now. They slid between her legs, his fingers everywhere—sliding through her slick crease, playing with her clit, dipping inside her tunnel with a pledge of what soon would happen.

"Please, Quinn…" she breathed behind closed lids. Her own hands plucked at her nipples. "Don't make me wait. I want your cock."

His strong fingers suddenly encircled her wrists. He placed her hands against the side of the stall, the new position bending her slightly forward. A split second later, the head of his cock probed against her lips from behind in search of her hole.

His body dipped slightly and he was in and fucking her, long hard strokes that tore the breath from her lungs. His thick cock throbbed as his hands slipped around her waist to finger her clit. Her knees began to buckle, but he supported her weight with his arms and thickly muscled thighs.

Quinn began to ram her with short strokes, each sparking the blaze that built higher and higher deep in the pit of her womb. Calli groaned aloud when the first pulse exploded. Her cunt was hot and shuddering and filled by his thickness.

Quinn gasped beside her ear and thrust forward as he came. He held her hips tightly against him, grinding into her body as he let himself go.

Calli panted heavily, her head swirling from the sensual position, her body trembling with the power of her release. Neither had been able to stave off the heated passion that had driven them to immediate orgasm.

His cock slipped from her. He turned her to face him, pulling her tightly into his arms as his mouth lowered. Calli's mouth sagged open. His tongue licked across her lower lip before he slanted his head and kissed her deeply. She clung to him and met each dart of his tongue.

The kiss began to slow, murmurs of love mixed with the spray of water as hands slid across the other's slick skin.

Calli could never remember being happier than she was. Even the love she had shared with Raine would never compare to what she felt at the moment. Quinn held her heart in the palm of his hand and she would never willingly relinquish it.

She loved the feel of her wet breasts pressed against his chest. She couldn't imagine a day, no...even a mere minute without knowing that she would always be a part of his life.

Calli squealed loudly at the same moment that Quinn let out a yelp as a cold blast of water hit them. Tripping over one another, they raced out of the stall, laughing hysterically and bringing down the curtain rod with them. Cold water sprayed everywhere as Quinn braved the icy spray once more and dipped into the stall to shut it off.

"Son of a bitch that's cold!" he yelped again. Finally he managed to spin the faucet until only a drip splattered against the floor.

Calli laughed heartily when he turned around with a comical wince on his face.

"Are you making fun of me?" His eyes narrowed.

She continued to giggle. "No," she managed to get out. "It's just that...I'm glad you had to go back in because there was no way I was going to."

"Well, maybe I'll just force you back in..." He took a step forward and made a grab for her. At the exact same moment, there was a snap and the showerhead fell to the tile of the stall. Water spouted out in a steady stream.

His arm was about her waist, but they both stared at the newest problem.

"Ah, shit," he muttered and then released her.

Calli tried to hide her giggle, but couldn't. "Can you fix it?"

"I'm going to have to try or risk burning out the pump and not having any running water at all. I better go see where I can shut off the main valve."

She scanned his long naked length, her gaze filled with desire despite how she shivered. She leaned against him and ran a hand across his chest. "You see what you can do about the water and I'll fix us something to eat. Then, who knows…" she added suggestively and ran a fingertip over his jaw as her hand drifted to his cock.

"You're a tease, Calli. I like that."

She giggled again, turned to grab her clothes and yelped when he playfully swatted her bare ass.

* * * * *

"How's it going in there?" Calli asked twenty minutes later. Quinn had found the main water valve in the pump house beside the cabin. The water had quit running, but the floor was soaked. Currently, he was muttering beneath his breath as he checked the faucet.

"I'm going to have to check the shed out back and see if I can find some parts. I'm hoping that Rocco's brother has plumbing supplies around. Shit!" He bent quickly and picked up his cell phone, which had slipped from his pocket and fallen into a puddle of water. Shaking it off, he used the end of his T-shirt to wipe it off and slipped it back into his jeans.

"I made sandwiches. Want to eat now or should I wait to heat the soup?"

"Give me a minute to run out back. I want to try calling Jenny at the hospital. If I can reach her, I'll come back in so you can talk to her, too."

"Are you sure that'll be okay?"

"There shouldn't be a problem. I don't want her to think we deserted her."

"Okay." The playfulness left her voice, however, when he picked up his pistol and leather holster from the back of the toilet and strapped it over his shoulder.

Quinn exited the bathroom with Calli, pulled her close and gave her a quick kiss. "I'll be right back. Why the frown?"

She shrugged. "I guess it was easy to forget for a while why we're really here. You picking up the gun instantly reminded me."

"Just a precaution. Give me five minutes while I fly out back. I won't be long."

She walked with him to the back door and watched his purposeful stride as he crossed to a shed built on the outer perimeter of the yard. He had the cell phone in his hand, and then to his ear a moment later. He disappeared inside the shed.

With a sigh, she headed back to the bathroom, located a handful of worn towels and spread them over the water to soak up what liquid she could. The emotion of complete contentment that had stayed with her the entire morning, into the afternoon, and even during the sex in the shower, was gone. Replacing it was a deep need to be gone from the cabin, to be done with hiding from the cartel. As she wrung out a towel over the shower drain, all she could think about was what the future would hold for both her and Quinn once it was safe to return to Boston.

She continued to sop up all the water, waiting for him to return. She'd finally wrung out the last towel and, still, he hadn't come back to the house. Deciding to hang the dirty towels outside to dry, she gathered them up and tossed them into an old plastic laundry basket that had seen better days.

She'd taken the first step into the living room when a gunshot rang out. She flinched, dropped the basket and slammed against the wall as her mind raced frantically.

Quinn!

Her gun! It was on the kitchen table. Darting her eyes to the window first, she took off. The front window exploded, sending shattered glass flying through the room. A bullet whizzed past her ear.

Calli screamed and fell to the floor to scramble on her hands and knees across the threadbare carpet as quickly as she could move, her chest tight and her heart pounding crazily. She literally skidded against the table leg in the kitchen, reached up to snatch the pistol and ducked back down.

Where was she going to hide? My god, Quinn! She crawled to a space between a cabinet and the stove, her wide eyes blazing with fear as they darted from the window to the open screen door.

A sob burst from her throat when another shot rang out from somewhere outside the house.

Her body began to shake as she clutched the gun in her fist, not knowing what to do or where to go. "Please, god…let him be alive," she murmured. She couldn't do this on her own. She couldn't face those men again. What if they had killed him? What if he was hurt and lying unconscious? He would be unable to protect himself or her. She cringed against the wall with her knees drawn to her chest and the pistol now clutched in both hands. She shook so badly that she could hardly keep the weapon gripped within her fist.

She blinked back the tears of panic, trying to get hold of her emotions. What should she do? Her watery gaze darted about the kitchen. She started wildly when another shot was followed by a series of bullets peppering the outside walls of the cabin and pressed tightly against the wall. A slug shattered the window above the sink. Shards of glass exploded across the countertop.

Calli cringed when she heard someone holler in the silent aftermath of bullets spraying everywhere. Was it Quinn? Another shot.

Stunned senses spurred her to crawl frantically to the doorway between the kitchen and the living room. Her head fell back against the doorjamb as she sucked in gulps of air. She had to keep a clear head. She had to be ready to run for one of the doors, depending on what happened outside.

She waited, straining to hear anything in the deathly silence that surrounded her, with a hand clapped over her mouth to keep down the terror-filled scream that threatened. The silence was more frightening than the gunshots. What should she do? She waited endlessly for something to happen, battling the urge to run frantically from the cabin, yet frozen as her eyes darted from one window to another.

A footstep scraped against the wooden back porch. Calli stifled her sob and scrambled around the corner, pressing her back tightly against the wall of the living room.

She froze in terror when the rusted hinges of the screen door screeched, signaling that someone was entering the house. She couldn't leap up and race across the room, because she would be seen. Her wild eyes scanned the room searching for a place to hide. She should have run to the bedroom immediately and hidden in the closet, but it was too late! She had waited too long to make a move.

Her fingers tightened around the gun. She shuffled quietly another two feet from the doorway, staying against the wall. Facing the kitchen entry, she raised the gun with trembling hands and tried to hold it steady. If she had to, she would shoot. Her eyes squeezed tight for a moment as she winced. How could she take another's life? She had no choice. With a silent deep gulp of air, she stared past the pistol's barrel. A shuffling footstep on the worn kitchen linoleum was like an electric shock jolting her body.

Calli swallowed and struggled to hold her hands steady. The breath caught in her throat. Her heart pounded so hard that it hurt her ears. She blinked back her tears to clear her vision. She had to shoot if she were to survive.

Another shuffle, then a loud thud and the clatter of something skidding across the floor.

She pursed her lips tightly and waited, blinking back her tears again, her disbelieving brain assailed by total confusion. If the intruder was Quinn, he would call out for her. The absolute horror of the moment sent a mind-numbing shudder through her body. Before she could shake it off, a deep gurgle echoed from the kitchen, then total silence.

She waited a full three minutes. Sporadic gunfire echoed in the yard, and then nothing. Every hair on her body stood on end. She had to do something! She just couldn't sit and wait for the lurking evil to find her. Taking a deep breath to find the courage she needed, she edged soundlessly against the wall and slid on her butt to the doorjamb. Her fingers gripped the pistol so tightly that they turned white. Slowly, she turned her head and moved an inch until her she could peer around the corner.

She fought the roar of fear inside her head. Diego lay unmoving on the kitchen floor. His dark-skinned fingers still clutched a pistol. Three feet in front of him, a sawed-off shotgun had skidded to a stop when he dropped it. The palm of her hand stifled a scream as she stared in horror at the pool of blood that widened as streams of red flowed in rivulets across the uneven floor.

Chapter Eighteen

‎80

Quinn winced against the pain in his upper left arm as he pressed himself against the side wall of the shed. His hand was numb. Warm liquid flowed down his chest where the bullet had ripped through his arm and was now lodged in his ribs. He was bleeding badly.

"Fuck!" he hissed behind clenched teeth and struggled to put his thoughts together. The first shot had taken him completely by surprise. There was nothing that he could have done about it. Someone had waited until he'd come out of the shed and tried to pick him off without the slightest warning. Before he had even crawled frantically to the side of the shed, he'd heard glass explode from a shot on the opposite side of the yard. There were two of them for sure and they had both the cabin and the shed in their sights.

His head pounded. Six bullets and at least two hit men. He had six bullets. That's all. Six bullets that stood between his and Calli's would-be killers.

He had to get to the cabin. She was in there alone, unable to defend herself, unknowing of what would unfold over the next hour. He worked frantically with one hand and his teeth to rip off a strip of his T-shirt. He cringed at the tearing sound, wondering if anyone was close enough to hear it. Quickly, he wrapped the torn strip around his upper arm and used his teeth to hold one end as he tied a knot. There was nothing he could do about the hole beneath his arm.

Wood splintered directly above his head. Quinn dove to the side, ignoring the rush of pain that sickened him, and rolled around the corner of the building. His head fell back against the wooden slats. How the fuck was he going to get to the cabin?

A sixth sense made him turn his head to the left. A dark-skinned man stepped from the thick tangle of brush with his sawed-off shotgun pointed directly at Quinn's chest. An evil smile resided in his eyes, easily affirming Quinn's death. Lightning-quick, Quinn swung his right arm up and pulled the trigger without thought. A look of surprise entered the Colombian's eyes as he dropped to his knees and rolled into the underbrush. Another spray of bullets peppered the wall above Quinn's head, stealing Quinn's opportunity to get off another shot at the wounded man. He ducked and scrambled around another corner feeling the sting of a bullet slice through the muscle of his thigh.

"Fuck," he hissed again once he had rolled to a stop inside the open door of the shed. The stray bullet had ripped through his jeans and peeled the top layer of skin, but the injury wasn't as serious as his arm.

Shots resounded again, but this time Quinn knew it was the cabin taking the brunt of the shells. He peeked around the corner to see the Colombian staggering toward the cabin's back door. He took aim and fired a precious bullet, noting how the man's body jerked, but still managed to stagger on.

Someone opened fire on the shed again. Quinn dove to the damp dirt floor and flattened himself against the ground.

* * * * *

Diego's lifeless eyes stared at her. Bile burned the lining of Calli's throat. She scrambled to her feet and sprinted for the bedroom. Her headlong, frenzied flight through the doorway was interrupted when an unseen hand seized her arm and yanked her sideways. The gun flew from her fingers and banged against the floor. A large hand clamped across her mouth as she was pulled against a hard chest. Her muffled scream was nearly soundless as she kicked out blindly and fought to escape.

"Calli! Shhh! It's me!" Danny's familiar voice hissed beside her ear.

Her wide eyes filled with tears when his hand dropped away. She spun and flung herself against his chest, her terror finding solace in the hope that she and Quinn would live to see the end of the day.

"Oh, god, Danny."

"Shhh. You've got to be quiet."

"Thank god you're here!" She sobbed quietly.

He flattened her against the wall beside him with his arm and peeked into the living room. "Where's Quinn?" he whispered over his shoulder.

"He went to the shed. I heard a shot. Then the window exploded when they shot into the house."

Danny hugged the wall beside her and checked the bullets in his gun.

"One of them is dead," she whispered.

His head snapped in her direction. "Are you sure?"

Her head nodded frantically. "He came in the back door. H-he's one of the men who kidnapped me. His name is Diego." Calli grabbed his arm. "Thank god you're here."

"Christ, word got out where you were. They've got spies everywhere. I've been trying to call on the cell phone. Why in hell didn't Quinn pick it up?"

"It...it never rang. I know it's working, because I saw him using it."

"Fuck..." his head fell back as his eyes closed. With a deep breath, he swung his head and glanced down at her. "Stay right beside me. We gotta get out of this house and find Quinn."

"Do...you think he's..." She pressed her knuckles to her mouth, afraid to say the words aloud.

Danny reached out and rubbed her goose-bumped arm. "He's smart, Calli." The glow in his eyes darkened. "He's one of the best detectives on the force. He's out there. I know it. I'll take this."

Calli watched him scoop up her gun and shove it into the tight space behind his belt.

He poked his head around the corner of the doorjamb. "Okay, this is it. Stay close. Ready?"

She nodded silently and followed him as he stepped lightly into the living room. He held up a hand, cocked his head and finally tipped his chin in the direction of the front door.

Calli did her best not to glance back at Diego's body, but some sense of morbid curiosity forced her eyes in that direction. She could see him through the kitchen doorway. The pool of blood was much larger now. A shudder ran up her spine as she froze on the spot. It could very well have been her lying lifeless as the blood drained from her body.

"Calli. Come on!" Danny hissed.

She spun from Diego's sightless eyes and reached for his hand. He clasped it just as a shuffling noise met her ears. She whirled back to see Quinn lean heavily against the doorway leading into the kitchen. His T-shirt was stained red on his left side. His face was white and drawn. Blood also discolored one leg of his jeans.

"Quinn!" She tried to shake off Danny's hand, but he wouldn't release her.

Quinn's pistol barrel was suddenly trained on his partner's chest. "Let her go." He cocked the hammer of his gun.

Calli resided within a horrible nightmare. Quinn looked like he was going to shoot! Suddenly, Danny yanked her back against his chest. The barrel of his pistol was icy cold against her temple as his muscular arm held her prisoner.

Calli's scream ended in a whimper as the cold metal dug into her tender skin.

"Shut up, Calli." Those were Danny's only words as his eyes bored into Quinn's and his grip tightened around Calli's waist.

"You fucking bastard..." Quinn's barrel wavered, but somehow he managed to stay upright. "I said let her go."

"I can't."

Quinn's expression was murderous despite the shiny beads of a cold sweat forming on his brow. "She's innocent in all of this."

"Danny!" Calli pleaded and tried to wrestle away. "What are you doing?"

The sound of a gun's hammer clicking back beside her ear sent a shock wave rolling through her body.

Calli whimpered with fear. "Quinn..." she pleaded desperately.

His eyes moved to her frightened ones. "It's all right, Calli. Danny. Let her go. It's not worth it."

Danny's jaw twitched. "How did you figure it out?"

Quinn shook his head, but kept his arm out, ready to fire the pistol. To the couple across the room, he looked composed even though his pallid features suggested he was ready to topple over. But, inside, he died a thousand deaths. He struggled against his best friend's betrayal and the horror of Calli being shot before his eyes. "You almost got away with it, but you made one tiny mistake."

Danny ran his tongue over his dry lips and remained silent, waiting...

Quinn fought against the nausea that churned his belly. His brain raced, his mind stayed sharp and he waited on the edge of a precipice for the opportunity to shoot Danny before he harmed Calli. The thought of killing a lifelong friend nearly made him gag. But he would do it. He would do it to release Calli from his clutches. He'd keep the man talking. His chance would come. His finger twitched against the trigger.

"When I went to the shed, I called Jenny. I decided to chance that the cartel couldn't trace a call. Why? Because this morning you told me she was doing wonderfully. It suddenly hit me. How can someone who's been an addict for so many years be doing wonderfully? That night at the hospital, the doctor told me that if she lived despite the beating, her detox could very well give her a heart attack. You made it sound like she was holding court from her hospital bed. Your attitude was too relaxed even for you. Have fun and don't worry about looking over your shoulder. That's what you told me, Danny. For fucking crissakes, there's a fucking Colombian cartel after us. A nurse helped Jenny with the phone. She was so weak she could hardly speak. She told me that a drug dealer was in her room, but she wasn't going to buy. She was going to get better. She promised me. I thought she was hallucinating until she asked why I had a dealer for a friend. I told her I didn't understand. She kept insisting the new dealer was a horrible man. He'd made her do things when she didn't have the money to get a fix. She recognized your voice that first night at the hospital — it was the same voice of the man who beat the hell out of her."

Quinn watched a shudder run through Calli. She anchored her gaze on him, her eyes silently begging for aid. He was their only salvation, if he could just talk Danny into letting her go.

"That bitch should've kept her mouth shut."

"I struggled against the truth of your deception, Danny. My mind rebelled when I first pointed my gun at you. I prayed that you would let Calli walk across the room. I doubted my own instinct, because you were my friend." His head wagged wearily. "I was certain when you didn't let go of her. That's when I knew I could never forgive you."

Danny stepped back toward the door, dragging Calli with him. Quinn tensed. How could he get off a shot when Danny used Calli's body as a human shield?

"Stay where you are!" Danny cried when Quinn lurched forward, the gun never wavering.

"Danny, please!" Calli sobbed and struggled to escape.

"I'll shoot her right here if you step any closer! Quit fighting me, Calli!" He shoved the gun hard against her head again.

"Danny! Think of Maggie. Think of the kids!" Quinn's shout resounded about the room as he took another dragging step forward. His brain spun. Warm blood made his shirt cling to the skin of his chest. He had to get the man's attention away from the woman in his arms. He had to watch for his chance. Danny hesitated, his eyes suddenly uncertain at the mention of his wife and kids.

Quinn pushed on. "Don't do anything foolish. Maggie loves you. The kids love you. They need their father."

A snort left Danny's mouth. "If I let the two of you live, I'll spend the rest of my life behind fucking bars." Anxiety was back in his voice.

Quinn had experienced desperate men in hopeless situations before. Danny would kill them, because in his mind he had no other alternative. He had to get to him first.

"Why, then? Why have you done the things you've done? Make me understand. At least give me that much before you end all of this." Quinn waited, his mind racing. Every time he looked into Calli's eyes, his heart nearly quit beating. Her entire body was a trembling mass of fear. He could smell her absolute terror in the air. It leapt from her eyes.

"I did it for them. Four kids? A house in an expensive part of town? How the hell else was I going to give them what they wanted? I'm in too deep, now. Maggie will never forgive me. I… I have to kill the both of you or everything I have will crumble."

Quinn caught the hesitation in Danny's voice and plunged on. "Did you know my brother?"

"What?"

"Did you know my brother? Were you and Raine Lemont in this together?"

Danny laughed, a high-pitched, anxiety-ridden chuckle that evidenced his growing uneasiness. His head wagged. "I never met him. No one but the cartel's top men knew who he was. I only heard of *El León*. That's what they called him, Quinn—because of his eyes. Eyes like yours. They made an example out of him. You don't fuck with the cartel. McMartin had no reason to believe that Raine Lemont's death was anything other than a simple accident because his identity was hidden so well."

Quinn struggled against his disbelief. "Everything was a lie. I trusted you. I trusted you with my fucking life. Is everything you've told me about McMartin a lie?"

"You made it easy. You never suspected that I could have been the mole. When you told me you thought John was behind everything, I almost laughed out loud that night in the bar. I had to keep you thinking he was the connection to the drug lords because you were getting too smart, too curious for your own good."

"Why then, Danny? Why did you continue with this whole charade? You could easily have handed Calli over when she called you. You could have let them know that I wasn't Raine. Instead you let us escape."

Danny shook his head and tightened his grip around the gunstock. "Jenny showing up made me think my cartel position differently. I didn't want them to know that you weren't Raine. I couldn't care less about the missing drugs. It was the money." He let out a strange high-pitched laugh. "If I kept my mouth shut, maybe you and Calli would lead me to it."

"Christ, Danny. You were playing the same deadly game my brother did?"

"That was the plan. Those bastards have plenty of money. I was going to get my hands on Raine's hidden stash, take Maggie and the kids and get the hell out of here. That was until Enrique Palacios asked why I was seen in the fucking parking lot when I picked up Calli. I didn't think they saw me, because no one followed us. I had to backtrack quickly, let them know that I was securing the two of you away from the city. That I had sent you to a place where a cartel murder wouldn't be suspected. They fucked up everything, Quinn. You and Calli might have lived if Diego and I weren't ordered up here to kill you."

"For how long, Danny?" Quinn questioned quietly. "How long were you going to let us live? Until the money was discovered?"

The room suddenly became quiet. The two men stared at one another, each certain they would do what they had to in order to survive another day.

"Or until it came down to this." Danny's voice lowered. "You made it easy for me by taking care of Diego. I didn't think I'd have to kill you, but you wouldn't leave well enough alone. You were bound and determined to keep pushing the edge of the envelope until the cartel was brought down."

Calli froze as the weight of the gun against her head lessened slightly. She couldn't let him shoot Quinn. She couldn't watch the man she loved die before her eyes. She took a deep breath.

The split second the pressure of the pistol's cold barrel disappeared, Calli sagged in his arms, letting her body go limp. She literally heard the bones of Danny's shoulder shatter when the bullet hit him. Out of the corner of her eye, she caught a flash of Quinn's body folding to the ground.

"Quinn!" she screamed. Danny's gun bounced off her shoulder and skittered across the carpet as his body slammed against the wall beside the door.

Quinn! She had to get to him. She had to tell him how much she loved him before he left her.

To her utter amazement, he wasn't lying motionless on the floor. He was crawling on his knees to reach her.

The door behind her crashed open. Two men dressed in fatigues leapt through the opening, their machine guns waving wildly about as another raced in behind them and tackled Danny who struggled to get to his feet. Between the three, he was instantly subdued. Four more men rushed into the room from the kitchen. Quinn grabbed Calli by the arm and clumsily dragged her out of harm's way. Bulky bodies continued to pour through the open doorway, but Calli was unaware as she clung desperately to Quinn, sobbing out the terror that refused to stay silent any longer. Somehow he was alive. She was alive!

His arm circled her shoulders tightly. She would never remember the soothing words he whispered beside her ear, only the rapid pounding of his heart against her cheek. She dragged in breath after sharp breath, her body trembling horribly as he held her.

"It's over, Calli. I love you. God, I love you." He kissed her tangled hair. "You're safe now."

His whisper reached through her shocked senses. The touch of his hand was gentle as he stroked her back. Chaotic shouts filtered through the buzz inside her head. She ignored all of it. The only thing that mattered was his strong arm around her.

"Quinn? How bad is it?"

The strange voice invaded her warm space. She opened her eyes to see a familiar face and tried to remember where she'd seen it before.

"I've lost a lot of blood, John. Thank god you got here in time. The bullet went through my arm. I think it's lodged in my rib cage because I hurt like hell."

"Get a paramedic in here!" John called over his shoulder.

Calli blinked and stared at the man who hunkered down beside them and busily checked Quinn's injury. John? John McMartin?

"I kept him talking as long as I could. I was going to take him out, because I thought I was on my own. How in the hell did you get here so fast?" Quinn winced when John pried his shirt away from his wound, but he refused to let go of Calli. "The bastard was going to kill both of us. Son of a bitch," he hissed with another wince as John's fingers gently felt along Quinn's rib cage. "I was hoping you would believe everything Jenny told you."

"Jenny?" Calli tried to concentrate on Quinn's words.

He looked at her, his face still contorted in a painful grimace as he nodded. "Danny called a second time when I was heading for the shed for plumbing supplies. His mistake. The cell phone showed he was calling from some phone booth in a different area code from this morning. Then when I spoke to Jenny, everything she mumbled finally came together. I didn't want to believe it, but I had no choice. Danny was the only person she could have been talking about. After we spoke, I called Maggie. She said Danny was on a case out of town. When I talked to him this morning, he said he was in the phone booth at the end of his block. And Maggie was surprised as hell that we were still at the cabin. Danny had told her that he'd moved us again last night. I knew then and there as much as I hated to believe it, that he was on his way here. I was just unfortunate enough to still be down at the shed when he arrived." His words trailed away to nothing as he watched three SWAT Team members haul Danny's struggling body from the cabin. He shook his head, still finding it hard to believe the events of the day.

"There's more to the story," John finally said. "I was already in a copter on the way here with the SWAT team when Jenny was patched through. Last night we caught up to Enrique Palacios. One of his men spilled his guts this morning about Danny and the fact you and Calli Lemont were up here in the woods. He laughed because he said we'd never get here in time. We've been watching Danny for the last year, Quinn. I first suspected his involvement with drug dealers when a report ended up missing last year after a homicide. He made mistakes, but none that pointed to his actual guilt. It's been a waiting game to catch him."

"And you never discussed it with me?"

"How could I? You two were partners and best friends. Would you have believed me?"

"Probably not. I'm still finding it hard even after everything that has happened."

"I gotta ask, Quinn. How does Jenny Johnson fit into the picture?"

Just then, three paramedics with a gurney entered the house. John stepped back, noting how the woman beside Quinn still clung to his hand.

Quinn's head shook again. "It's a long story, John. Come visit me at the hospital. I'll tell you all about it."

Epilogue
Two years later

&

Quinn hurried around the front of the car to open Calli's door, but she beat him to it. With a beautiful smile, she reached for his hand and they walked across the parking lot to join Jenny.

Quinn's mother turned and waved excitedly. She stood in the sun, her new dress crisply pressed, her dyed dark brown hair framing more youthful-looking skin. She clutched a sheaf of papers in her hand. Scores of TV and newspaper reporters milled about, checking their cameras and interviewing softly speaking women who looked like they didn't want to be the center of attention.

Calli released Quinn's hand when they reached the sidewalk and held out her arms with a huge grin. Jenny hugged her tightly, the gold flecks shining in her eyes.

"I was so afraid we weren't going to make it," Calli exclaimed. " Traffic was horrible."

Quinn chuckled beside his wife. "Don't believe it for a second. We would have been fine. Calli just had so damn much luggage that it took longer to pack the car. I told her all she needed was a bathing suit because I don't plan on doing a thing except lying around on the pristine Fiji beaches." He ignored the mocking expression Calli shot in his direction and bent to give Jenny a hug. "I wouldn't have missed today for anything. How you doing? Is everything on schedule?"

Jenny nodded her head. She turned to take in the large crowd and the newly painted building. Her eyes lifted to the white sign edged with gold above the door. *The Hope Women's Shelter.*

She couldn't help herself. Tears welled in her eyes. It had been a long road to get to this day, but she'd done it. She'd beat her addiction with Calli's and Quinn's help. It hadn't been easy. More than once she'd relapsed, but they had never given up on her. No matter the time of day, they were forever at her side when she needed them. She would miss them over the next two weeks, because it was the first time the couple would be gone from her side. Quinn had told her repeatedly that she would be so busy at the shelter that the days would fly by and they would be back from their vacation before she even realized they were gone. Jenny didn't think so.

It had been Calli's idea to put the cartel's drug money she'd hidden to good use. She'd written proposals for city hall, spearheaded fundraisers across the state and lobbied congressmen and state senators for grant money to help pay the initial salaries of trained counselors. She filed the necessary licenses and advertised in numerous newspapers for nurses and doctors to come to the aid of battered women whose lives were turned upside down by the horrific effects of drug addiction. She'd even sold her home and donated the money, cutting all ties to her past. Calli had been tireless in her effort to give Quinn's mother a future, to help those in need.

Jenny batted away her tears and clutched Calli's hand as the crowd hushed. The governor of the state stepped up to a podium at the bottom of the shelter's steps.

"Good afternoon, ladies and gentlemen. What a beautiful day to celebrate the grand opening of a dream." He turned and tipped his balding head to denote the building behind him.

The crowd roared its approval.

The governor held up his hand until the throngs of people quieted. "The state of Massachusetts is proud to support this wonderful endeavor. I had a speech planned, but this isn't my time. This day belongs to all those who worked so hard to see a dream come to fruition. This day belongs to all those who will walk through this door to seek aid and comfort. I'd like to turn the podium over to Ms. Jennifer Johnson, the manager and keeper of this fine facility." He stepped away, joining the applause of the many onlookers.

Calli squeezed Jenny's hand in support.

Quinn's mother met her son's eyes and accepted a gentle kiss against her cheek. "It shouldn't be me up there," she murmured to the two of them. "It should be you, Calli. It's because of your persistence that this all came about."

"Go on," Calli urged with a smile. "They're waiting for you."

Jenny took a deep breath and walked the short distance through the crowd to reach the podium.

Quinn glanced down at Calli and drew her to his side, his faced creased with a proud smile.

The crowd quieted again when Jenny stepped up, adjusted the microphone and unfolded the sheets of paper in her hand. She was infinitely thankful that no one could see how her hands shook. She cleared her throat and kept her eyes glued to her handwritten words.

"Good afternoon, everyone. I'd like to thank you all for helping us celebrate the grand opening of Hope. Our doors actually opened a month ago and to date we have filled our rooms to seventy-five percent capacity..." The words died in her throat as she stared at the sheets of paper filled with facts and figures. She'd worked so hard with Calli to gather the information for her speech — cold numbers, hard solid facts — a wealth of knowledge that would appease government offices, but never tell the true story of warm pride and heartfelt thanks.

She raised her chin and scanned the now silent and questioning crowd until she found Quinn and Calli. The earlier proud smiles had left their faces as they wondered at Jenny's sudden silence. Calli chewed nervously on her bottom lip, but her eyes blazed with quiet encouragement.

Jenny wet her lips, refolded the sheets and gripped the edges of the podium. "Excuse me." She cleared her throat. "I...I had my speech prepared, but it's not what I really wanted to say. Please bear with me." Murmurs ran through the crowd. She took a settling breath and began to speak from her heart.

"Nothing could have ever prepared me for this day. The wonder that I feel is overwhelming. You see, I was an addict for more years than I can count. I was a mess, to say the least, and at rock bottom, simply existing with the disease of addiction that led me down a path of self-destruction." Her eyes found her son's. She watched him place his arm about Calli's shoulders, but his smile was only for her. "I've made many mistakes in my life—errors before I even began to experiment with the drugs that helped to soften my everyday heartache. Drugs that made me forget the terror of being beaten by an uncaring husband—someone I'd been drawn to because my parents were indifferent to my existence and…" She faltered for only a second. "I'd been a sixteen-year-old mother who gave away her precious twin sons."

She spied the tears that suddenly sprang to Calli's eyes. Quinn's jaw tightened.

"Years passed. My life passed. I went from one bad relationship to another. I went from one horrible shelter to another. One day, I awoke and realized that I couldn't remember a lot of the awful details of my life because it was easier to reside within the haze of a drug-filled mind. The only thing I could call my own were the clothes on my back and the pain in my heart. I wanted to get clean, but it was too difficult to face the physical pain of withdrawal, to know that I had only myself to depend on. I was a worthless human being who would do anything, or steal anything just to feel the high."

The only noise to be heard was when someone from the audience coughed uncomfortably.

"The vicious cycle of addiction continued for years. I would try to stop my substance abuse but the drugs—be it meth crack, or marijuana—were simply too powerful for me to take on. They all became my keeper. They were slowly killing me." She shook her head. "No, I was slowly killing myself. Then, by some turn of fate, I found the courage to look into my past. I didn't want to die friendless and alone. Through many strange twists and odd turns, I was able to find one of my sons who had left my life when he was only two days old. I want to thank him…" Her voice cracked and it took Jenny a moment to struggle past the emotions that choked her. Finally getting hold of herself, her brow furrowed slightly when she realized more than one person on the crowded sidewalk wiped at their tears. The sight gave her strength.

"I want to thank Quinn Morgan and his wife, Calli, for treating me like the human being that I am. You cannot comprehend the peace and serenity I feel because they made me believe that I wasn't a bad person trying to get better, but a sick person trying to get well." She held the couple's loving gaze, raised a hand and pressed her palm against her heart. "They have given me my life back. Together we have created a family that will be bound forever. You've all read in the papers how hard Calli has worked over the last two years to bring us to this day. Hope was her dream and I will do my best to never let it die."

Suddenly, the written words now folded in front of her became clear in Jenny's mind. She dismissed the many numbers and dollar amounts, knowing they would be recorded for all time in the many newspaper articles yet to be written. Instead she went straight to the heart of why so many strangers had come together on this sunny afternoon.

"The mission here at the Hope Women's Shelter is to always provide succor to those women who need it. Anyone who walks through these doors and asks for help will be provided with the best counseling, the greatest respect and a network of hope that will turn their lives around. Thank you to everyone who has donated their skills and abilities for the refurbishment, the many government offices that always stood behind the idea of Hope until it actually became a reality and to every mother and father out there who shield their children from the awful world of drug addiction. Please come inside and see our wonderful facility." She stepped back and began to clap.

The crowd went wild. Cameras snapped, people cheered and reporters rushed forward to interview Jenny. Somehow she managed to duck past the many microphones waving in front of her face and push through the crowd. Quinn elbowed his way through the throng with Calli tucked close to his side. The newspapers all got their front-page picture for the following day of the three people most instrumental in creating Hope as they clung to one another, laughing and looking forward to the future.

* * * * *

Quinn's eyes opened behind the tinted sunglasses and he released a peaceful sigh. Warm tropical winds helped cool his body from the sizzling heat of the sun. He breathed in sweet, salty air and looked forward to the next two reclusive weeks with Calli by his side. They'd rented a tiny bungalow on the end of a private beach to finally celebrate a belated honeymoon, one he'd felt was long overdue, but his stubborn wife wouldn't have it any other way. Calli refused to leave Jenny until she was assured his mother was settled and on a complete road to recovery. Then all the plans and meetings for Hope had soon taken precedence.

A smile creased his face as he thought about the day before. Once he and Calli had taken Jenny's tour of the new facilities, they'd hugged her goodbye with promises to call. To his surprise, his mother's glowing face and happy smile were the last things he'd seen as they left for the airport when he had really expected tears.

He tucked his hands beneath his head in the white, warm sand and crossed his bare ankles. Wiggling his toes, he made a promise to himself that he wouldn't put on a pair of shoes until they boarded the plane for home, and then wondered where in the hell Calli was. She should have been back with the beer she'd promised him. He wanted the honeymoon to start because the evening before they were both so dead tired that they'd curled up on the bed and slept for hours.

A startled yelp left him when a splash of icy-cold liquid hit his firm belly. He jerked to a sitting position, hearing Calli's soft giggle above him.

"You shit," he teased and sloughed the beer from his stomach.

She flopped down beside him and grinned comically as she held out a cold bottle. "That's what you get for lazing around like a no-good husband and demanding his wife run beers for him."

He snorted his glee, grabbed his bottle and tipped it up.

Calli's eyes widened when he didn't take a simple sip, but chugged away until three-quarters of it disappeared. When the mouth of the bottle left his lips, he rested his fingertips against his chest and let out a loud carbonated burp.

Calli burst out laughing. "You pig!"

"Well, what the hell? If you did the same thing, you'd burp, too. God that was good."

A mischievous glint appeared in her gray eyes. "Okay, let's test your theory." She tipped her bottle and began to suck down her beer swallow after swallow.

Quinn chuckled when she started to choke and the icy cold liquid dripped across her chin and down to the deep vee of her small bikini top. Once she caught her breath, she sent him a scathing look. "Shut up, Quinn. I'm going to do this if it kills me." Once again, she tipped the bottle, this time taking it slower. Gradually, the beer began to disappear. With hardly any liquid left, she finally pulled it from her lips, copied his actions of earlier by placing her hand against her chest and let out a long, drawn-out burp.

They fell back in unison to the warm sand and laughed until tears wet their cheeks. The bout of hysterics finally came to an end, prompting Calli to reach out and take Quinn's hand. They stared at the turquoise sky and listened to the waves lapping against the beach.

"God, this is wonderful," Calli murmured. "I know I'm not going to want to leave."

Quinn sighed. "My sentiments exactly. How in the hell do people live here year round and get anything done?"

She rolled to her elbow and rested the side of her head on an upturned palm as she smiled at him. "Are there even any people here? I love the peacefulness of this place. I haven't heard a human voice all day except for yours." She reached out and punched his shoulder. "And then it was only when you called me a shit."

"I said it lovingly," he murmured, behind closed eyes.

He received another punch for his comment.

"I'm going swimming. Want to take a dip?"

Quinn mumbled, "No," and closed his eyes behind his glasses.

She leaned forward to study him. The idiot looked like he was going to fall asleep.

She rose quietly, flipped the clasp between her breasts and tossed the bikini top to the sand. Her bottoms quickly followed. She took three steps back, struck a pose and put one hand on a slender hip. "Oh, Quiiiiin… Are you sure you don't want to go swimming with me?"

He opened one eye behind the sunglasses and immediately followed with the other. Calli stood bare-ass naked, her breasts jutting out and a seductive smile on her lips. His glasses flew to the sand. "Let the honeymoon commence," he muttered as he leapt up and reached for her.

"Uh-uh," she spouted and backed out of his reach. "Get rid of the trunks first."

He slid them down his legs. "What if someone comes?" he asked as he kicked the suit away.

"Oh, someone's going to come all right," she laughed.

When she took off for the water's edge, Quinn sprinted after her. His long legs easily ate up the distance between them

even though she'd had a head start. Calli squealed with delight when he scooped her off her feet, tossed her over his shoulder and took the last few steps into the ocean. For good measure, he smacked her bare butt before he prepared to heave her in ass first.

"No! Don't you dare throw me!" she screamed playfully.

"And why shouldn't I? It's what you deserve for wasting precious beer just to get a rise out of me."

"Oh, I'll get a rise out of you," she laughed.

Quinn twirled her into his arms and let her body glide down the front of him. "Pretty much the saucy wench today, aren't you?" But even as he delivered the teasing comment, his eyes darkened until the gold flecks in their depths glowed molten. Holding her naked body in the sunlight without a care, feeling her small, firm breasts scraping across his chest and her fingers playing through his hair all combined to instantly put him in a hard state of arousal.

"I'm so happy, Quinn. And so ready to just bask in the sun with you by my side." Her body surged against his hard cock suggestively. "Now, what about that rise?"

His mouth lowered to capture hers. Calli met him halfway, clasping his sun-warmed shoulders. Water lapped at their feet and gulls screeched on the horizon, but they were only aware of one another.

His hands ran the length of her smooth back, his fingers in search of her round buttocks. Calli followed his lead, sliding one hand between them to caress his burgeoning cock.

They sank to the white sand, letting the warm South Pacific waters lap gently against their bodies as they kissed. Quinn's hand slid across the flat surface of her belly, down lower, and gently urged her legs apart. His palm lingered a moment against her thigh, but when Calli murmured his name, he parted her lips to stroke her clit.

Her hand slipped from his neck, followed the length of his arm until she coaxed a thick finger into her heat. A small, contented moan sighed against his mouth.

"I love you, Quinn..." she murmured, hips rolling slowly against his hand with the sensual tempo he'd set.

"Always," he whispered back. "Just you and me. I love you more every day, Calli." His teeth caught her lip and he closed his eyes, loving the feel of her slippery walls sucking at his finger.

"Now," she mumbled and nipped him back. "Together."

He rose up, slid over her body and loved how she spread herself as she waited for him. His muscled arms flexed as he supported his weight above her. The tip of his cock prodded against her, seeking her warm haven.

Her hands slipped down his back as she waited on the precipice of his entry.

Gray eyes turned a silvery shade.

Gold flecks glittered.

The sun glowed in the tropical sky, but was not the reason heat sizzled through their blood as he slipped into her welcoming sheath.

A warm wave rolled over their bodies, a physical delight that enveloped them as Quinn's hips moved slowly, sliding his cock in and out of his wife. Calli met each sensual glide with a gentle surge. They kissed between murmured words of love, their hands brushing the other with soft caresses as the water lapped against their skin.

Neither sought a climaxed peak to their joining. It would appear when they were ready. For now? The experience was a union of mind and body, an exploration of the familiar dips and swells of the other.

They kissed for an eternity. The rhythmic sex slowly and exquisitely built a fire of arousal. Quinn gently clasped Calli as he rolled to his back, his cock never leaving its warm haven as he settled her atop him.

Her eyes widened slightly, then took on a warm glow as she slipped down his full length. He filled her completely, tenderly. One of his hands treasured the sweet curve of her breast. The other slipped between her thighs.

Calli gasped in delight as a rush of pleasurable shivers tightened her clit. Her head fell back to greet the warm sunrays.

Her hips rolled sensually as a flame flickered higher.

His hands clasped her hips. Immediately, their sexual tempo increased. It was time.

Quinn buried himself deeply with a growl that accompanied Calli's breathless moan. She shuddered around his cock. When the pulses ebbed, she sagged forward to be greeted by his lips once again.

Quinn gathered her into his embrace, gently rolled her to her back and let his fingers drift across her mouth. His shuttered gaze coasted across the face that he eagerly and delightfully dreamed about nightly.

About the Author

இ

Picture Ruby with her hair on fire! Yup, that's her every morning when she bounds out of bed and heads for her home office. Ruby thanks her lucky stars that she's a full-time writer and a part-time matchstick. Although, there is a hint of a bulldog somewhere in there, too. Once she sticks her teeth into something, there's no turning back until it works. Her husband says she reminds him of that little mouse who stares up into the sky at a swooping eagle (this would be the mouse with his middle finger up) daring that darn bird, and just about anyone else, to screw up her day when she's got writing on the brain. Ruby loves to write, plain and simple. So much so that she took a leap of faith in herself and quit her 'professional' job, stuck her butt in front of a computer, and finally discovered what brings her true happiness in the wilds of Minnesota. Some might think that the life of a writer is glamorous and enviable. This is what Ruby has to say about that: "Glamorous? Think of me in sweats and an old t-shirt just beneath that flaming head of mine, typing with one hand and beating out the fire with the other. Envious? Most times my 'new' job consists of long hours of dedication and damn hard work, cramping leg muscles from sitting too long, and a backside that for some reason is widening by the week. But I wouldn't change my life for the world." Most people who fantasize about strange people and occurrences are sitting on the sixth floor of some psychiatric hospital. Not Ruby—she gets paid for it!

Ruby welcomes mail from readers. You can write to her c/o Ellora's Cave Publishing at 1056 Home Ave., Akron, OH 44310.

Why an electronic book?

We live in the Information Age—an exciting time in the history of human civilization in which technology rules supreme and continues to progress in leaps and bounds every minute of every hour of every day. For a multitude of reasons, more and more avid literary fans are opting to purchase e-books instead of paperbacks. The question to those not yet initiated to the world of electronic reading is simply: *why?*

1. *Price.* An electronic title at Ellora's Cave Publishing and Cerridwen Press runs anywhere from 40-75% less than the cover price of the <u>exact same title</u> in paperback format. Why? Cold mathematics. It is less expensive to publish an e-book than it is to publish a paperback, so the savings are passed along to the consumer.

2. *Space.* Running out of room to house your paperback books? That is one worry you will never have with electronic novels. For a low one-time cost, you can purchase a handheld computer designed specifically for e-reading purposes. Many e-readers are larger than the average handheld, giving you plenty of screen room. Better yet, hundreds of titles can be stored within your new library—a single microchip. (Please note that Ellora's Cave and Cerridwen Press does not endorse any specific brands. You can check our website at www.ellorascave.com or

www.cerridwenpress.com for customer
recommendations we make available to new
consumers.)

3. *Mobility.* Because your new library now consists of
   only a microchip, your entire cache of books can be
   taken with you wherever you go.

4. *Personal preferences are accounted for.* Are the words you
   are currently reading too small? Too large?
   Too...**ANNOYING**? Paperback books cannot be
   modified according to personal preferences, but e-
   books can.

5. *Instant gratification.* Is it the middle of the night and all
   the bookstores are closed? Are you tired of waiting
   days—sometimes weeks—for online and offline
   bookstores to ship the novels you bought? Ellora's
   Cave Publishing sells instantaneous downloads 24
   hours a day, 7 days a week, 365 days a year. Our e-
   book delivery system is 100% automated, meaning
   your order is filled as soon as you pay for it.

Those are a few of the top reasons why electronic
novels are displacing paperbacks for many an avid reader.
As always, Ellora's Cave and Cerridwen Press welcomes
your questions and comments. We invite you to email us
at service@ellorascave.com, service@cerridwenpress.com
or write to us directly at: 1056 Home Ave. Akron OH
44310-3502.

erridwen, the Celtic Goddess of wisdom, was the muse who brought inspiration to story-tellers and those in the creative arts. Cerridwen Press encompasses the best and most innovative stories in all genres of today's fiction. Visit our site and discover the newest titles by talented authors who still get inspired - much like the ancient storytellers did, once upon a time.

CeRRIDWEN PRESS

www.cerridwenpress.com

Discover for yourself why readers can't get enough of
the multiple award-winning publisher

Ellora's Cave.

Whether you prefer e-books or paperbacks, be sure to
visit EC on the web at

www.ellorascave.com

for an erotic reading experience that will leave you
breathless.